LEST WE FORGET
By George H. Edgley

ISBN-13:
978-1497332096

ISBN-10:
1497332095

This book is a work of fiction. References to real people, events, establishments, organizations, or locales are intended only to provide a sense of authenticity, and are used fictitiously. All other characters, and all incidents and dialogue, are drawn from the author's imagination and are not to be construed as real.

All rights reserved. No part of this publication may be reproduced, stored in a retrieval system, or transmitted in any form or by any means—electronic, mechanical, audio recording, or otherwise—without the written permission of the author George H. Edgley or publisher Ingram Books. For further information or to order books, please visit www.deaningram.com or contact ingrambooks@yahoo.com.

First edition: April, 2014

Copyright: George H. Edgley, Ingram Books, 2014 Worldwide

Printed by CreateSpace, An Amazon.com Company.

"Lest We Forget" is available on Amazon.com and Ingram Books at www.deaningram.com library.

Lest We Forget

About the Author
George H. Edgley

I was born and raised in Washington State. Following graduation from high school, I enlisted in the United States Marine Corps and served with the First Marine Division in Korea during the Korean War. I advanced to the rank of Sergeant and was trained in and assigned to Intelligence work. I was honorably discharged after the end of the war, when my enlistment was up.

After my military service, I attended junior college, where I obtained an Associate Degree in Engineering. I then attended and graduated from the University of Washington with Baccalaureate Degree in Physics(BS) and in Mathematics(BA). Employed by The Boeing Company as an Associate (Mid-Level) engineer, I worked in a variety of positions, most notably in Operations Analysis doing war gaming, research testing and writing for contract proposal teams and writing test manuals for various products related to missile programs. During this time, I was a candidate for the State Legislature, but lost narrowly to the Governor's son. I then decided I was not meant to be a politician. Later, I worked for the City of Seattle in Personnel/Civil Service, where I wrote and administered original examinations for employment testing of managers, engineers and skilled trades applicants and performed job classification analysis for the same groups.

During my years in Washington State, I hunted deer and elk and fished throughout the State and was involved in casual shooting sports, which I continue to enjoy. I maintained an interest in military history, primarily Civil War and World War II. Because of my employment background with the City of Seattle, I served on the Civil Service Commission for the Clallam County, Washington, Sheriff's office for several years following my retirement. I currently am living in Cottonwood, Arizona, where my wife and I enjoy researching the Native American culture and history of the Southwest.

George H. Edgley titles are available at Amazon.com.

ABOVE AND BEYOND: The compelling story that is a must read for those who love their country. "Above and Beyond", ordinary men and women rise above the call of duty and perform valiant acts of courage worthy of the Medal of Honor to defend their country. Following a soviet invasion of the United States, Colonel Fred Walker, U.S. Ranger, leads his men in courageous combat, finds love amid the carnage, and fights the invaders with daring and audacious deeds while facing near-impossible odds.

ESCAPE TO PAREJO: In "Escape From Parejo", neither the guilty nor the innocent emerge unscathed from the vicious civil war raging in the South American country of Vengaza. Captain Bob Olson, a mercenary, never imagined that all factions would degenerate into cruel, vengeful entities void of honor or integrity. As the dominant revolutionaries, led by Roberto Chiemi, terrorize the nation, the government retaliates with greater cruelty. In this savage environment, Olson must struggle not only to survive, but to maintain his personal honor. When the Government falls, he is in a precarious situation as he and others try to Escape from Parejo.

NORTH TO VALDEZ: Chief Troubleshooter and Private Eye Mitch Carson has investigated many challenging assignments but none as strange as this one. Before he learns that this assignment involves the oil pipeline in Alaska, faces two attempts on his life. Then he discovers that the two mob bosses he pursued earlier and who had vowed to kill him are apparently involved in some aspects of the oil operation. When one of the oil company's officers turns out to be a lovely woman who hates to be confined by clothing, he embarks on a perilous adventure that leads him North to Valdez.

Lest We Forget

CHAPTER ONE

Graduation Day, Marine Corps Recruit Depot, Parris Island, South Carolina, July 1998. I was filled with pride only because my grandson was in the graduating class of recruits. He was about to shed the degrading titles of shithead, boot, dumbbutt, and other, more despicable and earthy names. Today, he officially would become a Marine, an accomplishment limited to only a few.

In becoming a Marine, he would join what might be considered a family tradition. My son-in-law's father was a Marine and fought in World War II. I enlisted in the Marines and fought in Korea. My son-in-law was a Marine in Vietnam. At the time we were serving, all of us had been proud to be Marines. But somewhere along the line, from the Korean War through the Vietnam War, our esprit de Corps faded.

I had become disillusioned when I discovered that no one in my hometown knew or cared about what had happened in Korea. Many of them apparently did not even know we had fought a war there. I also learned that many of my friends from high school did all they could to avoid any military service and they laughed at me and called me a sucker for enlisting. I felt estranged from my former friends and even some of my favorite teachers because they never expressed an interest in the fact that I had served my country, come close to dying and had lost some good and true friends in Korea. When I mentioned the fact, they merely shrugged and walked away without comment.

I kind of figured those on the home front should have taken more of any interest in the war the nation was fighting.

After all, we were fighting to preserve their freedoms, also. At least, that was what we were told. After coming home, I began to wonder.

Likewise, my son-in-law had come home from Vietnam only to be spat upon, treated with disdain, ignored or called a baby-killer. He had difficulty obtaining employment because everyone considered him to be a drug-using junkie, a hippie or a psycho-maniac. That was the impression those on the home front had of men who served in Vietnam. Many of his friends and classmates had moved to Canada to avoid serving in the military and they laughed at him for serving his country. Others joined the so-called peace movements and marched against the war. They accused him of committing war crimes and murdering innocent civilians in cold blood. He had nothing in common with them and, had he not met my daughter, he likely would have withdrawn from society and become a loner or worse.

It was hard to reconcile out pride in having served in the Marine Corps with those attitudes. In fact, we felt we had been betrayed by the people at home, by our government and by the Marine Corps. They had fed us so much propaganda that we had come to believe it and now we doubted. Even so, we persevered over the years and didn't speak much about our service. When my grandson told his father he wanted to enlist in the Marines, it was a dark day. His father and mother and I discussed the possible ramifications at length. Yet, we gave him our support and, of course, we had to come to celebrate his graduation from boot camp with him. Despite our reservations, it was a momentous day for him and for us, too, in a way.

We had traveled all the way from Washington State to attend the ceremony. It was a long trip and a tiring one for all of us. We visited the base after getting a motel in Beaufort, South Carolina for our stay. The people at the visitor's center were quite gracious and we joined a number of other parents and relatives for a tour of the base. That was quite interesting, as we were able to see some old tanks and artillery pieces that were on display. Seeing some of the old equipment we fought with in Korea brought back a few memories. The tour guide took a count of those on the old bus who were veterans and it was surprising that so many of the parents had never served in the military. Silently, I wondered how many of them had gone to Canada to avoid joining the military.

We even got to see my grandson for a few minutes. Needless to say, he was well tanned and looked good in his fatigues. Then it was back to the motel for the night. We returned to the base early the next morning in order to get good seats in the visitor's stands.

Anticipating the start of the official ceremony with my daughter and son-in-law, I glance around the once familiar scene. I had taken my boot training in San Diego, but had been stationed at Parris Island for only a few months. A lot had changed since the late forties and early fifties. One new addition was the large monument when approaching the base -- a depiction of the flag raising on Iwo Jima in World War II. Seeing that was kind of awe-inspiring and it aroused a bit of pride in me. We had no memorials for those who sacrificed years of their lives to serve and for those who gave their lives in Korea and Vietnam. I guess, in the thinking of some, Truman's Police Action and the war in Vietnam didn't merit such a memorial. After all, we more or less lost both wars. It was a sore point with me and others I knew.

Now a slight morning breeze is drifting across the rectangular parade grounds, traipsing over the assembled ranks of recruits waiting on the manicured grass to my left. Along the opposite side of the grounds, across from the visitor's stands, the Marine Corps Band was assembled. On the end opposite the ranks of recruits and to my right, the official reviewing stand was filled with officers and a few dignitaries. Next to it, and extending around the corner and partially down the side, the visitor's stands were crowded with family and friends of the graduates.

A few visitors stood on the grass beyond the stands on the side, along with a platoon of recruits apparently being allowed to take a break from their training. They were lying on the grass, clearly enjoying the opportunity to relax. The recruits, with their short-cropped hair and their innocent faces, seemed to be so young and pure, perhaps even naive. I wondered how they would fare when they got out into the real world. Would they uphold the Marine Corps traditions if and when they became involved in a war and in combat? Or would they, also, be betrayed by our government and by the Corps? It was a nagging question I couldn't answer and I think no one else could, either.

The festivities began with the Marine Corps Band playing "Carolina in the Morning" as they marched the length of the drill field, turned in front of the reviewing stand, then marched in front of the visitor's stands and back to their original position. Then the color guard marched in and, with the playing of the national anthem, the colors were unfurled. The Stars and Strips began to ripple in the slight breeze and the globe and anchor on the Marine Corps flag undulated with pulsating power. The presentation of the colors was an emotional, inspiring sight and the visitors fell silent while the military men saluted.

I scanned the seemingly endless ranks, hoping to spot my grandson. In the sea of white covers, khaki blouses and dress blue trousers everyone looked the same. They all stood ramrod straight, with chins tucked in, chests out, eyes on a point and fingers lined up on the seams of their trousers. Their ranks were impeccably adjusted. Just looking at them made one feel proud to have shared the legacy of the Marine Corps.

I took a deep breath when the band began to play Semper Fidelis. My slouching stance straightened and a tingle of excitement bristled up my spine. Instinctively, my shoulders squared and my sagging gut crept back imperceptibly. My chin retreated into the extra folds of my throat and my fingers sought the seams of my trousers. Tears flooded my eyes as memories of former times invaded my thoughts.

Fifty some odd years ago, I never would have admitted to the tears. I was a Marine. Marines don't shed tears and they don't ever apologize for being tough. Marines are fire-spitting, beer guzzling, blaspheming, hell-raising lean and mean fighting machines. Man or woman, a Marine takes no crap from anyone. Marines are the toughest of the tough, the elite of the elite, the few good men and women.

That was then and this is now. I'm not as lean now nor as mean, but, despite my loss of faith in my government, my former friends and others, in my heart I'm still a Marine. As time elapses, however, things change. The body expands in the wrong places and muscles have a tendency to sag. Some memories inevitably fade, but Semper Fidelis brought the important memories back as vividly as if it were fifty or so years ago. There was a bit of naiveté in our generation. We came of age right after the big war.

Everyone knew someone who had fought in that war. Be it an older brother, an uncle, a brother-in-law, some other relative or just a friend or neighbor, those surviving veterans of the big war regaled us with their tales. We all listened -- those of us who gloried in their daring deeds, those of us who respected the courage displayed and those among us who had lost loved ones during the big war and longed to get an understanding of what it had been like. We all listened and wondered if we would ever face such a challenge.

It didn't matter which part of the war they talked about. The horrors of the jungle fighting on Guadalcanal were just as awe-inspiring as the landings and the flag raising on Iwo Jima or the struggles against the Japanese on Okinawa or the terrors of fighting in the Po Valley in Italy or the beaches of D-day or the hedgerows of France. But we discerned the tales were being told with an air of mystique. Parts of the stories were shrouded in an unspoken aura of secrecy never revealed, as if only the narrator and the Almighty were privileged to share the information.

We listened but we never really understood this aura of secrecy that implied that only someone who had been there could know or understand the intimate details. For five long years we listened and wondered. We entered the military still wondering.

In boot camp, the five of us discussed this secrecy and, sharing a common interest, we just kind of melded together into a group as friends. We really didn't have much in common other than the fact we were boots. We came from different parts of the country and had vastly different backgrounds. Becoming friends and buddies just seemed to be the normal thing to do. Others in our training platoon did the same. Having several buddies helped us over the rough spots and made life as a boot more tolerable. At least, we had someone to talk to. We were a proud and cocky bunch, perhaps even a little arrogant when we graduated from the trials of boot camp and became real Marines. However, we intuitively sensed that the training we had received really didn't teach us much, especially when we started more advanced lessons and discovered what we did not know. That, of course, made us wonder even more what it would be like in combat and why the veterans of the big war were unable to give us details on how it was. So, we continued to wonder about that aura of secrecy even as we began our tour of service. The five of us were lucky enough to stay together after boot camp and we hung out with each other on liberty. It was a fun time. Then, suddenly, we had our own war.

It erupted in a place called Korea only a few months after the five of us graduated from boot camp. We had survived the toughest training that can be given to raw recruits. The firm friendships we formed there made us feel there was nothing we couldn't do, even if we had to fight with our bare hands. It was good to know there were four other men we could rely upon when the chips were down.

When we were assigned to the provisional battalion,

we knew we were headed to Korea. None of us knew much about the place. We even had difficulty finding it on a world map or globe. We knew it was close to Japan in the Far East and that was enough. We also knew that, as Marines, we would be going there to fight. That's what Marines are trained to do, so we weren't too worried about it all. Besides, Marines are always the first to be called and our country was in a war and American men were being killed. It didn't matter that President Truman called our war a Police Action. To us, it was a war.

So we headed off to our generation's conflict and we went as cocky sons-of-bitches. Arrogantly, we boasted that we would straighten everyone out and stop the fighting in a few weeks. We were trained and knew everything.

It was on the ship that we first began to doubt. The troubling news that our own people -- soldiers as well as Marines -- were being kicked around along with the South Koreans and pushed back toward the sea by those upstart North Koreans was sobering. Perhaps the job would require a bit more time than we initially thought.

In that moment of somber reflection, we came to the awareness that men often become separated by the necessities of combat, that our group was not an official battalion, but only a provisional group. We were being sent in as a stop-gap measure to help hold the line until the First Marine Division could be outfitted and deployed. So the five of us vowed then and there to meet one year after the end of the war at our favorite restaurant in San Diego. We shook hands on it -- a binding vow to a Marine.

A few days later, our ship pulled into Pusan, South Korea. We had reached our war on that small peninsula in a different world and this is our story.

CHAPTER TWO

August, 1950. Pusan, Korea.

The five young men stood at the railing of the troop ship as it was eased toward the pier by a pair of tugs. An assortment of ships were in the harbor. Freighters, tankers, destroyers, cruisers -- you name it and it was likely floating somewhere amid the flotsam. But the men were not looking at the ships. Their attention was drawn to a group of dirty Korean children assembled in a small open area close to where the ship would be docking.

They were grubby little urchins, their pajama-like clothing stained, their heads uncovered, their hair unkempt, their dirty faces unexpressive. They were waving small American flags and shouting something. It was impossible to hear them. The nearby makeshift band was making too much noise.

It, too, was composed of Koreans. Older Koreans. No one could tell if they were musicians, however. The squeaky, weird tune they were playing on their motley assortment of instruments only vaguely resembled the Marine Corps Hymn.

Other Koreans, civilian and military, and American military personnel swarmed over the supplies stacked on the pier like an army of ants. Military Police were everywhere. They were shouting orders and counter-orders, seemingly trying to create mass confusion. It was a strange sight that greeted these young American Marines.

Gary Tilton stared at the baggy pants and strange hats the Koreans in the band wore. A small town boy from Iowa, he was a typical farm kid -- tall, husky, sandy haired -- who had never wandered far from the farm. Gary quit college to enlist and he left a promising tenure in Iowa football, but never told anyone why. He had been seasick for most of the voyage and didn't look too good now. His face was drawn and pale, his hands trembling slightly.

"They sure don't look like people back in Iowa," he mumbled to no one in particular.

"Kind of resemble some of the Indians in Washington," Glenn Martin nodded. A product of Washington State, Glenn was a quiet, studious type, his deep blue eyes always questioning. Even so, he had a quick smile and was well liked by everyone he met. He had been a scrawny lad when he enlisted, but, because of the regular regimen, had put on weight in boot camp. Like Gary, he, also, had quit college after a year to enlist. He admitted he and his girl friend, Carol, had broken up shortly before that. But he adamantly maintained that wasn't why he enlisted. No one believed him.

"Bullshit!" Jim Murphy snorted, "ain't no Indians anywhere that look so shitty! Look at them baggy pants and shirts! Even an unsuccessful New York pimp dresses better than that!" Jim came from the streets of New York City. He was used to the rough and tumble life there, the gangs, the crime, the pimps and whores, the corrupt police and the politicians who did nothing but line their pockets. He had never finished high school and still insisted that boot camp was a vacation compared to existing with the struggles against rival gangs and the brutality of the police. Quick tempered, he had already been in several fights. He usually won by fighting dirty. Standing a handsome six feet three inches tall, Jim had migrated west to escape the gangs and to try to get into the movies. Apparently he was too much of a trouble-maker even for the filmdom crowd, and, when that didn't work out, he enlisted in the Marines. He had taken some good-natured ribbing when his long, curly black hair was trimmed short in boot camp. Now, he kept it in a short crew-cut style.

"Yeah, really!" Glenn insisted, "in their ceremonial

dress, some do look like that."

"Well, they sure as hell look strange to me," Hank Brown shrugged, "but they do seem glad to see us." From Alabama, Hank seemed kind of slow to everyone, but he was sharp. With his brownish hair trimmed short, his ears protruded like large flaps and earned him the nickname "Ears" in boot camp. A good-natured, southern boy, he was about an inch shorter than Murphy, but a few pounds heavier. He had played a season of football for Alabama before he enlisted and had never explained why he joined the Marines.

"Why shouldn't they be glad to see us?" Jim growled, "hell, we're here to save their damn butts."

"You sound like you're pissed!" Harry Schein grinned. From Michigan, Harry was the shortest of the bunch, standing a mere five feet seven inches tall. A stocky man, his short, blond hair made his head appear small. Harry had a serious side to him, but he enjoyed a good time as much as any of them. He had insisted that he simply wanted to get off the family farm for awhile and do something different and that was why he enlisted. The reason didn't ring true, but no one questioned him. A genial sort, he nevertheless was as tough as they come and as hard as nails. Not even Murphy cared to tangle with him.

"Damn right I'm Pissed," Murph retorted angrily, "why should we risk our necks for them? Ain't they man enough to protect themselves? It's all Harry Ass Truman's fault. It's his war. Just because he screwed up ain't no cause to send us over here to die."

"Hey, man!" Harry laughed, "you ain't got a bitch coming. You volunteered!"

"That's right, Murph," Glenn echoed, "you volunteered."

"Don't throw that shit at me!"

"Scuttlebutt has it we're going straight to the front," Gary swallowed, "cause them North Koreans is about to break through and push us back to Japan."

"Don't believe everything you hear," Harry sobered, "I heard we were to go to a rear area and --."

"Who'd you hear it from?" Murphy spat sarcastically, "some one in the galley? Probably a cook, for god's sake."

"Well, stands to reason they'd give us a few days to adjust, don't you think?" Harry questioned, "I mean, we've been aboard ship for a long time."

"I hope they do," Gary replied.

"You scared, Tilton?" Murphy sneered.

"You aren't going to get sick now, are you?" Glenn anxiously asked.

"No, I'm not going to get sick," Gary scowled, "but I am scared."

"Don't worry, Tilton," Hank soothed, "we'll all be together."

"Yeah," Murphy giggled, "Ears can hold your hand. Anyway, I'll lay you five to one that we --."

"What in the hell are you damn boots gawkin at?"

The voice boomed out from behind them. Murphy shook his head. "Ten to one that's Sergeant Parker."

"You win, Murph," Glenn grinned.

They all turned to face Sergeant Parker. He stood with his hands on his hips and a scowl on his face, glaring at them. Parker was a vet of World War II, to them and Old Marine. He stood about six feet tall and his body was as hard as nails. His gnarled, leathered face underscored his age and his steely eyes seemed to penetrate whatever they focused on. His apparent old age and the five stripes he wore had initially earned their respect. Then they had seen the ribbons he wore on his blouse and knew he not only had seen a lot of combat, but had earned several decorations, including two Silver Stars, two Purple Hearts, and a Bronze Star. During training, they had learned that he knew his profession and that impressed them. They had come to trust and respect him completely.

"What's the word, Sarge?" Gary asked anxiously, "we going straight into combat?"

Parker snorted. "We're going to a camp, kid. Got it straight from topside."

"Told you!" Harry exulted, ignoring Parker's scowl, "pay up, Murph."

"For the night," Parker smirked knowingly, "we'll get provisioned and pick up some ammo, leave our excess gear and then haul our asses up to the front to relieve an Army unit. They got shot up pretty bad and need some rest. By 1200 hours tomorrow, you ladies will be baptized into combat. On a ridge near -- these damn names! Worse than those we had to contend with in the big war. It's near a village -- here it is! Changwon."

When he paused, Murphy held his hand out toward Harry. "Gotcha!"

"That soon?" Gary gasped.

"Yeah, that soon," Parker frowned, "you ain't scared, are you? Hell, you ladies is supposed to be Marines. What the hell -- you want a night off to play footsie with the Korean broads first? You're here to fight, dammit."

"But we've been on this boat for --."

"So? No reason to be scared, Tilton," Parker snorted, "Ears will hold your hand and, if you really get scared, old Sarge will shove his boot right up your --."

"That's right, Sarge," Glenn interrupted, a twinkle in his eyes, "you've been there -- in combat."

"Damn right I have!" Parker snorted, "and you ladies will soon discover that it ain't no picnic. It's --."

"Hell!" everyone but Tilton chorused, "really hell!"

Parker stared at them for a moment, barely able to keep from laughing. "In the old Corps we --."

"We know, Sarge," Murphy interrupted, "you've told us a hundred times."

"We don't need no lecture, Sarge," Harry added, "everyone knows the old Corps was tough."

"Damn right it was! Took me four years to get that first stripe and they give it to you ladies simply for surviving boot camp. The Corps ain't what it used to be."

"They just recognized how good we are," Ears smiled.

"Yeah?" Parker snapped, "well, let's see how good you are. Get below and get squared away. Stow your clothing, check your rifles and other gear and be ready to move out in ten minutes! Move!"

He chortled as the five men dashed for the hatchway and scrambled below. Their growth and development was almost amazing. When they had arrived at the training camp, they were all as naive as little children. Even Murphy, who hailed from the rough and tumble streets of New York, was a naive, innocent kid. The others? They were mostly from the farms and they had a lot of rough edges. Boot camp had turned them into disciplined Marines, but they had no idea of how to fight, how to use most weapons available to a Marine platoon or how to survive. These were things he and others like him throughout the Corps had to teach such recruits. Sure, they all thought of themselves as tough guys, as good fighters, as Marines. But he knew better. Fortunately, these five had wanted to learn. They listened to his instructions and did what he taught them. Now, they were being placed in a position where they would have to use that knowledge.

He nodded. He liked these men he had trained. Of course, he realized that no training ever teaches men more than the rudiments of combat. He breathed a silent prayer that these men might live long enough to mature and learn how to survive. If they did, they might become real Marines who could pass on their knowledge to other recruits.

The movement from the ship to the trucks went in an orderly manner. The men carried everything either in their sea bags or on their persons. Of course, they had no ammunition for their weapons at this time. As they filed from the ship, the Korean civilians assembled near the dock cheered them loudly. Then, when the trucks pulled out, the people waved and shouted encouragement.

The camp proved to be nothing more than a hastily erected tent city in a shallow valley protected from aerial observations by a few trees. There were few amenities. A pit with a wooden bench surrounded by canvas for a head, pipes stuck in the ground for a urinal, and a large tent for a mess hall. There were several smaller tents intended for use for sleeping. Clearly, the camp was only a place where they could drop excess gear, pick up some ammunition and get a hot meal. There really wasn't much time for sleeping, although some were able to squeeze in an hour or two on the hard cots provided in the smaller tents. Then it was turn out before dawn, grab a bite to eat and some coffee, then fall in ready to move out. It was still too dark to tell where they were going when they marched out of the camp. All they knew was that they were headed toward the front lines.

The sky had begun to lighten about a half-hour before the long column was halted. They had marched, in rout step, perhaps six or seven miles since they left the camp. Sergeant Parker glanced back and motioned the men off the graveled road. The men followed his command and started to settle in. Then they saw Colonel Bowman signal Sergeant Parker just before he and Lieutenant Brewster started up the steep hill in front of them. Parker nodded and waved for them to follow. Then he hurried ahead to join the two officers.

The hill was not extraordinary and had a bit of scrub brush here and there. It was typical of all the hills they had seen since dawn. As they neared the top, one could see that a few shell holes were scattered about amid the scrub brush that appeared to stop at the crest of the hill. Then, Parker dropped back and motioned for them to stop. He watched as they sprawled about, then moved on ahead to re-join Colonel Bowman and Lieutenant Brewster.

Glenn Martin dropped to his knees and scanned the area he could see. There appeared to be many more shell holes on the other side of the ridge, in addition to a lot of dead bodies spread about randomly. Even the scrub brush was torn up and mangled. Clearly, something had happened here. A battle of some sort. There was quite a bit of gunfire and artillery explosions audible from somewhere beyond the ridge. He glanced at the others. Apparently, they either hadn't bothered to look ahead or were too tired from the march to do so. No one seemed concerned about the sounds of a battle up ahead. He sighed and wondered what was up and whether they would be staying on the ridge. The three men were too far away for him to hear what they were saying.

Glenn studied the three men. Colonel Bowman had been their commander since the provisional battalion had been formed. He seemed like a good man, but no one except Sergeant Parker really knew him too well and it wasn't clear how well Parker knew him.

Lieutenant Brewster was relatively new to the unit. He hadn't been around much and really had pretty much ignored the men during their training. The Lieutenant seemed kind of strange, but perhaps it was just because he was an officer. Apparently, he didn't need the training.

Glenn eased back into a sitting position and closed his eyes. Sergeant Parker he knew pretty well, of course. Parker had conducted most of their training and was a man who could be trusted and that was gratifying. In a combat situation, he thought that it was absolutely necessary.

CHAPTER THREE

Faint wisps of smoke still rose from many of the shell craters that pocked the forward slope. Trees were torn asunder, their limbs ripped from their trunks and scattered among the myriad and blackened scrub brush. The dead littered the area, some curled and intertwined inside their foxholes, others lying amid the torn limbs and uprooted brush.

Colonel Lucius Bowman crouched at the crest of the ridge, his large frame shielded by scrub brush. His searching gaze was to the north, to the next ridge about a half-mile distant and the dust and smoke rising beyond it. The fighting clearly raged on there, the sharp cracks of rifle fire and the bursting of artillery and mortar shells still audible.

He took a deep breath and scanned the steep slope in front of him. The positions occupied by the former troops on the ridge set up fields of fire that covered the entire slope with overlapping sectors. Even so, the North Koreans had come perilously close to breaking through the line.

Had the line broken, an entire battalion with all of its heavy equipment would have been surrounded and trapped, likely annihilated. The dirt road just to the south of the ridge had been their only avenue of escape. The tenacious defense of the ridge and the ferocity of the attack on it attested to the fact that both sides were well aware of that.

Colonel Bowman glanced at the bodies inside the nearest foxholes. The faces of the Army men were etched with grim determination and their blood-stained fingers remained clenched about their blood-caked combat knives. Around the immediate area, at least sixty or more other bodies lay in various poses. They were the enemy, the North

Koreans. He had seen such scenes before, only then the enemy was the Japanese.

To the West, the graves registration teams were busy removing the bodies. It was about time, for, soon, the sun would rise and then --.

He lowered his head, removed his helmet, closed his eyes and thought a simple prayer. As he did, he heard the Marines behind him stirring restlessly. He ignored them. Someone had to pay homage to these brave, dead heroes who had held the line long enough for the counterattack to form. The Marines behind him were not old enough to know about such things.

The thought choked him up and revived suppressed memories of other times and other battles in the not too distant past. Battles on Guadalcanal, Tarawa, Iwo Jima, Peleliu and Okinawa. Brave men giving their last breath and fighting against overwhelming odds and for what? A dusty, forsaken few feet of crusty coral ridge on a remote island few had even heard about a month earlier? Or a few yards of slimy, insect infested jungle that no one really wanted. And all they got was a stark, white cross or tablet at some location where few would ever find them. He looked imploringly heavenward. Are we doomed to repeat this every few years? Will my young Marines have to die here?

To his trained eye, the sequence of the battle was clear. The men manning the listening posts in front of the main line either did not hear the infiltrating North Koreans and were overwhelmed before they could react or they heard and were not able to notify the main line of the enemy approach. He surmised they were surprised and overwhelmed. That was indicated by the fact their bodies were in or near their advanced positions.

The North Korean assault clearly hit the main line by surprise. Perhaps some of the enemy slipped around the ridge and attacked from the rear. Only the men who fought here could say and most, if not all, of them were dead. Regardless,

Lest We Forget

the Army men fought well. Their concentrated fire was able to hold the enemy at bay for awhile. Then ammunition began to run low. It always does. Some men were probably sent back to the rear for more. Without good radios, that was what usually occurred. Obviously, the resupply did not reach the line soon enough.

That was evident even to an untrained eye. Cartridge belts were empty, slides on pistols and rifles were open and bayonets on all rifles. Those armed only with pistols had their combat knives in their hands. That the men made good use of these primitive weapons was attested to by the number of enemy dead.

He swallowed and placed his helmet back on his head, covering his sparse, slightly graying hair. A pre-dawn counterattack pushed the enemy back a mile or so. That enabled the endangered battalion to escape. But the cost to retake the ridge was extremely high and the fighting continued to rage to the North.

Colonel Bowman pushed himself up, turned to Lieutenant Brewster and Sergeant Parker. He noticed Brewster was sweating and crouching low, as if he expected enemy fire. That puzzled him and he wondered if the Lieutenant was actually afraid. Parker, of course, was standing upright, his eyes scanning the battlefield, as a good Marine should. "They ran out of ammo," Colonel Bowman stated matter-of-factly, with a searching, evaluating glance at Brewster.

"Yes, sir," Brewster agreed, "it's obvious." He glanced at the dead bodies, his face showing a trace of contempt. Then he quickly turned his eyes to the North.

"See that our men don't."

Brewster glanced at Parker and then nodded. "Aye, aye, sir."

"Your platoon will be placed here, Lieutenant," Bowman continued, "and you'll be stretched thin. Any questions?"

"No, sir," Brewster shook his head. Again, he glanced at Parker, his eyes puzzled. *Why should I have any questions? Hell, I'm a Lieutenant! An officer! I know what to do.*

"How about you, Sergeant?" Colonel Bowman continued.

"Just a comment, sir," Parker replied, "it's just going to be us? My men are all green, sir. No more than a year out of boot camp -- most of them even less than that."

"So? I know they're just young recruits, but they're Marines, aren't they? Weren't they trained?"

"Yes, sir, but --."

"Then see that they fight and, if necessary, die as Marines. At least as valiantly as these men."

"Very well, Colonel," Parker nodded.

"The Army people are working their way up here to remove the bodies. Have your men give them a hand. Then occupy and hold this ridge at all costs. You probably won't get much help from anyone else. Hell, Sergeant, our lines are spread so thin --."

He shook his head and glanced across the valley. "I don't know how long we'll be here. Our purpose in this god-awful war at this time is to give the Army men a break. They've been fighting for god knows how long. Since this thing began and against overpowering odds. So chances are we'll be shuffled about and used to reinforce critical areas. That doesn't matter. One hill is as good a place to fight as any other."

Or to die, Parker thought.

Colonel Bowman paused and his rugged, taut face relaxed slightly. "Hell, Parker, I know your men are green boots. The whole damn battalion is with the exception of a few men like yourself. That's why you're wearing those chevrons. Your boots are simply going to have to mature damn fast."

"I understand, Colonel," Parker grinned, "they will." He glanced at the men clustered about twenty yards back.

"They're good men, sir."

"I know they are, Parker. We trained them. Clue them in and pray they stay alive until the First Division arrives. Get them into position, Sergeant."

He watched Parker walk back to the men, then turned to Lieutenant Brewster. "You're green, too, Lieutenant. Parker, here, fought with me on Iwo. He's a good Marine and he knows a helluva lot more than you do. You'd do well to listen to him and ask his advice. Just because you're wearing that gold bar doesn't mean you know everything. That's one thing you'll learn after you've been in combat for awhile. Experience in combat is far better than a gold or silver bar. I hope you can survive long enough to learn that."

"Yes, sir," Brewster replied, his lips tightening slightly. His eyes betrayed the fact he didn't accept the assessment of his knowledge. When Colonel Bowman turned away, he glanced at Sergeant Parker and snorted disdainfully. Hell, I'm a Lieutenant and I know more than any Sergeant.

Gary Tilton glanced at Murphy and swallowed. Wish I was as brave as he is. Hope I don't run when the shooting starts. I'm already scared and we ain't even seen no fighting. Just those dead bodies. Don't like to look at dead bodies and definitely don't want to touch them. Didn't even want to look at my Grand-dad's body when he died a few years ago, but had to when we walked by his casket. Still gives me the willies. Him lying there so life-like and all. No one else seems to be bothered by the dead bodies. Glenn ain't upset and Harry don't seem bothered. Ears is -- how can anyone handle them bodies? They used to be people like us -- alive! And now they're dead!

"Listen up!" Parker barked.

Gary swallowed the thick saliva in his mouth and looked at Parker. The others shuffled their feet and shifted their rifles as they moved closer.

"We've been assigned to hold this ridge," Parker

Lest We Forget

continued, "at all costs. You'll use the foxholes dug by the Army men, two men to a hole. Questions?"

"What do you mean by at all costs?" Ears asked.

"You've got to be kidding me!" Parker snorted. He glared at Ears for a moment.

"The, the dead men," Gary stammered, "what about them?"

"You squeamish, Tilton?" Parker snorted.

"Well, yeah, kind of, Sarge."

"You ain't gonna get sick, are you?" Glenn asked anxiously.

"No, I'm not -- what's with you guys? So I got sick on the damn boat! Hell, I hadn't even seen the ocean until --."

"Can it, Tilton!" Parker snorted, "you can relax. The Army people are coming to collect the bodies. You won't have to cuddle up to them."

"Might be kind of fun to cuddle, Gary," Murphy chortled, "they probably got more life in them than that broad I met in San --."

"Shut up, Murph!" Harry snapped, "you'll make him get sick and barf."

"Hell, Tilton," Hank shrugged, "ain't no different than handling a dead animal. Back home, we do it all the time. Pigs and calves and rabbits. Ain't no big deal."

"Yeah, Gary," Glenn noted, "I used to butcher rabbits at home. Even skinned and prepared deer a few times."

"It's not the same," Tilton insisted, "hell, I've butchered cattle before, too. It ain't the same."

Hank shrugged and tugged at his left ear.

"All right, knock it off. You guys pair up as you like," Parker directed, "there's plenty of holes to go around."

"Why not one guy to a hole, Sarge?" Harry asked, "like you said, there's a lot of them."

"You guys are green. I don't want you to get lonely and start talking across ten, fifteen yards. Okay, pair up."

"I'm not pairing up with Tilton!" Murphy blurted, "I

don't want to wallow in barf all night."

"You can stick with me, Gary," Glenn offered.

"Okay. Thanks."

"I'll pair up with Ears," Murphy announced.

"What about me?" Harry asked.

"Odd man out, Schein," Murphy shrugged, "you're okay, but I think Ears will be able to hear them coming better."

"Team up with one of the other guys, Schein," Parker grunted.

"Fine with me, Sarge. Real buddies."

"I'll be in the hole in the center," Parker declared, "and I guess the Lieutenant will be in the hole back behind me. Now remember. The rest of our unit is spread along the ridge to the left and right. The recon people are going to man the listening posts out in front. Apparently, they'll be going out later tonight. If they come back through our line during the night, try not to shoot them. If you do, you're going out in their place. Settle in and get some chow into you. As soon as the counterattack units withdraw, we're on our own. You'll get the password later."

"Think they'll attack again tonight?" Glenn asked.

"Have no idea," Parker shrugged.

"Maybe they've had enough, what with the counterattack and all."

"Don't count on it, Martin," Parker retorted, "they're trying to push us off the peninsula, you know."

"When they attack, will they bring up tanks?" Gary inquired with a concerned voice.

"Yeah, of course, Tilton," Parker laughed, "right up the hill after they swim across the damn river."

"How we gonna stop them with just rifles and grenades?"

"You dumb boot! No tank is gonna climb this steep hill. Besides, tanks can't swim a river like this one. They need a bridge, dummy. The only place you'll see tanks is on the road behind you -- if they flank us. If they do, then we'll be in deep shit. But remember -- tanks have to stay on the roads in this terrain and the only bridge is about three miles up river."

"Oh." How am I supposed to know that? Ain't nobody said nothin about no bridge and nobody has shown me a damn map. Dammit, Sarge, we don't know nothin about what tanks can do or where they can go. Y'gotta tell us these things.

"C'mon, Gary," Glenn grinned, "let's get the bodies out of our hole and get settled in."

"I ain't touching them!"

"It's okay, Gary. Nothin to it. Just think of it as handling a nice, thick beef steak."

"Damn you, Martin!" Murphy snorted, "you had to mention food! When all we got is these damn C-rations."

"Sorry, Murph."

"Your people all squared away, Sergeant?"

Everyone looked at Lieutenant Brewster, who had just walked up. The tone of his voice and the expression on his face as he glanced at them revealed his scorn for enlisted men.

"Yes, sir," Parker replied, his eyes narrowing.

"Make damn sure they are!" Brewster snapped haughtily, "I don't want to have to answer for an ill-prepared line." Then he turned and strode away.

I don't like him, Parker mused, he's an arrogant ass. Thinks he's a hot shot just because he's got Lieutenant's bars. He'll learn the only thing more despised than a Second Lieutenant is a damn boot. I sure hope he doesn't screw us up. Wonder if he'll break and run. Hope no one in the unit does. Tilton is scared shitless, but he's a good man. So is Martin and Ears. Schein is okay. The one I'm most concerned with is Murphy. Usually, it's those who show a lot of bravado that break in combat. Well, we'll see what happens.

A few hours later, the Army unit began to withdraw

around the ridge and through the forward line of troops. There appeared to be no enemy pursuit. The men carried their dead and wounded, some on standard stretchers, others on improvised stretchers and a few on a friend's back or helped along by friends. Clearly, there were too many casualties and some of the men looked as if they were about to fall over.

An Army Sergeant paused at the base of the ridge, watched his men stumble by and then looked up to examine the platoon's positions. He spotted Sergeant Parker and wearily climbed up to speak to him. Everyone stopped what they were doing and listened in.

"Name's Thompson," the Sergeant offered, "Company A of the First Battalion."

"Parker. Pleased to meet you, Thompson," Parker responded with a smile, "how was it out there?"

"Pretty rough," Thompson shrugged, "but we pushed them back well beyond the river and the next ridge. Colonel figured we couldn't hold the advanced line, so I guess we'll have to fight them here again. They didn't seem to want to fight us in the daylight, anyway. Prefer nighttime, I guess. They're probably reorganizing for tonight's attack. Determined bastards and not bad fighters." He paused and studied Parker's face for a moment. "You've been there, I see."

Parker nodded. "Iwo, Okinawa, among other islands."

"Yeah, rough duty. Was in France, myself. D-Day up to the Bulge."

"That was no picnic, Thompson. Glad you made it. Notice any armor coming down?"

"Didn't have any when we hit them. Heard that air spotted some up north. Might get here by tonight. They have to stay on the roads, you know, and the only bridge is up river a ways."

"Right," Parker acknowledged, "ground is too soft."

"The Gooks are good at infiltrating," Thompson added, "so you better keep your men alert all night. Last night, some almost got around us. They come at you from all sides." He glanced at the men around them. "Your Marines all green?"

"Yeah. Green as hell and so is our Lieutenant. Don't know how they'll do once the shooting starts. Thanks for the advice. I'll put it to good use. Uh, here comes our Lieutenant now. He's kinda strange."

Thompson looked at Brewster and grinned. "Lieutenant. Was just filling in Parker on what he might --."

"Doesn't the Army teach you to salute officers, Sergeant?"

"Hell, Lieutenant, one thing we've learned is that snipers love to shoot officers when we salute them. Those bars make a great target -- shiny and they stand out real well."

Brewster instinctively reached up to finger his gold bar. His face paled and his eyes widened in fear. Quickly, he glanced to the north.

"But, hell, Lieutenant," Thompson continued, "if you insist --."

"No! Don't salute! I, I mean, uh, it's okay, Sergeant. I didn't know."

"Yes, sir. Whatever you want me to do."

"Yes, of course. What were you telling Parker?"

"That the Gooks may have tanks in here by tonight and that they're pretty good at infiltrating. So best stay alert."

"We know that, Sergeant!" Brewster snapped contemptuously, "hell, we're Marines. We know what to do."

Thompson glanced at Parker, who slightly shrugged and rolled his eyes. "I understand, Lieutenant."

"Next time, Sergeant," Brewster directed, "speak to the officer in charge first." He spun around and walked away.

"Whatever, Lieutenant," Thompson said to Brewster's back. He turned to Parker. "Good luck, Parker."

"Thanks, Thompson. We'll need all the luck we can get."

"He's a real ass, isn't he?"

"Yeah," Parker nodded, "all wrapped up in the fact

he's got a gold bar and is a Marine. They all aren't like that, thank god."

"I know. Hope you guys can hold 'em here. We're heading back for a night or two of rest. First in almost a week. We sure need it. Everyone is totally worn out. It takes a lot out of a man, especially someone our age. We just hope and pray we won't be called out tonight."

"I know what you mean. We'll do our best to hold the line, Thompson. Good luck to you and your outfit, man. You guys obviously have earned it. Enjoy your rest and get some hot chow. Take care, man, and I hope I get to see you again."

Lest We Forget

CHAPTER FOUR

Everyone had been quiet as they watched the Army unit move by. It was sobering to see the many wounded and dead and to realize there was no one else to defend the ridge, no reinforcements to call up should they run into too much trouble. The thoughts caused a bit of doubt.

Faint sounds of activity drifted in from the North. No one could determine just what was going on. Occasionally a lone shot would shatter the stillness and, now and then, a cry for a Corpsman would be raised from another area along the ridge. Obviously, there was a sniper somewhere up ahead of them and he apparently was a good shot.

Everyone listened to the sounds, but no one could make out what exactly they were hearing. Ears thought he could hear the rumble and clanking of tanks from the North, but Parker scoffed at the idea. Gary thought it sounded like a gaggle of geese and Murphy thought he could hear men talking. Schein thought it sounded like some cattle lowing and Martin simply shrugged and said all he heard was noise.

Lieutenant Brewster was noticeably absent from the main line. He hadn't been seen since he upbraided Sergeant Thompson for not saluting him. It was just as well. Everyone felt more comfortable with Sergeant Parker in charge.

The heat and humidity soon became intolerable as the sun climbed into the sky. There was no shade in the foxholes. On top of the heat was the stench from the rice paddies. No one had really noticed the smell when the unit advanced earlier. Now the odor was quite strong as the breeze blew it toward them. Even so, the men began to break out their rations.

Gary Tilton looked at his and his face turned a pale green. His lips twisted and his stomach churned. He put the box of rations down and closed his eyes.

Glenn took one look at him and caught his breath. "You ain't gonna be sick, are you?" he asked anxiously.

"No," Gary shook his head, "at least I don't think so. It's just -- well, got this knot in my stomach and the sight of these rations just -- this ain't at all what I thought it would be like."

"Yeah, I know what you mean," Glenn replied knowingly, "if they showed a situation like this in the movies, there would be a band playing the Marine Corps Hymn in the background."

That thought made Gary laugh and eased his tension. "Won't hear no band out here."

"I know." Glenn paused and glanced to the North. "Hard to imagine, ain't it? I mean, the possibility of them charging us -- hundreds of them -- and us shooting at them. Be hell to get caught taking a crap, wouldn't it?"

"Right," Gary chuckled, "they never show that in the movies, either."

"Right now, I don't feel too brave," Glenn admitted, "I just hope I don't let you and the others down. I'm wondering if I'll be able to keep from running or wetting my pants."

"Know how you feel," Gary nodded, "kind of wonder about that myself. I'm more scared of what you guys might think of me than the North Koreans. You're all already pissed off at me just because I got sick on the boat"

"No one's upset about that!" Glenn protested, "we've been kidding you about it, that's all. We all felt queasy out there. Most of us had never been on the ocean for that long a time before. Besides, it got kind of rough at times, what with the wave action and the winds."

"But I was the only one who really got sick."

"You weren't alone, Gary. Lots of other guys got sick. Don't know if you noticed, but Murph was awful quiet while we were at sea. Even Harry -- did you see him trying to walk along the deck?"

"No. I was too sick to notice."

"He was wobbling and staggering along like a drunken gob."

"Really?" Gary questioned.

"Yeah, only he's so short no one noticed him."

"You mean he was like he was in L.A. that time?"

"Exactly," Glenn nodded, "I didn't know anyone could drink that much booze."

"Well, Harry and Murph did. Good thing we didn't run into the MP's."

They both turned as someone eased up alongside the hole. It was Sergeant Parker.

"Hi, Sarge," Glenn grinned.

"Hi, my ass!" Parker snorted, "I could hear you guys talking clear down on the other end of the ridge!"

"You mean we were talkin too loud?" Gary questioned.

Parker rolled his eyes heaven-ward. "Why? Why me?"

"Sorry, Sarge," Gary swallowed.

"Just hold it down," Parker snorted, "you can't hear the enemy approaching while you're talking. Stay alert."

"Okay, Sarge," Gary nodded. He looked sheepishly at Glenn.

Glenn shrugged and glanced at Parker, then looked across the valley when Parker left. *Hell, ain't nothing gonna approach us in broad daylight. Reminds me of the first time I went deer hunting.* A smile crept across his face as the thought of that day. He was only twelve and his brother Chuck was eighteen.

Chuck and the others had been quiet as they drove out into the woods along the old logging road. It was still early and a light mist drifted down on the landscape. Finally, Chuck

Lest We Forget

stopped the truck and everyone piled out. Chuck simply motioned for him to follow and headed out into the woods. In a few minutes, they came to a small clearing.

"Sit here," Chuck ordered, pointing to an old, half-rotted log, "and stay alert and don't squirm around. Keep still."

"Okay, but what am I supposed to be alert for?"

"Deer, y'farthead! Deer with antlers."

"D'ya mean they come right up to you?"

"Can you believe it?" Chuck protested to the others, who giggled, "why did I bring this runt along?"

"Cuz Dad told you to," Glenn snorted, "and he tole ya to let me have a good shot at a deer."

Chuck sighed. "Yeah, he did. That's why I want you on this log. You have a good clearing out this way." He pointed to the cleared area which had only a spotty growth of brush. "Just watch the clearing area."

"Okay. You want me to sit here in case a deer with antlers comes along. What do I do if one does? Do I shoot it or yell for you?"

"You run up to it and kiss its -- of course you shoot it, farthead! Right were I told you. Remember that?"

"I remember what you said. What are you guys gonna be doing and where will you be?"

"We're going to be moving around over there in the trees. We'll try to drive a deer toward you. And be sure you don't shoot one of us. Okay?"

Glenn nodded. "If I do shoot one, a deer, do I call you then?"

"We'll hear the shot, farthead, and we'll come over to see if you got one."

"You don't like having me along, do you?"

"It's okay, Glenn. If you do see one, just don't miss. Okay?"

"You know I'm a good shot."

"At targets. This is different. Try not to move too

much. Deer see movement. Do as I told ya -- raise your rifle slowly and aim. And don't flinch. That 30-30 don't kick as much as some rifles. Understand?"

Glenn swallowed. He'd shot the deer the others drove toward him. A real nice four point buck. One shot was all he needed and it fell about fifty yards away. Chuck was well pleased over that. In fact, he bragged about it for a week. It was the last time he went hunting with Chuck. Three months later, Chuck entered the Army Air Force. He became a fighter pilot and was shot down over Germany not long before the end of the war. His death hit the family hard.

He, too, had been deeply hurt by Chuck's death. In spite of the normal brotherly competition, they had been close. Even when Chuck got a girl friend, they remained close. The day Chuck went on his last date before entering the service, he had borrowed ten dollars. Of course, Chuck never paid it back, but that was okay. That was the way they were. He never expected to be repaid.

Glenn knew his father had been hurt by Chuck's loss, too. His father had great hopes for Chuck. His mother -- well, she kind of held them all together during the hard time. Perhaps Chuck's death had hit her the hardest, however, even though she never spoke about it. That was the way it was with mothers.

Then, when he said he was going to enlist in the Marine Corps, all his mother could do was weep. His father looked at him for a long moment, then nodded his assent. He knew they didn't want him to enlist. That was written all over --.

"Glenn -- did you hear that?" Gary hissed, his voice wavering.

"What?"

"That sound -- like a rock rolling down in front of us."

"No, Gary. I didn't hear anything," Glenn shrugged. He raised up slightly and stared down the slope. There didn't seem to be anything there. "Maybe you just imagined it."

"No, I heard something," Gary insisted. He glanced at the other holes and the men in them. No one seemed to be concerned about anything. Then he heard it again!

"Did you --."

"Yeah, Gary," Glenn replied softly, "I heard it this time. Keep quiet." He checked his rifle to make sure a round was in the chamber, then eased the safety off. A glance at Gary told him Gary was scared. His face was pale and his eyes wide and he moistened his lips nervously.

Glenn nodded to himself. Funny. I thought I'd be scared shitless, but I don't feel that way. It's just like when I was out hunting deer. He heard a scraping noise and eased his head up again. Then he saw it. A movement about a hundred and fifty yards out. It wasn't much. Just a small swirl of dust and a brownish piece of what appeared to be earth sliding sideways and then coming toward him. He slid his rifle over the rim of the hole and aimed it toward the piece of earth and waited.

As he watched the area around the piece of earth, he tried to recall the instructions of the Range-master when he was firing in boot camp. The man was a stickler for detail and for controlling one's breathing. That was what made for a good shot, he always declared. Glenn smiled slightly. It was true. He had learned to control his breathing and was able to attain an expert's level, which made him feel good. He had also learned to squeeze the trigger and not jerk it. That helped him control the rifle better. Now he wondered if he could take a man out with one shot. If he hit the man, surely the shot would kill him. But, what if it was an American? Could it be a straggler who was trying to get back to his outfit? Perhaps it was a wounded man simply trying to survive! Was it possible to tell? How could he determine if it was another American?

A movement beside him made him catch his breath! He rolled his head so he could look -- it was Sergeant Parker.

"See you're on him, Martin," Parker hissed, "none of

our people out there in this area at this time, so take him out."

"Okay, Sarge, if you say so," Glenn breathed. He aimed his rifle again, waited. The piece of earth shifted again and he squeezed his trigger! There was a short cry and grunt and then the sound of something sliding down the slope.

"Good job, Martin," Parker commended, "good shot."

"Sure, Sarge," Glenn replied. He looked at his hands and noticed they were shaking. "It was Gary who heard him first."

"Good. Stay alert. There may be more of them."

Glenn nodded. He had always wondered what he would do when actually confronted with the possibility of killing another man. It made no difference that the man was an enemy. He was still a human being. But, he believed the Bible did not condemn killing in defense of one's country or oneself. As a member of the military establishment, that was what he was supposed to do. His pastor had told him to simply put the enemy in God's hands and do his job. It was not an easy thing to do, however. A person had to reconcile the facts in his own mind.

"Nice shooting, Glenn!" Gary enthused, "you got him good."

"I guess." He clicked on the safety and eased deeper into the hole. "Only thing now is that they know where we are."

"I suppose they already knew," Gary shrugged, "I mean, someone else dug these holes for the battle last night. So if they fought here, they for damn sure know where the holes are."

Down the line, Murphy looked toward Glenn and Gary with a touch of envy. Damn! I wanted to be the first to take a shot and get a Gook, so I could brag about it. Hell, Glenn isn't going to brag. He's too nice a guy. If I had taken that shot, I'd be able to parlay it into a couple of free drinks, maybe even a broad. Dammit! Why couldn't I have taken that hole?

Sergeant Parker slithered back into his hole and glanced around for Lieutenant Brewster. If he was in the foxhole he should have been in, he was crouching so low no one could see him. Could he actually be hiding?

Parker considered crawling over to inform him of what happened for only a second. He knew Brewster didn't care. Besides, the Lieutenant was probably too scared to want to know. So why bother him with details. If he wanted to know, he could come and ask for the information. Otherwise --.

Martin did all right, he mused. Nice to know some of my people are squared away. Pretty cool guy, too. At least on the outside. I bet he's all tensed up inside. Martin is that kind of guy. Like another Marine I used to know.

They were pinned down in front of a pill box on the beach. There wasn't much they could do about it. Maybe burrow a bit deeper into the sand. It took very accurate fire to hit the slits in the pill box and one had to expose himself to even fire at it. So he and Jack Richman, along with thirty others, stayed put. It was tough to just lie there and wait as bullets dug up the sand around you. The sun was hot on their backs and the waves lapped close to their feet, threatening to come up higher when the tide rolled in. Once that happened, there would be no place to go but ahead.

He was only a Buck Sergeant then and Jack was a Corporal. They had gone through boot camp together at Parris Island and then, when the war broke out, had been shipped out to join the First Division. Jack had gotten married just before they were sent overseas. As Jack's best man, Parker knew Jack was extremely happy, as was his bride. She was a pretty woman, about Jack's height, with auburn hair and a radiant smile. She had asked him to watch over Jack while they were in the South Pacific. Jack often talked about making Sergeant someday. The extra money would go far for he and his wife and the family they hoped to have.

It was strange. After they were rescued from that

predicament, so to speak, when a flamethrower took out the pill box, they advanced inland. Of course, the Japanese had planned their defenses well. Overlapping fields of fire from every position made it hazardous to move and any movement, even a slight nod of the head, drew enemy fire. But they made it through the day without getting shot and then settled in for the night. That was when Jack was hit. He was sitting behind a log with a cup of coffee when the sniper fired. Jack died a few days later. It seemed unfair, in a way. They had survived intense combat all day and then Jack was hit during a quiet spell when he finally had a chance to relax. It was only the first buddy of Parker's to get shot. There were more after that. Combat was tough on friendships and buddies.

Parker tuned in to the present and shrugged. Perhaps that was why Brewster tried to act so tough or remained so aloof. Maybe he didn't want to become friendly with the men under him. Hell, I was that way for awhile after losing Jack. Then I realized it didn't help any. Losing anyone in your command is just as hard as losing a close friend. Even if you don't know them well, you have a kinship with them. So I figured I might as well make some friends and to hell with it. Life became a bit easier then.

I like Martin and the other guys. Good men all. Brewster -- I hate to even think it of a fellow Marine. But the man appears to be a coward. Damn! Why did I have to end up under the command of a --.

A flurry of fire erupted from the line and he rolled forward, scanned the hillside. Clearly, the enemy group was pulling back. Here and there, he could see them moving through the scrub brush, out of range. He nodded. This, obviously, was just a reconnaissance to locate their positions and to test their strength. The real attack would come later, after dark. It was unfortunate that the men fired back at the enemy. That was his fault. He should have imposed some fire discipline along the line. Well, the damage was done now.

The men would soon learn to hold their fire under such circumstances.

He glanced around to see where Lieutenant Brewster was, but the Lieutenant was not to be seen. With a shrug, he rolled from his hole and moved along the line. Murphy was quick to point out he had hit one of the enemy soldiers. Hank merely rolled his eyes as though to say so what. Schein and his partner were very quiet. Tilton and Martin simply nodded when he explained the situation to them. They evidently understood it might be a long night.

Parker smiled to himself. He was right not to comment on the lack of fire discipline. These guys were new to combat and they would learn. Right now, they didn't especially need a lecture from him. Had Lieutenant Brewster been around, they might have gotten one from him, however.

CHAPTER FIVE

All hell broke loose about 2 A.M. Enemy flares lit up the slope and rocket and artillery fire slammed into the area. Fortunately, the barrage landed about fifty yards short. Even so, the ground shook incessantly and dust swirled close to the ground and drifted up the slope. Glenn choked back a cough and wiped his nose on his sleeve. He leaned forward, fully aware that, if they chose to, the enemy could easily crawl extremely close under cover of the dust. He turned toward Gary and nudged him.

"What's up?" Gary hissed.

"Nothin. Just stay alert. They could crawl up close through the dust."

"You kiddin? Hell, they'd be coughin their heads off."

"Maybe no," Glenn shrugged, "it worries me."

"Yeah, well, okay. I'll keep my ears peeled."

Glenn smiled and nodded. Do that, Gary. Me, I'll watch and listen. I don't want no bayonet slicing through me.

A few minutes later, Glenn heard a rock roll down the slope to his right. He tensed and shifted his gaze in that direction, stared into the lingering dust. There seemed to be nothing to see. He frowned and was about to turn away when he remembered a statement by one of his instructors regarding night vision. The man had told them not to look directly at an object, but just off to the side.

He let his eyes drift to the left slightly. What appeared to be a shadow of a man slowly took form. For what seemed an eternity, he watched, resisting the impulse to look directly at it. When it finally moved, he shifted his rifle and squeezed the trigger. He saw the man fall and felt Gary jump beside him.

"What you doing?" Gary hissed.

"A gook. Got him," Glenn whispered back, "stay alert. They're sneaking closer and infiltrating our lines."

"Uh, yeah, okay," Gary grunted.

It seemed as if the night lasted forever. There was some firing down the line, but nothing else came toward them. Then the pre-dawn glow began to filter over the area and trees and bushes started to take shape. The sky displayed a reddish streak or two in the east and Glenn sighed in relief. He checked out the area to his right and spotted the body of the North Korean he had shot. The body had rolled partway down the slope. With a deep sigh, he turned away.

Near the center of the line, Sergeant Parker rose from his foxhole and moved along the line away from them. Parker paused by each hole and spoke briefly with the men. At the one where Harry Schein was, he motioned to the rear and waved a Corpsman forward! Glenn held his breath and watched as the man knelt beside the hole and seemed to be administering aid. Then a stretcher team came up and the body of one of the men was placed on it. He swallowed and looked at Gary, hoped it wasn't Harry. Gary apparently had not noticed the scene.

Later, when Sergeant Parker reached their foxhole, he asked who had been hit. Parker studied him for a moment, glanced at Gary, whose face now was pale and whose eyes were wide. "Al Horwood, Harry's partner. Rose up at the wrong time, I guess. He only got a flesh wound, but had to be taken back to the hospital. Harry is a bit shaken up. You two okay?"

"Yeah, we're fine," Glenn replied, "I didn't know Horwood too well. Thankfully, that's all it was. He seemed okay enough and nice."

"He's a nice kid," Parker shrugged, "you're all nice kids. Soon, you'll become real Marines. If you live long enough."

Glenn grinned. "Yeah, we know, Sarge. Where's Lieutenant Brewster?"

"I don't know, Glenn."

"Oh."

"You worried about him?"

"Not really, Sarge. Just thought he'd be doin the checking."

"Well, that's the way it goes. Got enough rations?"

"I think we got a couple of meals -- isn't that right, Gary?"

"Uh, I think so."

"We'll be fine, Sarge," Glenn grinned, "of course, a good, juicy steak would be better."

"Some other time," Parker smiled.

"Shot a gook last night. He's over there," Glenn motioned with his head.

"Keep up the good work. I'll send the graves registration team over to pick up the body," Parker nodded.

An hour later, Lieutenant Brewster appeared at the top of the ridge. He spotted Sergeant Parker and, crouching, moved toward him. Parker saw him coming and stood.

"All's well, Lieutenant," Parker reported, "we only lost one man. PFC Al Horwood. Good man. He was wounded and had to be evacuated."

Brewster nodded and glanced anxiously toward the enemy held area. He swallowed and moistened his lips. "The Colonel thinks we might stay here for a few nights," he offered, "so I guess the men will need some rations."

"That would help, Lieutenant," Parker nodded, "and a resupply of ammunition might help some."

"Ammunition? Did they get into a firefight?"

"How do you think Horwood got wounded?"

"Well, I thought --."

"Too bad you weren't here, sir," Parker noted, "it was a good fight. Martin got a couple of them. I guess it was quiet

45

down in the command post."

"Uh, yes, it was. I wasn't there, however. I was -- I'll see to the resupply, Sergeant."

"Thank you, sir."

Brewster turned away and hurried back to the cover of the scrub brush before standing erect. He glanced back at Parker, then along the line. With a deep breath, he turned and went down the slope.

Parker watched him go, his face expressionless. He thought he saw a touch of wistfulness when the Lieutenant looked along the line, as if Brewster really wanted to be a part of the platoon. Perhaps the man could overcome his touch of cowardice in time.

The rest of the day was uneventful. Occasionally, a North Korean sniper would fire a round or two toward the line. Fire discipline among the Marines, by now, was such that only a few would fire back blindly out of frustration. No one was hit by the fire.

Ammunition and rations were brought up by later afternoon. Lieutenant Brewster, however, did not show his face on the ridge. At dusk, Parker moved along the line. He clearly was shifting the positions of the men. "Move into this other foxhole," he directed when he paused at Glenn and Gary's hole.

"Why, Sarge?" Gary questioned, "we just got this one broken in."

"Because after last night, they know where you are," Parker explained, "we have a surplus of holes, so move. Chances are they've been mapping our positions all day and they won't be able to see you move now."

"Oh."

"Makes sense," Glenn agreed. His eyes searched Parker's face. "Is the Lieutenant coming back?"

"Just take care of yourself and Gary, Martin," Parker growled, "don't worry about the Lieutenant. That's my job."

Glenn simply nodded. It was evident Parker was irritated by the question and by the actions of Lieutenant Brewster. His absence placed a greater responsibility on Parker's shoulders.

About midnight, flares again brightened the already moonlit slope. Bugles could be heard blaring from the North. Then an artillery barrage slammed into the hillside. Only a few shells hit close to the foxholes and, again, most of them fell short.

The men hunkered down as deep as possible in their foxholes. They knew only a direct hit or really close near miss could harm them if they stayed low.

His back pressed against Glenn's, Gary closed his eyes. He recalled the first time he had heard the sounds of explosions and witnessed the destructive power of dynamite. It was when his Dad and a neighbor were clearing some land and had to remove some huge stumps. Neither the team of horses nor the tractor could budge them. So his Dad got some dynamite.

At the time, the red, round sticks merely looked like large firecrackers. He had often played with firecrackers, placing them in the ground around his toy lead soldiers and toy tanks and trucks. It was great fun to play war and blow up his toys. Me even made believe he was an engineer and used firecrackers to blast out roadways and hillsides.

"Gee, Dad," he said, "those are just big firecrackers!"

"Much more than that, son."

"Y'mean they'll really blow those stumps out?"

"Depends on how many we use. They can make a pretty big hole. We'll probably just use enough to loosen the stumps."

"But they're so small!"

"Yeah, sure. You get back now, son."

"Do I hafta?"

"We'll all get back once I light the fuse. So you go on back aways."

I didn't believe him at first, Gary mused as dirt and rocks fell on him from a close hit. But when the dynamite exploded -- wow! The stump was still there, but it had been loosened. The hole was much bigger than I thought it would be. And the smoke -- it smelled a lot like it does now.

He felt the ground shudder again. Wonder if we should move. That last one was really close. He felt Glenn move and twisted his head.

"You okay, Glenn?"

"I'm okay," Glenn grunted.

"That last one was close!"

"Hit our old foxhole -- or close to it."

"It did?"

"Yeah. We'd be dead now if we had stayed there."

"Damn! Sure glad we got Parker with us."

"Right. Be quiet now. The ground troops will be sneaking in once the artillery lifts," Glenn predicted.

"Do you hear trucks -- or tanks -- up North?" Gary asked.

"Hear something," Glenn nodded, "just remember what Sarge said. They can't swim the river."

Both men fell silent, their senses straining to see or hear or even feel the presence of the enemy. The darkness seemed to close in around them. In such a situation, the imagination goes wild. One could almost construct a bogeyman next to the foxhole ready to cut one's throat or stab one with a bayonet. The skin tingled with the thought that someone could be near, that eyes were watching from out of the darkness, that hands were reaching out to kill. It was enough to make even a strong person jittery and many men eventually broke under the strain.

The entire slope was now dark and the area was covered by a thick haze of dust. For what seemed like hours, they waited tensely, wondering what peril was lurking only a few feet away. Then, up the line, a rifle shot shattered the silence, followed by a burst of fire! Almost instantly, the entire line erupted in fire! Then, once again, flares burst overhead, bathing the slope in a brilliant glow. These, however, were friendly glares and they revealed a horde of North Koreans starting to climb toward them!

Gary started to aim his rifle when Glenn nudged his arm. Gary twisted his head slightly, irritated by the interruption. Glenn shook his head and nodded to Gary's left. Gary barely moved his head -- there, partially outlined in the shadows, kneeling quietly, apparently waiting for the glow from the flares to subside, were three North Koreans! Their eyes were focused on the foxhole Glenn and Gary had previously occupied. Each of them held a gleaming knife at the ready. As the glow started to fade, they carefully put their rifles down and eased forward, encircling the hole from behind!

When the North Koreans reached the edge of the hole, both men raised their rifles and fired twice. The three men toppled into the foxhole head first.

"Got 'em!" Gary enthused.

"Stay alert," Glenn hissed, "may be more."

A rock clattered noisily down the slope to his right and Glenn twisted around. He saw the man rushing him from about ten yards away and fired instinctively! The man tumbled to the ground about six yards from the foxhole. As he raised up slightly to look at the man, a shot exploded next to his left ear, the report making his ear ring!

"What're y'doin?"

"Another one," Gary gasped, pointing with his rifle.

Glenn caught his breath when he saw the second man. He had been slightly behind the one he shot, hidden from view. He glanced down the slope. "Here come some more!"

Both men began to fire. The entire line erupted and, down the slope, grenades started exploding as the men lobbed them into the mass of the enemy. The sea of North Koreans surged forward despite the toll taken by the grenades and rifle fire.

"We ain't stoppin 'em," Gary gasped, his voice tinged with a hint of panic.

"Keep firin!" Glenn grunted as he threw a grenade into the massed ranks.

The enemy masses seemed to pulsate like a throbbing heart beat. Time after time, they surged ahead, seemingly unstoppable, only to slow and then drop back. After a brief respite, they would charge forward again, shouting and screaming, oblivious to the fire from the Marines. Their shouts were unintelligible and unnerving and the occasional blare of the trumpets was shrill and piercing. But no one had time to even think about the cacophony.

From his foxhole, Harry Schein squeezed off rounds as rapidly as he could. The men on either side of him were firing as fast, also, but he didn't hear their shots. He watched the bullets knock the enemy soldiers to the ground, only to see the fallen replaced by another. As he reloaded his rifle with another clip, he wondered if his ammunition would last.

After what seemed an eternity, the enemy withdrew out of range and Harry sighed with relief. He checked his supply of ammo -- it was adequate. As he settled back into his foxhole, for the first time he felt the ache in his shoulder.

Damn lonely here by myself, he mused. Too bad Horwood got hit. Stupid ass wouldn't stay still. Kept popping up and down, trying to see what was at the bottom of the slope. Guess he was kinda scared of them sneakin up on him. Wonder how the others are doing? He glanced wistfully toward the area where Glenn and Gary were. They couldn't be seen, but he figured they were all right. His thoughts turned to another night when he had been alone.

It was summer and he had gone fishing with his Dad. Somehow, they had become separated -- he found out later he had followed a side stream instead of the main one. When dusk came, he realized something was amiss. His Dad was nowhere to be seen. There was no time to backtrack, as darkness fell rapidly and the bank was too rough to traverse in the dark.

So he found a fairly sheltered spot near the stream and tried to make himself comfortable. Of course, he had no matched to make a fire and was only wearing a light jacket. At first, he wasn't really afraid to be alone, despite the fact that bear and mountain lions and other wild critters roamed the area.

The night turned chilly and it was difficult to stay warm. He wrapped his arms around his chest and wondered what his Dad would think or do. Obviously, his Dad would not panic. They had spent enough time in the woods together that they each trusted the other. So, likely, his Dad would wait until morning and then look for him.

Then he began to hear strange noises. The popping of branches indicated it might be something big! It was also approaching him! He tensed -- the animal let out a blood-curdling cry! It took all his strength and will power to remain still and not jump up and run! The noises continued throughout the night. Once, something definitely had come real close to him. He had both seen its shadow in the moonlight -- it was huge -- and smelled it. After it had gone, the stench lingered.

He must have fallen asleep despite the bone-chilling cold and the animals. For, the next thing he knew, he was being shaken and he could hear his Dad calling his name.

"I'm okay, Dad," He mumbled as he struggled to wake up.

"I ain't your Dad, but I'm glad you're okay," a gruff voice answered.

Harry looked up -- Sergeant Parker was kneeling beside the foxhole. "What're you --."

"You must have fallen asleep," Parker chortled. He gave Harry's shoulder a reassuring squeeze and moved on.

Harry grinned and nodded. He looked around -- the

sky was beginning to lighten up and he could see to the base of the slope. It was littered with enemy dead. He saw one of the men move as if trying to crawl back to his lines. For a long second, he considered shooting the man. Then he merely turned away. It wasn't necessary and the man would likely die soon anyway. A glance to the east told him sunrise was not far away. He twisted around sharply when one of the men nearby cried out!

"Hey! One's still alive!"

Harry opened his mouth to speak -- the man's rifle cracked loudly! He saw Fred, another man in the platoon, staring down the slope.

"Why did you shoot him, Fred?" Harry challenged.

"He's a damned gook, that's why."

"A human being," Harry snorted, "there was no need --."

"What's going on?" Sergeant Parker questioned. He had hurried over when he heard the shot and the two men arguing.

"Fred -- the dumb bastard shot a wounded, helpless gook," Harry explained.

"Who you callin a dumb bastard?"

"Knock it off!" Parker snapped.

"Wasn't no need to shoot him," Harry continued.

"We could have used a prisoner," Parker told Fred, "might have given us some information."

"Never thought of that, Sarge," Fred replied with a shrug, "sorry, Harry."

"It's okay, Fred. Guess I was just tired. I never thought about taking him prisoner, either."

The next two days were much the same. Come midnight, the North Koreans attacked en masse, trying desperately to push the Marines off the ridge. During the daylight hours, they tried to infiltrate the lines or their snipers fired at anything that moved. It was difficult to get any rest and the men soon became quite irritable.

Parker watched them change and smiled knowingly. He had seen it before -- on the beaches and islands during War II. Trained men seemed to rise about the weariness and remain strong, though irritable. Those not so well trained allowed the tedium and the accompanying stress to get under their skin, causing them to act rashly at times. They were the ones who usually became casualties. He knew he had trained these men well.

On the morning of the fourth day, Lieutenant Brewster reappeared. He stood well back in the cover of the scrub brush and scanned the ridge and the area beyond it carefully, as though trying to spot the enemy. Then he moved warily to Sergeant Parker's foxhole. After the two men talked briefly, Lieutenant Brewster ran in a crouched posture back to the cover of the scrub brush and disappeared.

CHAPTER SIX

Shortly before noon, Lieutenant Brewster returned. He again paused at the edge of the undergrowth and carefully scanned the line before crossing the open area to Sergeant Parker's foxhole. Once more, the two men spoke briefly and then Brewster quickly left, repeating his movements as he crossed the open area.

Jim Murphy watched the exchange from his foxhole, his eyes squinting in the sunlight. He nodded to himself. It was clear to him that Brewster was likely a coward. He had seen them in the city -- cops who brag about their exploits and act tough when among their own and then pistol whip a kid when backed up by another cop; new kids who arrogantly boasted of their alleged deeds elsewhere, but refuse to prove their courage; gang members who act tough as long as they have a gun or a knife and their opponent has no weapon. Put them in a corner, unarmed and by themselves, facing a strong opponent and they begin to whimper and cry like a lost puppy. He had no respect for people like that.

It wasn't just fear or terror that made a man act that way. Sometimes it was just misplaced pride or a sense of having to prove their manhood or a desire to be accepted by their peers. Some men simply had to have others think they were tough guys. Then there were men who felt inadequate or felt insecure or who had lost their will to continue unless they could gain the approbation of others. A few were simply so beaten down by circumstances that they lost any self-respect and they just gave up.

His Dad had fought in the Great War and had come home with a few medals and some new friends. One lived in

Lest We Forget

New York and the man convinced Murphy's Dad to move the family there. The man had grandiose plans and hopes for the future in the financial end of the stock market.

For ten years, his Dad worked hard and learned much about the financial business. He advanced nearly to the top and held a great responsibility for the company and his employees. Then the crash of 1929 occurred and he lost everything. He was a proud man and deeply in debt. The experience of being unable to provide for his employees or his family apparently broke his spirit. It was a very difficult time.

Murphy barely remembered moving out of the nice home they had acquired and into a tenement flat. He recalled his Mother having to get work -- menial work -- to put some food on the table. Of course, he was only a child at the time, but he soon learned to borrow a potato, tomato or an apple from the neighborhood fruit stand without getting caught. It was wrong, but it put a bit more food on the table.

He could not forget the nights his Dad came home so disheartened that he would sit in a corner and weep over his failure to get work. There was nothing anyone could do to help him. Then, one night, his Dad didn't come home.

Murphy was devastated until, after a few weeks, he learned his Dad had simply stopped trying and had joined the ranks of the homeless hoboes. Then he felt a sense of utter disdain for his Dad's weakness.

As time passed and he learned more about life and taking on responsibility, he began to understand how such events could affect a man. How the inability to provide for his family could devastate a man's being. He began to wonder if his Dad had failed or if it were something else. Then, when his Mother passed away, it dawned on him that his Dad had simply reached the limits of his ability and had done all he could do.

That was when he wished fervently that he could have helped his Dad more. The feeling of disdain gradually was replaced by a sense of pride, but it was too late to find his Dad and tell him.

He saw Sergeant Parker rise and a wry grin crossed his face. Now there is a real man. I think my Dad would've been a lot like him before --. He nudged Ears as Parker approached.

"Murph," Parker greeted, "you awake, Ears?"

Hank Brown twisted around slightly. "Yeah, I'm awake."

"Good. Lieutenant was just up."

"Saw him, Sarge," Murph grunted.

"We're being pulled out. Be leaving the hill as soon as we're relieved by the Army guys. In case you're wondering, the unit is being split up among the regiments of the First Division."

"The First?" Murphy questioned, "they comin' over here?"

"Already here, I guess. They were getting organized to load up when we left the States. Just needed to get some equipment from the equipment park."

"Yeah, forgot," Murphy nodded, "they landing at Pusan?"

"Don't think so," Parker shrugged, "Lieutenant thought they might have stopped in Japan."

"The brass didn't let us do that," Murphy snorted, "I'd have liked to see what the Japanese broads were like. Some of the guys that had been in Japan after the big war said they were real nice lays. Pretty, too, so they said."

"Well, I guess they needed us more right here."

"Any chance our gang can stay together?" Ears asked, "you know -- us, Glenn and Gary and Harry."

"Don't know, Ears," Parker replied, "we'll have to wait and see."

"Figures they'll break us up," Murphy growled, "get a group of guys who fit together, fight well as a group and like each other, they always break them up."

"You guys go through boot camp together?" Parker

asked

"Yeah. Stayed together ever since, too."

"Well, I'm sorry. Wish I could do something to keep you all together, but -- I do have to tell the others we're being pulled out."

"Right, Sarge," Murphy shrugged.

"You guys will do okay," Parker stated. He squeezed Murphy's shoulder, nodded, then moved on. Murphy let a tight grin cross his face. I like and respect him.

Glenn Martin swallowed when he heard the news. He shot a glance at Gary, then shook his head. "Any chance of us --."

"I don't know, Glenn," Parker sighed, "Murphy asked the same question. Have to wait and see."

"Yeah, I suppose," Glenn agreed, "we thought it might happen. After all, we ain't an organized outfit, at least not officially."

"Right," Parker nodded.

"We made a vow, you know. The five of us. Promised to meet at Rossini's place in San Diego when it's all over. A year later, actually."

"Nice restaurant. Hope you all make it."

"Us too," Glenn sighed, "hey, there's always room for one more. Want to join us?"

"We'll see," Parker smiled, pleased he was asked, "anyway, get ready to move out." His thoughts shifted to Jack Richman -- they were buddies before and during the big war. Like these men, they had promised to meet again after the war. Jack, of course, did not make it. Having to go meet Jack's wife when he got back to the States ad tell her what had happened was the most difficult duty he had ever drawn. Perhaps that was why the Lieutenant --.

"What about the Lieutenant, Sarge?" Glenn was saying.

"What about him?"

"Well, everyone knows he ain't been much use to us

around here. I haven't even seen him up here except when he --."

"Martin, cut the man some slack. He'll come through when he's needed."

"I sure hope so," Glenn noted, "hope I don't end up under him when they split us up."

Parker met Glenn's earnest gaze and nodded imperceptibly. Then he turned away and growled. "Be ready to move out as soon as the relief arrives."

Glenn bit his lip nervously. He knew he was out of line speaking up about the Lieutenant, but he had felt he had to say something. Clearly, Sergeant Parker wasn't too pleased. Maybe the Lieutenant would turn out to be okay. Maybe all he needed was some slack. Then, again, if he really was a coward --.

As he descended the hill after being relieved, Hank Brown glanced at the other men with an odd sense of respect and pride. It was an emotion he had felt only twice before.

He lowered his eyes and stared at the ground. Fortunate to be able to enroll at Alabama, he had made the football team as a freshman. It wasn't a very good team. They lost their first four games by wide margins. Their coach patiently encouraged them even while he increased the intensity of their practices. A few guys couldn't take the heat and the pressure and dropped out. The rest simply tried harder.

They won their fifth game -- a real squeaker against a team they should have rolled over. Even so, it was an exhilarating moment. Then, back into despair as they were shut-out by their next four opponents. There wasn't much team pride left by then. Just a bunch of guys practicing and playing hard to preserve their own dignity.

In their tenth game, something started to click. It didn't show on the scoreboard, but they all sensed it. Even the coach relaxed his drill somewhat. After all, their last game was against the powerhouse of Auburn and they were expected to lose big.

Leading the league, Auburn was unbeaten. They had simply massacred every other team by large scores. Sportswriters were saying they were the best team ever assembled. There was noting to indicate that wasn't true.

Prior to the game, the guys were quiet and pensive. Their coach omitted his usual pre-game exhortation. He simply said it had been a long season and, despite their one and nine record, they had done well and he was proud of them. Hopefully, they could do even better next season when things would be different.

Hank smiled to himself. It would be nice to be able to say we went out and beat Auburn, but we didn't. We did make them fight for the game, almost stopping them on that winning drive. But they won and we ended up one and ten. However, we came out of that game with a sense of pride and respect for each other and our coach. We knew we had accomplished something special. That season, that game, all the many hours that went into it, the sweat and tears and bruises -- it made men out of a bunch of boys.

He looked around at the others. The second time he felt that way was in boot camp. It was when he and the others suddenly realized they had made it through some of the toughest training given to military recruits. They had survived to become real Marines. It was a great feeling.

This was similar, but more intense. He and the others had been baptized into combat. Had joined an elite and exclusive fraternity of fighting men. To be sure, they had only been in one battle which was so insignificant it would never be noted in a newspaper or anyone's history book. Likely would not even become a postscript in some officer's weekly report. Nevertheless, it was a battle -- their first taste of combat -- and they had met the enemy head on and prevailed.

Hank studied the faces of the other men. They seemed older and more mature now. Certainly showed more fatigue than they had earlier. Murphy's eyes reflected more respect for the others than before. Tilton's face was set in a stern expression, but his movements portrayed more confidence than he had shown since embarking. Schein appeared to strut a bit more and moved with a subtle swagger. Glenn wore an anticipative expression -- as if he were ready to enter a football game.

The other men nearby displayed similar expressions. Jenkins, Wilburn, Fonseca, Paul and McNeil -- they all walked with a barely discernible swagger and a confident stride. Strangely, no one attempted to verbalize the new-found confidence. It was a tacit sense that could not be adequately expressed.

Hank pondered the feeling and slowly began to get an inkling of understanding of the aura that had enshrouded the tales told by the veterans of the big war. How does one explain or relate such feelings to those who were uninitiated? How could he explain to someone who had never experienced it how it felt to be shot at or to shoot a fellow human being, even an enemy? What words can you use to describe the olio of horror, fear, exultation and relief? Sure, the enemy was trying to kill him, but that didn't make it any easier to explain nor did it eliminate the emotional aspects. The relief felt over the fact that you survived and the enemy didn't was not enough to overcome the horror of taking a life.

Hank took a deep breath and nodded. He felt more of a kinship with these men now. He knew he -- and they -- could and would hold their own in any future combat situation. They may not always prevail and some of them may not come out alive, but they would fight to the utmost for each other, their country and for the Corps.

Sergeant Parker twisted about and scanned the faces of his men. To be sure, he was proud of them. He noticed the new-found strides, the squaring of the shoulders despite the fatigue, the looks of grim determination and confidence. Even a small, insignificant battle will transform boys into men. He knew, from his own experiences, that they would face greater, more horrific battles. They would see friends fall or be maimed, might taste the fear of being wounded and not knowing how seriously. But they would fight on and would come through. They were now Marines.

He turned to the front and eyed the back of Lieutenant Brewster. The Lieutenant had hidden out somewhere and had not been in the battle. Did that mean he was a coward? Not necessarily, although it was not a good sign. His actions were not what was expected of a Marine officer.

It was obvious Brewster was a cocky asshole. If he survived a few battles, he might become a good officer. That, however, was a mighty big if. First, he would have to get up to the line and participate in the fighting. That would require some guts.

Then, if he was assigned to a group of veterans, he would have to convince those veterans under him that he knew his job in order to avoid being fragged. Veterans do not like officers who are assholes -- especially Second Lieutenants -- and they seldom tolerate them for very long. It was simply a matter of survival. An officer who did not know what he was doing would endanger the entire platoon. The men knew that and they would not put up with it.

Parker sighed. Hopefully, he'd be assigned to a different unit than the Lieutenant. It wasn't like they were passing on a problem, although they were. It merely was a matter of getting out of a bad situation. Then the brass could take care of the Lieutenant and his problem. That was a sentiment Glenn Martin had also expressed. Likely, everyone else felt the same way. It was the best solution they could hope for. Perhaps it was the only solution short of actually ensuring the Lieutenant would not return.

CHAPTER SEVEN

Traditionally, every Marine is a rifleman first and foremost. That is the emphasis of all training. Therefore, with few exceptions, the men in the provisional battalion were assigned tot he rifle battalions of the First Division. There was no real effort to keep friends of squads together.

At the assembly area, the men were given their individual assignments. Then, as the trucks had not arrived to take them back to the ship or to their new units, the men gathered in small groups to wait. Sergeant Parker and the others clustered together.

"I'm going to the First Battalion, Fifth Marines," Hank Brown offered to Sergeant Parker and the other four men, "I've heard it's a good outfit. They aren't too far up the road, so I don't have a long way to go."

"Got a good reputation," Glenn Martin agreed, "me, I'm assigned to the Second Battalion, First Marines. Someone said they're still in Japan. I guess the brass will figure out how to get me to them."

"Both good assignments," Sergeant Parker noted, "used to know a few people in those units."

"Well, give us their names," Glenn suggested, "so we can tell them we know you and get in good with them."

"Chances are they're all gone now. Hell, that was a good five, six years ago."

"Dammit! Oh well, it was a good try, Glenn," Hank shrugged.

"I'm going to join the Second Battalion, Seventh Marines," Murphy stated, "I guess one outfit is as good as any other. But they ain't here yet. Still at sea, I guess."

Sergeant Parker nodded. "You'll do okay with them, Murphy. Just don't brag about your exploits. These guys in the Seventh, if they've been around much, are tough as nails. It's a good outfit."

"Y'think I can't handle them bums?" Murphy challenged, somewhat taken aback.

"You could handle them, Murph," Parker grinned, "but they could also make things miserable for you. Just play it cool for awhile."

"Okay, Sarge," Murphy growled and looked at Parker thoughtfully. "Do y'think I really brag too much?"

"Sometimes."

"C'mon, Sarge!" Glenn laughed, "he's always dreamin up stuff to brag about."

"Ya guys are just jealous," Murphy snorted.

"If anyone cares," Schein interjected, "I'm going to the Third Battalion, First Marines. Like Martin said, they're still in Japan."

"Hey! That's great!" Glenn exclaimed, "at least we'll be in the same regiment."

"Big deal," Harry shrugged, "so am I supposed to rejoice?"

"Gee, Harry -- we're buddies, ain't we?"

"Well, you didn't -- up on the ridge -- oh, hell, I suppose so, Glenn. Come visit me if you get the chance."

"You too," Glenn nodded, "where you going, Gary?"

"First Battalion, Seventh Marines," Gary responded, "same regiment as Murph."

"That's good, Tilton," Murph stated, "we might get to see each other now and then."

"Hope so," Gary grinned, "be nice to have someone I know close by."

"How about you, Sarge?" Glenn asked.

"Third Battalion, Fifth Marines. Like Hank said, just up the road a spell."

"Know anybody there?" Murph inquired.

"Doubt it. They've changed a lot of people around since the war. From what I've heard, a lot of men coming over are drawn from recruitment stations and reserve outfits across the country. Don't think anyone knows how much experience they have. Some, like some of us before we came over, haven't seen any fighting."

"Man, that scares me," Tilton sighed, "y'expect it with a group like ours."

"Yeah," Brown echoed, "they could be even greener than we are. That is frightening."

"What about the Lieutenant?" Murphy questioned, "d'ya know where he's going?"

"Does anyone even know where he is?" Gary laughed, "haven't seen him since we left the ridge. Never saw him up there until all the fighting was over and we were ready to leave. Does anyone even care where he goes?"

"Well," Parker stated softly, "I ain't supposed to say nothin."

"C'mon, Sarge! Y'can tell us." Glenn encouraged.

"Yeah, Sarge," Murphy nodded, "we can be trusted.>"

"The Colonel didn't want me to say nothing."

"He talk to you about the Lieutenant?" Glenn questioned.

"Yeah, and I hate to be pinned down by a Colonel, especially one I know and like and respect. The Colonel and I -- we go way back, even before Iwo. Had to tell him Brewster wasn't up on the ridge with us. Colonel wanted to know why. What could I say?"

"Wish he had asked me," Murph sneered, "I'd have told him the truth -- that Brewster is a damned coward."

"Y'can't say that about a Marine officer," Parker protested, "at least not to another officer. Especially not to a Colonel. I mean, Brewster got his commission."

"Doesn't matter. We all know it's true," Glenn added, "hell, we could see how he acted up on the hill. It was pretty obvious. He's just a real asshole. Was more concerned about his pretty brass bar than about the troops under him. I even wonder how he got his commission."

"Well, he did get it," Parker shrugged, "and he is an officer, so they say."

"So what did Colonel Bowman say about him?" Brown inquired.

"He just said he'd take care of it. Didn't want me to say any more than that."

"Well, thankfully we didn't need the Lieutenant up on the ridge," Gary noted, "besides, we'd rather have you in charge than Brewster."

"Thanks, Tilton," Parker smiled, "thanks for the vote of confidence."

"You know we all feel that way," Glenn added.

"You're a great bunch of guys. Could have used you in the old Corps. Hope y'all make it to Rossini's after the war."

"You know about that?" Murphy exclaimed, astounded.

"Yeah, Glenn told me, I guess."

"Oh. Y'know you're welcome to join us," Murphy continued, "ain't he, guys?"

Everyone nodded agreement.

"Thanks," Parker smiled, "we'll see. Anyway, I guess I can tell you. Brewster is being sent to the G-3 Section of the Eleventh Marines."

"Artillery?" Schein laughed.

"Right. His, uh, attitude probably won't do any harm there. In fact, he might become a good supply officer."

"Probably best for everyone," Glenn commented, "even the Corps."

"Well," Brown noted, "the bastard didn't come by to say good-bye."

"Yeah, well, he's an officer," Schein noted, "didn't really expect him -- you guys won't forget our date, will you?"

"One year after the end of the war," Glenn nodded, "at

Rossini's in San Diego."

"Right," Murphy agreed.

"The one with the most medals buys the first round," Hank Brown laughed.

"And the one with the highest rank buys the second," Gary grinned.

"Sounds good," Murphy nodded.

"You guys set a time for your meeting?" Parker asked.

"Seven P.M." Schein stated.

"Okay. You guys take care. Stop by if you get over to my outfit."

"Will do, Sarge," Glenn nodded. He looked at the others. "Wish we could have stayed together. Don't nobody forget."

"Tenshun!" Parker barked when Colonel Bowman approached.

"At ease, men," Bowman growled. He glanced at the others and nodded, then turned his attention to Sergeant Parker. "Wanted to say good bye, Sergeant, and wish you luck."

"Thank you, sir. Do you know where you'll end up?"

"Yes. I'm going back to Camp Pendleton. A training command. Guess they think I'm good at training recruits and instilling some pride in them. Besides, I'm too old to be fighting out here."

"It's good duty at Camp Pendleton, Colonel," Parker commented.

"I guess." He glanced at the five men. "You men did well on the ridge. Proud of you. You're a bit seasoned now and I know you'll do as well with your new outfits."

"Thank you, sir," Gary responded quickly, speaking for all of them. The others grinned in appreciation of the compliment.

Colonel Bowman nodded and eyed each man carefully. "I suppose you're wondering about Lieutenant Brewster."

"Yes, sir, we are," Glenn answered with a quick glance

at Sergeant Parker, who held his breath.

"Going to the Eleventh. Artillery. He should be able to handle that. Also, with my comments on his fitness report, I don't think you'll ever see him in a line outfit. I hate to do that to a Marine officer, but I think it was necessary."

"Probably a good solution, sir," Parker added quickly before anyone else could speak.

Bowman smiled tightly. "Well, someone, somewhere, saw something good in him. Maybe he had some solid, courageous qualities at that time that will manifest themselves later. I don't know."

Again, he eyed each man thoughtfully. "Good luck, you guys. You each earned it up on that ridge." He saluted them, then turned to Sergeant Parker and extended his hand.

"Sergeant, you take care. You've already expended a few of your nine lives on Iwo and the Corps needs men like you. Stop by when you get back stateside."

"Will do, Colonel," Parker assured, shaking the extended hand.

Bowman nodded and turned, walked away.

"Good officer," Parker commented.

"Looks like the trucks are here," Schein noted, with a wave of his hand toward the gate, "I'll miss you guys."

"Yeah," Brown admonished, "don't take no chances."

"Don't forget the meeting," Glenn reminded. He swallowed the lump in his throat as they walked away.

CHAPTER EIGHT

Sergeant Parker smiled slightly as he scanned the earnest faces of the four men assigned to him. They were standing near the temporary Command Post, about two hundred yards behind the line. The men had been pulled out of the line so he could meet them.

They were all Privates. The one seemed to carry himself with an air of authority. He was tall, fairly husky, his helmet throwing a faint shadow across his stern face. His stance seemed to indicate a bit of aloofness. In fact, the other three looked at him as if they expected him to speak for them. One of the others seemed familiar to Parker -- as if he had seen him before. The other two were typical Marines, their faces clean shaven and a bit dirty from being in the field, their hair short, their weapons held informally. There was little to distinguish them from any other Marines.

"Understand your previous Sergeant was wounded," Parker stated to no one in particular.

"Yeah," the tall one replied, "two days ago."

"Bad?"

"Any wound is bad, ain't it, Sarge?"

"I guess. What's your name?" Parker asked.

"PFC Ron Lofton."

"Well, Lofton, who's been leading the team the last two days?"

"I guess I have," Lofton stated with a shrug and a glance at the others.

The other men nodded wordlessly.

"Apparently, you did a decent job," Parker commended, "I just left a group of new men -- we came in as a provisional unit and happened to be assigned to hold a ridge and give an Army unit a chance for some rest. Down near Changwon."

"Hey! I heard about that! You guys fought off a whole regiment!"

"And you're --."

"PFC Hall -- Dennis Hall."

Parker nodded and turned to the other two men. "Which of you is Worrell?" He looked at the man who seemed familiar to him.

"I am." The man who spoke was of medium build, a bit taller than either Lofton or Hall, but not as husky. He had a quietly confident air about him and met Parker's gaze with an inquiring look.

Parker studied him for a long moment before speaking. "I knew a man named Ogdon Worrell in War II, at Iwo."

Worrell caught his breath, his eyes squinting. "My brother," he stated, his eyes searching Parker's face, "they gave him a Silver Star -- posthumously, of course -- and a Purple Heart. Not much for a life."

"I know," Parker smiled, his voice soft and reassuring, "I got the same medals. Sorry he didn't make it. We all thought he'd at least get a Navy Cross for what he did." He paused and looked at the fourth man.

"I'm Jackson," the man offered, "PFC Aaron Jackson."

"Okay, Jackson." He scanned their faces again. "You guys did all right on your own. Chances are you don't need me, but the brass thought you might, so I'm here. Sorry you didn't get promoted to Sergeant, Lofton. You probably deserve it."

He fell silent and stared at the ground for a moment. "I suppose you want to know about me. I was in the last war, on Iwo and a few other islands. I'm no glory hunter, if you're worried about that. We do what we have to do to survive and complete our mission. There's scuttlebutt that we'll be pulled out and be shipped up North to land somewhere in the enemy's rear. That's what we're trained to do. As far as my authority goes, just do as I say and you'll be fine. Right now, as long as we're here, we have a line to hold."

"That's right, Sarge -- just like you guys held that ridge before," Hall enthused.

"We heard rumors that your Lieutenant there wasn't of much help," Worrell ventured.

"We don't need to talk about that, Worrell."

"Okay, Sarge, I understand."

"Now, you guys want to clue me in on what piece of real estate we have to hold?"

Sergeant Lyons had his nose in a well-worn book and only briefly glanced up at Hank Brown when he approached. He jerked his head toward an adjacent dirt bank and went back to reading. Lyons had a squarish face and short, black hair. He was of medium build, shorter than Hank and appeared muscular and stocky. Hank shrugged and eased his pack to the ground, held his rifle. He squatted beside his pack and glanced at the title of the book. 'Lee's Lieutenants.' A faint grin spread across his face. It was heavy reading, but, perhaps, this guy was a southerner. That might prove to be interesting.

He took a deep breath and glanced around the shell-pocked area. A few officers and men were huddled over a map spread out on a makeshift table about thirty yards away. Another twenty years beyond stood a sentry with a Thompson submachine gun. In the other direction, three men were lying in the shade of a gnarled tree. A few cans of C-rations littered the ground around them. Further on stood another sentry, the one who had questioned him about his purpose and unit and had directed him to Sergeant Lyons.

"Sorry," Lyons offered, putting the book aside and looking at Hank, "wanted to finish the chapter. Don't get to read too much up here."

"No problem," Hank smiled, "heavy stuff."

"Not too bad. Ever read it?"

"Started a few years ago. Never finished it. I'm Hank Brown, the new guy."

"Pleased to have you aboard, Hank. Mike Lyons. Did I detect an accent?"

"From Alabama," Hank replied.

"Really? Virginia, for me. Home of Robert E. Lee."

"He was a good defensive General," Hank shrugged, "but I liked Longstreet better."

"Longstreet was okay," Lyons conceded.

"Might have won the war if Lee had listened to him at Gettysburg."

"Could be. College?"

"Year plus at Alabama."

"Virginia Tech. Two years," Lyons noted.

"We played Tech my first year -- they clobbered us. We weren't very good. One and ten."

"Football?"

"Yeah."

"Never went out for sports in college," Lyons admitted, "but played some football in high school." He paused and studied Hank's face for a moment. "Hear you guys got into a scrap before they sent you here."

"We did," Hank nodded, "four nights -- they usually attacked us at night. We held the ridge for four days and nights. Gave some Army men a chance to get some rest."

"The experience changes a man," Lyons breathed softly.

"Sure does."

"Well," Lyons brightened, "I got a nice bunch of guys under me. Sure you'll like them. They're not southerners, however. All Yankees. Damn Northern Yankees."

Hank laughed. "That mean I'll have to fight the war again?"

"No, not really. Let's see -- Gilbert is from Maine. A proper New Englander, lots of money in his family. Nice guy, though you wonder why he's in the Corps. He's the brown haired one on the right over there. Schultz, the blond, in the center -- he's of German stock out of Pennsylvania. Hard working and as honest as they come. Beck, the other brown haired one of the left, is from Arizona -- Flagstaff, I think. Good man to have around. I swear he can hear a fly land twenty feet away." He paused and his eyes shifted to Hank's ears. "I suppose you got a nickname already."

"Yeah. They call me Ears," Hank shrugged.

"Do you mind it? I mean, does it make you sore when anyone uses it?"

"No, I'm used to it. DI in boot camp pinned it on me and it kinda stuck. You know how that goes."

"Okay," Lyons smiled, "pleased to have you aboard. We didn't get much sleep last night, so they're sacked out over there. When they wake up, I'll introduce you. Some say we're gonna be pulled out soon for something up the coast."

"I've heard that, too. Know where it might be?"

"Don't have a clue. They'll tell us soon enough."

Sergeant John W. Kimball eyed Glenn Martin skeptically. "You say you've been in combat?"

"Right. We held a ridge. To give Army guys a break."

"How long did you hold it?"

"Four days and nights. They attacked every night."

"Okay. You've done more than I have."

Glenn nodded and raised his eyebrows a bit at the statement. Kimball was a large, husky man. His hair had a reddish tint and his eyes a piercing gaze. He moved easily for a large man. Glenn wondered how he ever fit into one of the bunks.

"I got into the Corps in forty-five," Kimball explained, "just got out of boot camp when they dropped the bomb. That damn Truman could have waited until I got some combat experience. Didn't vote for him in '48, either. The bastard cost me a chance to get into the war."

Glenn grinned sympathetically. "That's too bad, Sarge."

"Ended up -- after more training -- in a recruitment office in Chillicothe, Ohio. That's why I got these stripes so soon. They -- the brass -- wanted only officers and NCO's our recruiting. Even sent me to a couple of places so they could give me some ribbons to wear to impress the new recruits. Don't know why I'm griping so damn much. Actually, it worked out great for me. The pay was better and I really liked the duty. I just wanted to get into combat, you know? Then, when they called me back -- you know, Martin, you forget the fine points of military life when you're in a small office like that. Shit, I walked right by a Colonel without saluting my first day at Pendleton. He chewed me out royally, he did. Thought I might lose a stripe or two."

Glenn laughed, the act drawing an appreciative glance from Kimball.

"Anyway, the rest of our group is on deck gettin fresh air. You'll meet them for mess call. Corporal DeWitt is a cowboy from Montana. Rode the bulls in the rodeo before he enlisted, I guess. Said there wasn't much money in it and the bumps and bruises were too much for him. He's kind of a small man, I guess you could say. Good fighter, though."

"Used to do a lot of horseback riding, but not in the rodeo."

"Well, maybe you'n him will get along right well. Granger, he's our BAR (Browning Automatic Rifle) man. Kinda strange. Loves that rifle so much he won't let no one close to it. I think he's a bit psycho, myself. But he's a good man to have around in a fight. Tough as nails, short and stocky, hard-headed."

"That's good to know."

Kimball nodded. "Masters, the fifth man, is greener than either of us. He's only been out of boot camp for six or seven weeks. Real friendly guy -- plays a good game of poker, too. I'd be real careful playin with him. Bluffs you outa your socks. Has green eyes, kinda strange for a man, but I've never learned to read them. Black hair and green eyes -- odd combination. I'm sure you'll like him. Any questions?"

"Know anything about where we're going?" Glenn asked.

"Not yet. There's word about a landing up North somewhere. All I know now."

"We heard that, too. Is MacArthur going to lead us?"

"Dugout Doug? I suppose so. He's really a good General, you know. Suppose Truman ain't too happy with him and if Truman ain't happy with him, I love the guy. Truman is an ass, anyway. All democrats are."

"I wouldn't know," Glenn admitted, "not old enough to vote so I don't pay too much attention to politics."

Kimball snorted. "Strange, ain't it? Not old enough to vote or buy a drink, yet old enough to fight and maybe die for your country. Seems kinda wrong somehow."

"Know what you mean."

"Well, Martin, y'can buy beer here, y'know. But iff'n y'want somethin stronger, I snuck some good booze in when we had shore leave. Iff'n y'want a snort, just let me know."

"I'll do that, Sarge. Hell, used to drink at home some. You know -- beer, wine and what not."

"Let me tell ya, boy!" Kimball exclaimed, rolling his eyes, "this crap is a helluva lot stronger than that! A good snort of this piss will knock your damn head off! Take two snorts and you'll be in sick bay for a week!"

Glenn laughed. He was beginning to like Kimball a lot. At least, the man was no stuffed shirt. Maybe being separated from the others wouldn't be as bad as he thought.

"Being last man in, Martin, you get the lower bunk," Kimball added, "tough lot, especially if anyone above you gets the heaves. So far, no one in this group has. It's a bit crowded down there. Hope you don't mind enclosed spaces."

"It's okay, Sarge." Glenn looked askance at the tiny space between the lower and next higher bunk. There wasn't much room. At least, he thought, it wouldn't be for very long. Word was they would be sailing in a day or two.

Harry Schein scowled when he saw Sergeant Jack Brady. The man's face told everyone who was at all discerning that he was a bitter man. He was of medium build, about six feet tall, with dark hair. The name Brady gave a hint of his Irish background.

"So you're Harry Schein," Brady sneered, "well, glad to have you aboard, I guess."

"Thanks, Sarge."

"Y'get any good experience in that rag-tag outfit y'was with?"

"Yeah, I guess. We got into combat."

"Really? S'pose that makes y'thing ya is somethin special."

"No," Harry shrugged, "we'll all be there before this is over."

"Right and it really pisses me off, too."

"Why is that, Sarge?" Harry questioned.

"Let me tell y'somethin, Schein. I was in on the last action of War II -- saw enough to make me barf. Then they tell me I gotta stay in the reserves -- not enough points to be discharged. Points? Who in the hell said anythin about points? Anyhow, six years they hold me to. Six damn years."

"I guess a lot of men had to go into the reserves."

"Well, it sure fucked me up. Got a good job, got married and had a kid. Even bought a house. Was doin real good, y'know. Then this thing blows up. Another freakin was! N'me with only a bit over a year t'go. They called me back, they did. Said they needed trained men. My ass."

He paused, his lips curling in disdain. "Then the stick me with the likes of you guys -- guys straight outa boot camp who don't know shit about fightin a war."

Harry could only shake his head. What have I gotten

into? This guy is dangerous! Hell, he could get all of us killed!

"Anyway, s'pose y'wanta know who the other guys is," Brady snorted.

"Uh, yeah," Harry replied, anxious to change the subject.

"Mason is my BAR man. Y'do know what a BAR is, don't ya?"

"I know."

"I'm surprised," Brady spat sarcastically, "Mason's okay, I guess -- good shot. He's the shortest guy in team. Well, maybe not now that you're here. Edwards -- he's in sick bay now, but you'll meet him in a day or two. Got some kinda crud, probably from those Jap broads he picked up. All in all, he's okay. Thinks he's real handsome, but he ain't. Nugent's a tall, husky guy -- played basketball for his high school -- in Indiana, I think. Mason's from Texas and Edwards is from New Mexico. Forgot to mention that. Where you from?"

"Michigan."

"Oh. Well, Nugent -- was I talkin about Nugent?"

"Yeah."

"Right. He's a pleasant fellow, I s'pose. I actually think he's kinda dumb. Well, that's it. Any questions?"

"Not really. What's my role?"

"Do what I tell y'do do," Brady snarled, "and do it fast. Don't give a rat's ass about your experience up on that there ridge. Here, you'll do things my way. Unnerstood?"

"Gotcha, Sarge."

Sergeant Terry Greenberg was a small man, wiry, with an unruly mop of dark hair. His features branded him as a Jewish believer. He seemed a nervous type, always fidgeting with something -- a button, a pencil, his glasses. Because of that, he certainly did not exude confidence. He eyed Gary Tilton questioningly.

"You a Christian?" Greenberg blurted.

"Uh, yeah," Gary nodded, "does it matter?"

"Not to me. I am Jewish, you know."

"I kinda thought so, but wasn't certain. Don't make no difference to me."

"Good!" Greenberg grinned with relief, "some guys don't like Jews -- especially in positions of authority. Tobin -- you'll meet him later -- he's also a Jew. But I don't play no favorites! That ain't right."

"Fair enough," Gary agreed.

"Tobin's a good man. Smart -- started college. You go to college?"

"For awhile. Quit to join the Corps."

"Oh. I ain't had much education, 'cept in the Corps. Learn't my job here well enough, so they say."

"That's good to hear," Gary shrugged, wondering where all this was leading, "a formal education isn't always what it's cracked up to be."

"Franklin, now, he's also a high school dropout," Greenberg continued, ignoring Gary's comment, "but a good man with a knife. You get much training in close combat?"

"A little."

"Too bad. You'll learn. Don't get into a fight with Franklin. He'll pull a knife and slash ya. Hot tempered. From Chicago, I think. Withrow, now -- he's the other guy, y'know -- meek as a lamb, so to speak. About as ignorant, too. Poor bastard got a Dear John letter from his gal just before we sailed. Was afraid he'd jump ship. He's still trying to get over it. All this for one gal -- don't make no sense at all."

"Guess some men get more upset than others," Gary grinned.

"No woman is worth screwin yourself up over," Greenberg grunted, "heard y'saw some fighting afore y'was transferred."

"About four days. They attacked every night."

"Good fighters?"

"Well, very persistent."

"Persistent?"

"Kept coming," Gary explained, "masses of them. Shoot one and another takes his place."

"Oh. Well, we should do okay against them, I guess. Know anything about where we'll be landing?"

Gary shook his head. "Thought you might know."

"Don't have a clue. Us peons is always the last to hear." He paused, glanced at Gary's gear. "C'mon, I'll help you get settled in. Ain't much space on this here ship, but we'll manage for a few more days."

"Thanks," Gary smiled. He was beginning to like Greenberg.

Jim Murphy squinted in an effort to see in the dim light. He scanned the area, looked at the four men sitting or lying on their bunks in the troop area of the ship. The air was hot and a bit smoky. Murphy's eyes narrowed as he looked at their faces and he swallowed apprehensively, wondered what he was getting into.

"Lieutenant said I'd find Sergeant Roletto here."

One of the men looked up. "I'm Roletto."

"Good," Murphy grunted. He moved closer to get a better look at the man.

Sergeant Curt Roletto was definitely of Italian descent and he looked tough. His eyes were hard and his gaze penetrating. A long scar marked his right cheek. He would have fit in with any of the Italian gang members in New York's Little Italy. Roletto was cleaning a 45 automatic pistol.

"You must be the new guy. What's the name -- Murphy?"

"Yeah, I'm Murphy."

"Okay. About time you got aboard. Listen up, you guys. This is the new man, named Murphy. That guy there is Corporal Robb Martinez."

Corporal Robb Martinez was clearly Hispanic. He was

of small build, but wiry. He looked up briefly from the M-1 rifle he was inspecting, smiled a short greeting, then returned to his task.

"Guy next to him is Mark Banks," Roletto continued.

PFC Mark Banks, on the other hand, looked like a poster boy for the Corps. Handsome, yet rugged looking, he epitomized the military stereotype. Short blond hair, squarish face, high cheekbones and a firm mouth. Yet, the easy grin he threw in Murphy's direction indicated he would get along with anyone.

"Over here," Roletto stated with a nod of his head, "is Walter Thornquist."

"Walter T. Thornquist," Walter snapped.

"Yeah, sure, Walt. Sorry," Roletto grunted.

Murphy nodded.

PFC Walter T. Thornquist obviously came from a wealthy family. His mannerisms, some of them quite effeminate in the way he sat and moved his head and arms, spoke of a soft life of indulgence. He seemed out of place in Marine dungarees and merely gave Murphy a disinterested snort after specifying his correct name.

Roletto glanced around. "You guys go get some fresh air while I chat with Murphy."

"Okay, Sarge," Martinez grunted, "come on, you boots. Sarge wants to speak frankly to the new guy."

Roletto waited until the three had left the area, then nodded to Murphy to sit on an adjacent bunk. "How long in the Corps?" he demanded.

"Almost a year," Murphy replied, focusing his attention on Roletto.

"Boot, huh?"

"Been in combat."

"Oh? Where?"

"Korea. Four, five days we held a ridge near Chang-won that was under attack."

"Never heard of it."

Murphy shrugged. "That's too damn bad."

Roletto looked up sharply. His steady gaze seemed to be sizing up Murphy. Then he nodded. "Okay, Murphy. Tough guy, huh? Shoot any?"

"Got a few. Quite a few."

"Good."

"You got any combat experience, Sarge?"

Roletto nodded. "I got into the fighting at Okinawa long enough to win the Bronze Star and a Purple Heart. Satisfied?"

"Think so," Murphy stated.

"Good. Rest of the guys is greener than you, but they're tough. I trained 'em."

"I see," Murphy nodded, his thoughts on Thornquist.

Roletto grinned. "Thornquist. He may look and act like a wimp, but don't underestimate him, Murphy. Boxing champ of his college league before he enlisted. A few people who tangled with him have come to regret it. He's tough."

"Impressive."

"I guess. With his upbringing, they shoulda sent him to OCS -- that's Officer Candidate School, y'know. Don't know why they didn't -- well, that ain't exactly true. Man ain't assertive enough and don't show no confidence in himself. I think his upbringing wore off all the rough edges. He's a good Private, though. Be a good man if he got some confidence."

"The rest?" Murphy shrugged.

"Yeah. Suppose you oughta know. Martinez is the best shot on the team. He does some sniping. Banks, he's a good gofer. Not too bright, but very likeable. At least he looks like a Marine. So, having an Irish, spud-growin street bum like you rounds us out quite good."

Murphy opened his mouth to protest, then chuckled. "Fair enough. You from New York, too?"

"Yeah, I been there. Little Italy is a nice place to be from."

"Gotcha. Any idea what's up?"

"They won't tell us for awhile. Some have said we're going to land somewhere behind their lines -- probably a hundred miles of so up the coast. But who knows what Dugout Doug is up to."

"Dugout Doug?"

"MacArthur."

"Oh. Okay, from War Two."

"Right."

"Where do I sack out?"

"Show you. Then you can tell me about your fight on the ridge. Okay?"

"Be glad to, Sarge."

CHAPTER NINE

Security was so lax at GHQ in Japan that the word filtered down through the ranks long before any official destinations were issued. Everyone from the rank of General to that of Private knew that MacArthur was going to invade behind the lines to cut off the North Korean supply line. They also knew he was planning to go in at Inchon and that the First Marine Division was going to lead the invasion. To hell with such facts that Inchon was decidedly the worst possible place to mount an amphibious landing, with its extreme tides and large, extended mud flats, not to mention the sixteen foot high seawalls in the landing area. Also to be glossed over was the fact the initial landing group would be on its own for at least twelve hours or until the next high tide, that the North Koreans held Kimpo Airfield a few miles inland and might have a superior air capability. Then there was the fact that the enemy probably had a large force available in Seoul.

The thinking at GHQ was simply this: MacArthur wants to land at Inchon and, by god, that's where the Marines are going to land. It didn't matter what the enemy had available nor did it matter what the logistics were. That was all irrelevant to the General's staff.

Still on the line around Pusan, the 5th Marines were chosen to land first and take the Island of Wolmi-Do. The success of this venture determined not only the strategy, but the tactics of the entire operation. The island dominated the harbor and its approaches and effective resistance from it could disrupt everything. It was connected to the mainland by a narrow causeway. If Wolmi-Do could not be taken and held, the operation was doomed to fail.

The Third Battalion, 5th Marines was selected to lead the landing. They were to advance quickly to the causeway and hold it. Part of their force would secure the rest of the island. Other elements of the 5th would land just to the north of Wolmi-Do and were to circle around on the mainland to cut-off any reinforcements that might come form Seoul or Inchon proper. This, too was a critical part of the invasion plans.

Once Wolmi-Do was secured, the 1st Marines would land to the south of Wolmi-Do, at Won-Do. They were to swing northward, enter the city of Inchon and secure that area while the 5th Marines drove toward Kimpo Airfield.

The operation itself was well-planned by the brass at GHQ. The main problems were simple. There was no place to practice and less time in which to practice. Improvised ladders were to be used to mount the seawalls, but no one knew if they would work. In addition, the 5th Marines were still manning positions in the Pusan perimeter and would have to be withdrawn, board ships, and be resupplied to get ready for the landing. That posed other problems such as who would replace them in the perimeter.

The other troops of the First Marine Division, for the most part, had been aboard ship for nearly two weeks. Whether or not they were in physical condition to mount a large amphibious operation was never considered. The assumption was that the Marines are always ready to fight anywhere.

Sergeant Parker could tell Lieutenant Bradford was leery of the idea of landing at Wolmi-Do. He didn't know much about the Lieutenant, having only met him once when he was transferred in. From what he could discern, Bradford was fairly sharp and knew his business. The fact he sported a silver bar instead of the gold bar of a Second Lieutenant said something about the man.

"What do you think, Sergeant?" Bradford asked."

"Tough job, sir."

"Yeah, I guess." Bradford paused, his eyes meeting Parker's for a long moment. "I'm sorry, Parker, but you're my most experienced Sergeant. Hell, the other guys are babes in the woods. I don't even know how a couple of them came by their stripes."

"Thank you, Sir."

"Don't thank me yet, Parker," Bradford snorted, "surely you know I've got to give you and your men the task of leading us ashore. I hate like hell to do it, but I have no choice. Those other asses would --."

He looked away, the frustration evident in his face. "Parker, you know that, if we -- you -- meet determined resistance, you're expendable -- we're expendable. The rest of those damn asses on the ships can just turn around and sail back to Japan. We're going to be on that island for twelve hours with only what we carry in, come whatever. If we run into a damn division, we've got to fight it -- with our bare hands."

Parker nodded. "It looks bad, sir. What are the estimates of the enemy strength?"

"From what the aviators say, there's some caves to the north and a lot of machine gun emplacements along the higher ground near the beach. Those have all been shelled or bombed. What we don't know is how well fortified the place is. You know, hidden pill boxes, bunkers, the like. We won't know until we land."

"It can probably be done, sir. Surely, it can't be as bad as some of the islands in War Two."

Bradford nodded and smiled. "That's what I liked about you the first day I met you. You have such a positive attitude. I just feel like a damned heel giving you this assignment. Hell, Parker, you should be back in Pendleton teaching youngsters how to fight instead of out here. You're too valuable to risk and, yet, I have to risk you. I don't like it."

"It's my job, sir. If you think I -- my men and I can do it, then we'll do our best. Would you mind explaining exactly what you want my squad to do, sir?"

"Not at all, Sergeant."

Thirty minutes later, Parker gathered his men around him. They were about fifty yards behind the line, in a somewhat sheltered hollow. Parker scanned their faces, noted their concern. Clearly, they knew something was up.

"Okay," Parker said, "we're going in at Inchon."

"Oh hell!" Lofton snorted, "we knew that."

"Yeah," Worrell added, "we thought we might be losing you."

"That was what worried me, too," Hall affirmed, drawing an agreeing nod from Jackson.

"I'm not going anywhere," Parker grinned, "but thanks for the vote of confidence. It's our assignment I want to talk about."

"I suppose we're going to lead the battalion in," Worrell joked, drawing nervous laughs from the others.

"You said it," Parker confirmed, "we are the point for the battalion."

"Oh shit!" Worrell exclaimed.

"Why us?" Lofton questioned.

"We're the most experienced -- or, rather, the Lieutenant thinks I'm the most experienced Sergeant," Parker acknowledged, "and he thinks we can do the job. Want to withdraw the vote of confidence?"

"Hell no!" Worrell snapped, "but they're fuckin us. Just like they did my brother when they -- oh shit. I guess it's okay."

"What do you think, Sarge?" Lofton speculated, "We go in first and we hit something big, they gonna get us off that island?"

"I doubt it," Parker conceded, "at least not for twelve hours. We'll be stuck there that long unless the enemy pushes us off first."

"Shit! The rest of them pogies is gonna be on the damn boat and we're gonna be fightin who knows what!"

"That's possible, Lofton," Parker nodded with a slight smile

"Ain't nothin we can do about it, I suppose," Lofton continued.

"I guess not," Parker sighed.

"Well, I suppose we can do it," Lofton sighed, "what do you guys think?"

"Sure we can," Worrell shrugged with an amused grin.

Hall and Jackson both nodded. They had been listening with frowns on their faces, realizing Lofton was talking himself into accepting the fact.

"Okay, here's the plan," Parker stated, leaning forward seriously, "we land and push inland once we get over those seawalls. We are to cross the island to the causeway and hold it, keep any reinforcements from coming across or any enemy on the island from reaching the mainland. The rest of the regiment is landing here -- called Red Beach. They'll circle the landward side and seal off the causeway from that side."

"Anyone else landing?" Jackson questioned.

"The First Regiment -- just south of Won Do -- on Blue Beach. They'll drive into Inchon proper from there."

"That's Chesty Puller's command, ain't it?" Worrell asked.

"Yeah. I know Chesty and he'll do right by us," Parker nodded.

"Well," Lofton sighed, "should be interesting."

Hank Brown fixed Lyons with a puzzled stare. The Sergeant was explaining their role in the Inchon landing and he was no longer the book-reading southerner. His attitude was cold, authoritative and knowledgeable.

"Lieutenant Pitney said we're going in on Red Beach -- here," he stated, pointing at the map, "and the Third

Battalion is going into Wolmi-Do. Our job is to circle to our right and secure the landward end of the causeway. They say there's a high seawall we'll have to scale. Regiment told the Lieutenant they'll provide some ladders for us. We'll see."

"What kind of opposition do they expect us to meet?" Beck questioned.

"No one really knows."

"Ain't they been flyin over the area every day?" Gilbert asked, "they must have seen somethin."

"All they -- the reports -- all they say is there's lots of emplacements and defensive positions in our sector. There may be something in them and there may not. Also some caves. They think most of the emplacements are empty."

"They don't seem to know much," Schultz snorted, "hell, I wouldn't trust them bastards. They ain't goin in -- we are. Chances are, they didn't get low enough to see if anyone was in them emplacements."

"Could be," Lyons shrugged, "what do you think, Ears?"

Hank smiled. It hadn't taken the team long to pick up on his nickname. He had found the whole team to be real nice guys. Even Gilbert, with his moneyed upbringing, was a right guy and not afraid of work. "Don't see that we have much say so in any of it, Sarge. We'll be goin in with the rest of the regiment, won't we?"

"That's right and there's security in numbers."

"Numbers ain't gonna help us none," Beck snorted, "we're almost landin in the city proper."

"It'll go fine," Lyons assured, ignoring Beck's comments. "Gilbert -- you haven't commented. Any ideas?"

"I'm not worried, Sarge," Gilbert stated, "we've been in worse situations since this war began."

"Yeah, we have," Lyons acknowledged, "only problem I see is gettin over that seawall. Even with ladders, we ain't gonna get more than one or two, maybe three outa the boat at one time. Ain't no way to make a landin."

"What's our objective -- other than gettin ashore and securin the causeway?" Brown inquired.

"Observation Hill. Cemetery Hill will be on our left as we advance -- and the brewery will be in front of us. We should be okay. Beyond the brewery, well, no one really knows what to expect."

"Cemetery Hill?" Gilbert repeated, "helluva place to go through. Suppose we could stop at the brewery and have a drink or two."

Everyone laughed at the comment.

"You superstitious about Cemetery Hill, Gilbert?" Brown grinned.

"No, just thirsty. I like the idea of taking the brewery."

As Lieutenant Gilford finished his presentation, Sergeant Kimball glanced at his men. They seemed to be listening carefully, especially Granger. Martin was clearly a bit apprehensive, perhaps distrustful of Lieutenants following his experiences with his last officer.

"That's it," Lieutenant Gilford shrugged, "our landing is on Blue Beach. By the time we hit it, the 5th will likely have secured Wolmi-Do. Any questions?" He scanned the faces of the men in his platoon. "Okay. You all know what you have to do. You Sergeants get your men organized."

Sergeant Kimball drew his men aside and waited until the officers and other men had drifted away. Then he shook his head in disgust. "Y'gotta believe these guys who plan this stuff is crazy! They call me back from a recruiting office and then tell me I'm goin t'lead you guys into battle. They gotta be crazy!"

"It's okay, Sarge," Martin grinned, a bit more relaxed now, "piece of cake. All we gotta do is leap over a fifteen-foot wall, engage an enemy who is probably numerically superior and keep moving inland. Nothin to it."

"Just get me on top first," Granger snorted, "I'll take care of the enemy with my BAR."

"Sure," Kimball rolled his eyes, "we'll put you on top, Granger. You can take on the whole fucking North Korean Army."

"The engineers ought to be able to figure out something," Martin noted, "they're s'posed to be smart."

"Sure. Four years of education or more and they can't even design a proper piss pot," Kimball laughed.

"Hey! Martin exclaimed, "talkin about piss -- maybe you could break loose with a couple swigs each of that damn horse piss you got hidden away, Sarge! Then we wouldn't care about that damn seawall or the enemy."

"Yeah," Kimball snorted, "you wouldn't care at all. You'd all be dead."

"Best idea I've heard so far," DeWitt offered.

Harry Schein frowned when Captain Brinton, the Company Commander, walked before the assembly. He was accompanied by their platoon leader, Lieutenant Odell. Schein glanced at Sergeant Brady and saw the scowl on his face.

"Listen up!" Brinton commanded, "Y'all know about the Inchon landing, I'm sure. Word gets out before we even make the decision."

There was a ripple of nervous laughter within the company. Brinton grinned and nodded.

"Okay. Straight scoop. Our company will lead the 3rd Battalion in to Blue Beach. That's just south of Won-Do. Lieutenant Odell's platoon will lead the company ashore. There's supposed to be an exit from the landing area through the seawall. Hopefully, we can secure it and use it rather than having to scale the fifteen foot wall. You'll be told the landing date soon. Questions?"

He waited and scanned the ranks. No one spoke. "Very well," he stated, with a glance at the platoon leaders, "your platoon leaders will meet with you immediately to provide more details. Good luck, men."

"Tenshun!"

Brinton turned and strode away.

"At ease," Lieutenant Odell commanded, "break up by platoons and assemble around your platoon leaders. Dismissed."

Harry eased closer to Lieutenant Odell, glanced at Brady, then at Nugent, Edwards and Mason. In the short time he had been with the squad, he had learned that Nugent wasn't as dumb as Brady assumed he was and that all Mason had was an innocuous skin rash on his arm. He had also come to believe that Brady, as bitter as he was, was a good Marine and quite knowledgeable.

"Okay," Lieutenant Odell stated, "got the scoop for y'all. It ain't all roses and what-not. Brady's squad will lead the way. His squad will secure the exit as quickly as possible. The rest of us will pass by them and move inland to counter any resistance. Any questions so far?"

"If the exit can't be secured --."

"We'll secure the damn exit!" Brady snarled.

"If it cant be, for some reason," the man continued, ignoring Brady's comment, "how do we get over the seawall?"

"I told ya, we'll --."

"Can it, Brady!" Odell snapped, "it's a good question. I understand the engineers will have ladders available as well as nets."

"Nets?" Nugent asked.

"Yes, landing nets," Odell replied. He looked puzzled as he read their faces, then grinned. "Sorry. Forgot some of you are boots -- most of you, in fact. The engineers plan to use the cargo nets to help us scale the sea wall. We usually use them to board the landing boats. Okay?"

"Oh, like in the John Wayne movies," Nugent nodded.

"Yeah, like John Wayne. Anything else?"

"How they gonna get the nets secured to the tops of the sea walls? Mason inquired.

"I guess Brady's squad will have to do it. They're going in first and leading the way. What about it, Brady?"

"We'll get the damn things secured, Sir," Brady snorted.

'Okay, then. That's solved. Any other questions?"

No one spoke up.

"Okay, dismissed."

Sergeant Brady didn't speak until most of the men had cleared the immediate area. Then he snorted in bitter disgust. "Why in hell they picked my guys is beyond me."

"They know how good you are, Sarge," Harry chortled, "besides, you're the only Sergeant who has combat experience."

"All the more reason to select someone else."

"We'll be okay," Nugent assured, "y'know we're the best squad in the platoon -- even in the company."

"Yeah, that's why they screwed us," Brady lamented. He paused and took a deep breath. "Okay, gather around. I'll show ya on the map where we'll be. Pay attention. Might save your life."

Gary Tilton caught his breath when Sergeant Greenberg cursed loudly. He had never heard the man use any foul language. Even Withrow and Tobin had shocked expressions on their faces. Franklin looked up with mild amusement.

"What's wrong, Sarge?" Gary asked.

"We've been fucked! The damn brass have screwed us royally!"

"How?" Tobin questioned.

"They ain't sendin us in! Just got the word from Lieutenant Trowbridge!"

"What d'ya mean?" Gary replied, his face puzzled.

"We ain't landin until the twenty-first, if then. The assault's gonna be made by the First and Fifth only. That means we'll be sittin on our duffs while they grab all the glory! That ain't fair!"

"Could be that they're more ready than we are," Tobin speculated, "besides, the whole regiment ain't here yet."

"That's a bunch of bullshit! Don't matter none if the whole regiment ain't here. They could still find a spot to put us."

"Well, they seem to know what they're doing," Gary shrugged.

"Geez!" Greenberg spat, " the damn war might be over before we even get into it!"

Gary laughed. "I suspect there'll be plenty of fighting to do even after we get in. Where is the Division gonna land?"

"At Inchon. The 5th and 1st are goin in -- they'll advance through Inchon to Kimpo Airfield and Yondong-Po -- on the outskirts of Seoul. The 5th might even cross the Han River, depending on what they run into. Dammit! We should be in on that!"

"Well," Tobin shrugged, "not much we can do about it. Just get our weapons ready for when we do go in."

Greenberg stared at him for a moment. "You guys is sure takin it better than me."

"We aren't in any great hurry to get shot at," Gary replied, "you know, that could be dangerous."

"Of course it's dangerous!" Greenberg snorted, "why do you think -- oh, I see. You think I'm being a bit of an ass over it."

"Just a bit of one, Sarge," Tobin acknowledged.

"I guess it won't hurt us none to wait and get some more training," Greenberg mused.

"Training?" Franklin queried, "what kind of training?"

"Yeah," Withrow agreed, "what kind of training? We already know how to pick up Japanese girls."

"In how to fight, stupid," Tobin explained.

"Oh, that kind of training," Franklin laughed.

"We already know how to fight stupid," Gary joked.

"Okay, guys. That's enough," Greenberg smiled.
Tilton grinned. The Sarge was himself again.

The news that they would not reach the Inchon area until September 21 was devastating to everyone. Having come nearly halfway around the world, they wanted to get into the fighting right away. No one really cared that it was Truman's war or that Dugout Doug MacArthur was in command. They were Marines and they wanted to send these upstart North Koreans to hell in a hand-basket.

Sergeant Roletto frowned and fingered the scar on his face as if it would help him concentrate. Captain Tyler, the Company Commander, was explaining what their assignment was. They were to defend the flank of the 5th Marines once they got ashore.

Roletto snorted. Protect the flanks, my ass! That ain't much of a way to fight. He snapped to attention when the Captain finished, then moved to where his people were when the company was dismissed.

"You guys hear all that crap?" He questioned, speaking to no one in particular.

"Yeah," Murphy growled, "damn war will be over by the time we get into it."

Martinez laughed. "Murphy, you New Yorker's is so na -- what's the word?"

"Naive," Murphy stated.

"Oh, yeah. Y'don't know what in the hell is goin on."

"Tenshun!" Roletto snapped.

Lieutenant Kenton returned Roletto's salute and nodded to the others. "At ease. Well, you heard the news. We'll get there eventually."

"Sir?" Roletto asked, "how come we is goin in so late?"

"Takes time to get the entire regiment her, Sergeant," Kenton shrugged, "most of it is still at sea. Not enough of us here to do any good." Kenton paused and scanned their faces.

He was a tall man, with a sturdy build and an air of confidence about him. Roletto, from Little Italy, was his favorite Sergeant. "We'll do okay when we get in. It's going to be a long war, possibly. We may have to drive clear up to the Yalu -- the border with China. Quite a distance, you know, and rugged."

"Yes, sir," Roletto sighed.

"You men clear on what's going on?" Kenton asked.

"Yes, sir," Murphy nodded, speaking for the others.

"Very well. Carry on, Sergeant."

Roletto watched him walk away. The idea of fighting all the way to the Yalu River was intriguing.

"Hell, Sarge," Thornquist ventured, "I don't mind going in late like this."

"Shut up, Thornquist."

"Sorry."

"Shit, Walt!" Banks growled, "must you apologize every time you open your damn mouth?"

"Well, I am sorry!"

"Knock it off!" Roletto snapped.

"Tell y'what, guys," Murphy suggested, "let's go on liberty tonight and get us a few Japanese broads."

"Great idea!" Martinez agreed, "some a'them broads is really nice!"

"I'll even go in with you," Thornquist enthused.

Everyone stared at him in shock.

Thornquist frowned. "I will go with you -- really."

"You ain't ever gone in with us," Martinez gasped.

"Well, this is our last chance at liberty here before we land. You all know we'll be over on that damn peninsula for a long time without any -- well, someone said we should be wary of Korean girls, so -- ."

"Hell," Banks snorted, "you've been so wary of any girl I was beginning to think you were queer."

"What?" Thornquist exclaimed, "me? No way! Did you guys really think that? I can't believe it!"

"Well, that's good to know," Roletto chortled.

CHAPTER TEN

News of an ill-fated South Korean guerrilla operation on the East Coast of Korea ripped through the Marines preparing to land at Inchon. Just north of Pohang, the Republic of Korea guerrilla force ship ran into heavy surf and strong currents approaching an unfamiliar beach. The ship, an LST, broached on a sand bank and came under heavy enemy fire. Anti-tank guns, machine guns and mortar fire took a heavy toll. To aid in the rescue of these men, the battleship Missouri and the cruiser Helena were detached from the landing force and sent to the east coast. The Marines would have to land without the benefit of the heavy guns of these two ships.

Everywhere, the troops gathered in little groups to talk about the guerrilla operation. Most saw the similarities between the two operations and that frightened even the experienced Marines. Those who had never participated in a landing on a defended beach could only look at the fear in the eyes of the older Marines and wonder.

"Same thing is gonna happen to us," Worrell fretted, "we're gonna get on that damn little island and be stranded there. Left to die! They're gonna screw us! That damn Dugout Doug don't give a shit about Marines."

"C'mon, Worrell," Lofton snorted, "ain't nothin at all like our operation. Hell, they're Korean soldiers, not Marines."

"Y'think that damn little painted globe and anchor is gonna protect ya?" Worrell challenged.

"Hell, no," Lofton admitted with a perplexed glance toward Hall and Jackson, "but it's different with the ROK.

They don't get the training we get, for one. They probably didn't plan it like our guys do, for another. They didn't know what they were getting into."

"Yeah, well, I do know and it scares the shit outa me!"

"What if we do get stranded, Lofton," Hall questioned, "can we get out of there?"

"Well, you know what Parker said. We'll be there on our own for close to twelve hours. Unless we get pushed off, of course."

"So Worrell could be right," Hall concluded, "they could very easily screw us and sail straight back to Japan."

"Look, Hall," Lofton pleaded, "they ain't gonna let us be wiped out or taken prisoner. They just don't do that, even if MacArthur is in command. You know there's Marines on his staff and they won't let it happen."

"Well, I'm scared," Worrell admitted, "and I don't know if I want to go or not."

"Hell, y'gotta go," Lofton snorted.

"Do I? Why do I have to go? Tell me."

"Worrell, I know you ain't no coward. You bug out now, your whole career will be shot."

"Better my career than me."

"I didn't mean it that way," Lofton sighed. He looked helplessly at Hall and Jackson, who seemed a bit bug-eyed. "If your brother were alive, he'd tell ya not to bug out."

"Leave him out of it, you bastard."

Lofton meet Worrell's angry glare for a moment, then nodded. "Sorry. It wasn't right of me to bring him into it. I'm going up for some air. If you ain't here when I get back, I'll know you decided to bug out. Sick bay is --."

"I know where it is."

"Yeah, sure," Lofton nodded. He glanced at Hall and Jackson, then turned and headed for the deck. It was just a bit before dawn and the sky appeared clear. He fished in his pocket for a cigarette, extracted a crumpled one from the pack, then remembered the smoking lamp was out. He cursed, stuffed the cigarette back into the pack, stepped to the rail and stared at the still shadowy land masses. They seemed rather forbidding.

Maybe he's right. Maybe we're all fools to go in under such conditions. Maybe -- shit! This is what we trained for, what we're supposed to do, how we're supposed to fight. If we all quit just because of a small danger, we'd never win a battle. Sure he's scared. So am I, but I couldn't tell him that. Damn! Worrell's a good Marine. We need him. I need him. He --.

He turned as someone moved up beside him. It was Worrell. He examined Worrell's face with questioning eyes.

"I'm not buggin out, Lofton," Worrell stated softly, his eyes staring at the deck.

"I'm glad. I wasn't gonna say anything to anyone, you know."

"Never figured you would."

Lofton nodded.

"Hall and Jackson -- they're okay, too. We had a short talk after you left. Wouldn't be fair to you or Sergeant Parker if any of us bugged out."

"I know," Lofton agreed, "it wouldn't. I like Parker. A good Marine." He paused and looked at Worrell with an admiring expression. "Thanks, Worrell. Took a lot of guts to make your decision."

Sergeant Parker studied the faces of his men as they came aboard. He wondered how the information of the ROK disaster would affect them. Such news often could turn a courageous man into a frightened man. Besides, prior to a landing or before going into combat, some men seem to be pre-disposed to accepting the possibility that they were going to be killed or become a casualty as fact. They simply knew it was going to happen to them regardless of what they did. Often, they wrote letter home stating the fact that they believed they would not survive the battle. Others simply did not worry about such things. It was always different for each man for each landing or battle situation. He had learned that in World War II.

He looked first at Lofton, the presumed leader of the men. There was something about Lofton that had bothered him from the start when he first met the man. Now, Lofton wore an expression of gleeful anticipation, as if he was eager to close with the enemy. That worried Parker, who had seem men react so to imminent danger. They usually ended up casualties. He mentally filed away his impressions for later use.

Worrell looked a bit worried, his face drawn and his lips taut. His body seemed tense and his eyes had a fatalistic expression in them. Very likely he was really frightened.

Hall and Jackson also appeared to be scared, but not as much so as Worrell. Parker eased closer to Worrell. He had seen men like Worrell, also. They initially were unable to grasp the reality of going into combat, of having men shooting at them, until the first shot was fired. Then they usually came around and were okay. This seemed to be different. Worrell, like the others, had been in combat already.

He caught Worrell's eye. "Relax," he suggested, knowing it was essentially impossible, "you've been under fire."

"Yeah, I know. But, somehow, this seems different."

"How?" Parker asked.

Worrell laughed. "Hell, I don't know, Sarge. All I know is that I'm scared shitless."

"Who isn't?"

"You, too?"

"Of course! Sergeant's stripes don't offer much protection -- could even be a target -- and my dungarees aren't any thicker than yours."

"I guess not," Worrell admitted, "see what you mean."

"Good. Feel better?"

"Yeah, Sarge, I do. Thanks." Worrell pursed his lips,

lowered his eyes, then met Parker's wondering gaze. "I was seriously thinking about bugging out, going to sick bay so I wouldn't have to land."

"That wouldn't have been very smart," Parker shrugged, "they would know you weren't sick. It would have been a black mark on your record. Might have led to a discharge or court martial."

"Yeah, I know. It was just -- well, that fiasco on the East Coast -- the ROK troops. The same thing could happen to us."

"Possible," Parker nodded, "but not likely. These Navy guys are pretty good. I've been through quite a few landings with them. They've always taken care of us. Just like the Corpsmen."

"Y'don't think they'd abandon us if the shit hit the fan?" Worrell questioned.

"No."

"Well, I'm glad you're confident. Me, I'm too scared."

"But you came, didn't chicken out. Neither did any of the others."

"They almost did," Worrell noted, "only -- well, Lofton gave me a pep talk and then Hall, Jackson and I talked it over and we decided to stick it out. We didn't want to make you look bad."

"Well, thanks for telling me, Worrell. You didn't have to, you know."

"I -- well, we all like you, Sarge. We've got a good chance with you leading us."

"Thanks for the compliment. Now tell me about Lofton. How did he act before your Lieutenant was hit?"

Worrell glanced toward Lofton and shrugged. "He's a courageous man, Sarge. Almost fearless. Asked for the tough and dangerous assignments. Didn't take cover as fast as most of us when under fire."

"And after the Lieutenant was hit?"

"Much the same, except, perhaps even more so. He just said he would take over and he did. None of us wanted to challenge him. We didn't want the job. Y'know, I think he really enjoys war and being shot at . Me, I don't like it at all."

"Me, neither. In our business, we have to endure it once in a while. Lofton scares me. He's too damn brave, almost to the point of being foolhardy."

"That's just the way he is, Sarge," Worrell noted.

"Yeah. Where's Hall and Jackson -- there they are. I'm going over to talk to them. They look scared, too."

"I'm sure they are."

"You'll be okay, Worrell."

"I know and thanks, Sarge."

Parker nodded and eased through the troops to the side of Hall and Jackson. "You two okay?"

"Scared," Hall answered for both of them.

Parker studied their faces for a moment. He could tell they were scared, but not overwhelmed by their fear. Most Marines in this situation were like that. He nodded. "You guys will do okay. Just follow my lead and keep moving."

"Right, Sarge," Jackson grinned weakly, "y'think those damn ladders will work?"

Parker glanced at the ladders lashed tot he loading ramp. The theory was that the ramp would not be lowered. Instead, the craft would nose up to the wall, hold its position there while the men positioned and then climbed up the ladders and got out on top of the seawall. It sounded reasonable and there was no real reason it wouldn't work.

"Well, Jackson," Parker shrugged, "it's a helluva lot better than trying to climb a sheer, fifteen-foot wall."

Jackson laughed. "I guess so. Ain't none of us that tall."

"True. Okay, we're approaching the landing site -- no fire yet. That's a good sign. Now, follow me when I go up." He glanced around caught Worrell's gaze, then met Lofton's wide-eyed stare and nodded.

The landing craft nudged against the wall with a bang, the metal scraping on the concrete as the backwash lifted the craft. For a second, it seemed it was going to drift back out to sea, even though Parker was on the third rung of the ladder. Then the coxswain revved the engine and the water behind the craft began to churn. The ramp nosed up to the wall again and stayed there.

Parker scrambled up and jumped ashore. There was only sporadic fire, most of it apparently unorganized and seemingly directed towards other areas. As he hurried ahead, he glanced back quickly. The men were following him. After about thirty yards, he dropped to the ground in a slight depression. The others slid in beside him.

"Everyone okay?" Parker asked.

"Worrell okay."

"Hall okay."

"Jackson okay."

There was no response from Lofton and Parker twisted around to look at him. "You okay, Lofton?"

"Huh?" Lofton grunted. His eyes were almost glazed with excitement. Then he focused on Parker. "Oh, yeah, I'm fine."

"Then stay alert and listen for voice commands," Parker snapped.

"Yeah, sure."

"Okay. Let's move out!" Parker jumped up and moved ahead. There was no fire from the enemy. On either side of him, other teams kept pace with him. As the squad cautiously moved inland, they could see the remains of machine gun nests along the higher ground. Apparently, the naval bombardment or the air strikes had knocked them out. It was eerie to be moving through enemy territory in sight of strong emplacements without seeing any enemy soldiers or receiving hostile fire.

Pushing on toward the causeway, they suddenly came under small arms and machine gun fire. This appeared to be coming from some caves to the north. The fire seemed ineffectual and wild, but they took cover regardless. All except Lofton.

"Get down!" Parker snarled.

Lofton, still standing erect, either ignored the command or didn't hear it. His eyes gleamed with excitement and he raised his rifle and fired several rounds. Then he dropped to one knee to reload.

"Stay down!" Parker commanded.

"I'm okay, Sarge," Lofton grunted, "think I got one."

"Dammit, Lofton! Stay down!" Parker snapped. He saw Lieutenant Bradford catch up with the lead and drop to the ground. The Lieutenant glanced at Lofton, then scanned the field before meeting Parker's gaze.

"Keep moving, Parker. Get to the causeway. The rest of us will catch up. We can handle these guys here."

"Yes, sir," Parker nodded, "move out! Keep moving!" He made certain the members of his squad responded to his order, then hesitated so Lofton could charge into the lead. He moved ahead and fell in beside Worrell, his eyes watching Lofton.

"Handled yourself well back there, Worrell."

"We probably should have stayed to help the others," Worrell blurted.

"They're fine. Don't need us. The Lieutenant has it under control. It isn't a large group of enemy anyway."

"I know. See how Lofton is?"

"I see."

"It's just the way he's been doing things. Probably get himself killed one of these days."

"You know, Worrell, it usually isn't his type that gets hit. It's the men with them. They see a man like Lofton get up there and take unnecessary risks and think they can do it, too. Then they get shot. I've seen it before. Just do what you can."

The sounds of firing slowly faded as they moved on toward the causeway. Several times, Parker looked back. He could see parts of the platoon following them at a distance of about a hundred yards. That was close enough should they run into any trouble. Finally, the causeway came into view. The team slowed and approached the area cautiously. There appeared to be no enemy emplacements or troops defending the area or the causeway.

Parker scanned the area for defensive positions and decided to set up to the left of the approach. There was a hill there to provide some cover and room enough to spread the men out. It also gave him a good view of the causeway and of Inchon beyond. He signaled the men and watched them take their positions. So far, all was going well.

About twenty minutes later, Lieutenant Bradford brought the rest of the men up. He looked puzzled for a moment, then walked up to where Parker was.

"Seems quiet, Sergeant."

"Yes, sir. Not a thing stirring. Understand we have some tanks ashore back there. If we had one or two up here, we could move across the causeway and help out the other guys coming in from Red Beach."

"Interesting thought, Parker," Bradford nodded, "I'll contact Headquarters about that possibility."

Parker nodded. From the looks of the situation, they could go right into the town proper, secure it and the others could land without any opposition at all. He smiled as he heard Bradford explaining it all to Headquarters.

He glanced at Lofton, then Worrell. He was pleased with how Worrell had handled himself. Both Hall and Jackson had done well, also. He was about to speak to Worrell when the Lieutenant returned.

"Well, Sergeant," Bradford shrugged, "they said no. Not even with the tanks. They just want us to sit here on our butts and watch the war proceed without us. Stick to the plans, they said. Just stick to the plans."

"You sound a bit bitter, sir."

"No, not really. Hell, s'pose there was a company or a

battalion hiding down there waiting for us to commit ourselves. We'd be kicked around pretty good, even with tanks. Might even be stranded on the other side of the causeway. No, I'm not bitter. Kind of disappointed, though. We'll stay here where they want us and let the other guys find out what's there."

"Whatever you say, sir."

CHAPTER ELEVEN

The Navy coxswain saw the breach in the sea wall and twisted around to tap Sergeant Lyons on the shoulder. He pointed to the breach questioningly. Sergeant Lyons raised up to look, noted the breach and nodded his approval. Then he glanced back at his men.

Hank Brown was crouching just to his right, his rifle cradled in his arm, his face set in a stern expression. Hank looked up and acknowledged Lyons with an anticipative grin.

Gilbert was checking his rifle and seemed to be ignoring the erratic motions of the boat. He didn't seem very concerned and had no idea Lyons had looked back to check on him.

Schultz was watching Gilbert. A slightly amused grin softened his lips. The two men were good buddies. Schultz looked at the condom over the barrel of his rifle and shook his head with amusement.

Beck was obviously chewing either a large wad of gum or tobacco very vigorously. He appeared to be the most worried of them all and that was likely why he was chewing so fast. Beck also carried the portable radio and, because of that, he was critical to communications with the platoon.

They all looked up when the coxswain revved the engine to run his boat into the breach. Following the heavy lurch as the boat hit the ground, Lyons waved the men forward. He was halfway up the lowering ramp even before the boat completely stopped. His men followed his lead and darted from the boat. They were met by sporadic and wild fire from the manned trenches not far behind the sea wall.

They were fortunate the fire was not accurate. The five

men ran to a slight hollow twenty yards inland with bullets churning up the dirt at their feet. All five slid into the hollow and hugged the earth. Sergeant Lyons counted noses and then cautiously raised his head. He saw immediately that they were in a good position that essentially flanked the enemy in the trenches. In fact, the men in the trenches had to expose themselves to even fire at them. He caught the attention of his men and motioned to them to charge inland a few more yards and then turn to outflank the trenches. He held up five fingers to tell them when to go.

On the count of five, the men leaped up and rushed inland. The North Koreans in the trenches were so surprised they could offer no fire. Then, when the five men suddenly turned toward them, they panicked! Some desperately tried to twist around to open fire -- they were shot before they could raise their weapons! Others, seeing their hopeless situation, simply threw down their weapons and raised their hands. Their wide eyes adequately expressed their terror and they cringed in anticipation of being shot.

Sergeant Lyons grinned as he waved the prisoners from the trenches. He noted that another team from the platoon stood ready to escort the prisoners to the beach. With a nod to them, he turned to his team.

"Good work, men."

"Yeah, thanks, Sarge," Hank beamed, "almost as good as General Lee could've done."

"What d'ya mean?" Gilbert scoffed, "that tactic was straight outa General U. S. Grant's book!"

Schultz laughed and Beck snorted before turning his attention to the front. It appeared to be clear of enemy troops or emplacements.

Lyons saw Lieutenant Pitney scrambling through the breach in the wall and stepped toward him. "They surrendered, sir."

"Excellent, Sergeant!" Pitney commended, "take your team and move out as a point."

"Aye aye, Sir," Lyons responded. He glanced around for his team members, saw them already facing the front, their weapons ready if needed. "Okay, you guys, let's move out."

Warily, the men stood and moved into a wedge formation. They advanced over the uneven ground, the buildings of Inchon proper looming ominously ahead. Any building, any window or door, any fence could be concealing enemy soldiers. Yet, there was no direct fire, although shots could be heard from other sectors.

After some fifty years, Lyons looked back. The rest of the platoon was still milling about at the landing site. It wasn't a comforting thought to know they were so far back. He wondered if they would close the gap enough to provide support should his team run into serious opposition.

To their left was Cemetery Hill and Lyons, as well as the others, glanced at it apprehensively. Although his orders were to advance as the point -- and that meant moving on to scout out the enemy -- he wondered if he should halt the team and wait for the others to catch up. He looked back again -- the platoon was over a hundred yards back now, but it was beginning to form up preparatory to moving out. That was a good sign, so he decided to keep moving.

Ahead ay two sets of railroad tracks that curved toward the docking area. Lyons signaled his men to stop and take a break. Hank Brown was in the lead and he moved up to him.

"See anything, Ears?"

"Don't see anything threatening, Sarge," Hank replied, "just the brewery up ahead. Doesn't seem to be anything around it, either."

Lyons drubbed his chin thoughtfully. "Okay, then, let's move out toward the brewery."

Just as they stepped over the second set of railroad tracks, gunfire erupted from Cemetery Hill, followed almost immediately by fire from the brewery. The team instinctively hit the dirt and squirmed next to the tracks to use them for cover. It was clear they were pinned down as far as advancing up the hill on their left was concerned.

"Anyone hit?" Lyons inquired, "Brown? Gilbert? Schultz? Beck?"

"I think we're all fine," Brown grunted, "but they sure as hell surprised us."

"Yeah, they did," Lyons agreed, "Beck, contact Pitney. Tell him we're coming under fire from a bunch of enemy on Cemetery Hill -- looks like they're in caves and well armed. Ask him for directions as to what we should do."

He listened as Beck outlined the situation, then heard Pitney's voice over the radio.

"Tell Lyons to move on ahead to the brewery and wait for us there. We'll take care of the positions on Cemetery Hill."

"Roger, sir. Out."

"You all heard him," Lyons snorted, "move out."

The men ignored the ineffectual fire from the hill and moved ahead. The firing from the hill ceased after they had moved a few yards. Sergeant Lyons looked back and saw the platoon approaching slowly and cautiously. He nodded and glanced ahead. They were now about fifty yards from the brewery. He could see what appeared to be trenches in front of the building. It looked like some men were moving in them. Suddenly, the troops in the trenches opened fire and, again, the men took cover. Lyons crawled up beside Brown.

"What do you think, Ears? How many men?"

"Only about four or five, I think," Hank responded, "and they don't seem to be good shots. Had us cold."

Lyons nodded in agreement. They were almost in the town proper. The presence of buildings made his situation more precarious. After all, a fire team by itself couldn't be expected to fight a house to house battle. However, he had been directed to take the brewery.

"Okay, you guys, you know what to do," he directed, "we want that brewery. Let's take them."

"Pickett's charge all over again," Hank snorted.

"Hope there's not too many of them inside," Lyons added, "go!"

All five men scrambled up and charged the trenches, firing as they ran. There were only a few shots fired at them from the trenches. As they neared the positions, the North Koreans seemed confused and frightened. The men shot them quickly and coldly. Then they flattened themselves against the wall of the brewery on either side of the big door.

"Anybody notice any fire from inside?" Gilbert asked.

"Didn't see any," Hank replied.

"There's no windows on this side," Beck commented dryly, "so they couldn't fire from inside."

Lyons stepped away from the wall and examined it. "By god, you're right, Beck! There ain't any windows. Never noticed that."

"Yeah, well," Beck grinned, "what d'ya think we oughta do, Sarge?"

"Don't know," Lyons shrugged, "but I guess we oughta go in. Gilbert, you go left. Schultz -- right. Beck, cover our ass. Hank, come with me."

"Gotcha, Sarge," Hank grinned.

"Okay, here we go!"

When Gilbert and Schultz eased around the corners of the building, Lyons and Brown threw their shoulders into the door -- it flew open! They jumped inside, weapons ready. There was no fire from the interior -- in fact, the area appeared empty.

Hank Brown looked around with a confused expression. "Where's the booze?"

"Maybe they drank it all," Lyons shrugged, "let's look around and make sure the building is secure." He started toward the nearest inner door -- suddenly, it flew open with a loud crash! Schultz stepped into the opening! The two men stared at each other for a long minute, each with a sick expression on their faces, their weapons half raised. Then Lyons lowered his rifle.

"Oh, it's you, Sarge," Schultz quipped weakly.

"Yeah, it's me. Where's Gilbert?"

"He's checkin out a room back here. Hey Gilbert! Everything okay?"

"Okay!" Gilbert called.

"I think the building is empty, Sarge," Schultz shrugged, "we didn't see anyone."

"Good. Hank, call Beck in. Let's see what's ahead."

Lyons and Schultz walked to a window facing Observation Hill. The top of the hill was visible above the roof tops of the Korean buildings. Lyons looked at the streets and alleys leading to the hill and shook his head. "A single team -- we're not going in there without some help." He glanced to his right. "What's that building over there?"

"Looks like a church of some kind," Schultz replied, "there's a cross on it."

Gilbert entered the room and looked out the window over Schultz's shoulder. "Yeah, I think it is a church building. Noticed it when I came around outside. Probably safe enough. I don't think anyone would use a church for cover. Seems kinda -- what's the word, Sarge?"

"I don't know the word, but I know what you mean. Wonder where the rest of the platoon is?"

"They ain't out here," Gilbert asserted.

"Hell, asshole!" Lyons snapped, "they ain't gonna be in front of us! Schultz, go look behind us and see if they're coming up. I don't want to get stuck here alone in case the North Koreans counterattack."

"Right, Sarge." Schultz moved to the door on the side of the building facing the church and glanced around warily. Then he stepped outside -- a machine gun chattered noisily and Schultz was spun around as bullets ripped into his body! He clearly was dead before he hit the ground.

"What the -- damn! Anyone see where that came from?" Lyons exclaimed. He hurried to the door and looked down at Schultz's body. "Damn!"

Hank Brown moved to the window where Gilbert was and looked out. There was no cover other than the church building.

"I, I didn't see nothin," Gilbert lamented, "didn't see a thing! I was watchin him. Why Schultz? Why?"

"I don't know," Hank comforted, "Sarge, it almost had to be the church building. No other cover out there and there don't appear to be any other emplacements in the area, no other troops."

Lyons wiped a tear from his face. "I ain't too religious, but if that don't take the cake. Being shot and killed by fire from a damn church. You'd think God -- what do you think, Ears? Can we take them out? I ain't leavin here until I get whoever did this. I think we owe Schultz that much."

"I think we can take them, Sarge," Hank nodded, "two of us can go out the way we came in -- which is hidden from their view, I believe -- and two of us can go out this side to draw their fire. Then, the other two can circle around and get the drop on them."

"Sounds like a good plan," Lyons agreed.

"But what about your orders to hole up here until the platoon comes up?" Hank inquired.

"We'll take care of them assholes and then come back. Hell, Lieutenant Pitney won't know the difference. We got time to do it." He paused and stared at Brown for a moment, then spoke without turning his head. "Beck, you and Gilbert go out the way we came in and circle around to the church. Hank and I will go out here and draw their fire. Okay?"

"Sure, Sarge," Beck replied with a glance at Gilbert.

"Sounds okay to me," Gilbert added.

Hank looked out the window and then turned to Lyons. "There's a bit of cover about sixty feet from the door. We should be able to reach it."

"Let me see," Lyons snorted. He moved to the window and looked out, his eyes scanning the terrain, noting the depressions and cover available. Finally, he turned from the window.

"You've got a good eye, Hank," he stated, "okay, we'll do it. Beck, you and Gilbert wait until they fire at us and then you go out. Circle around and get close enough to lob a couple of grenades into the building. Don't want no so-called emotional, heroic stuff, understand? Can't afford to lose another man. Just get a couple of grenades in there. Now, in the meantime, Ears and I will be working our way toward the gooks. For heavens sake, don't shoot us."

"Hell, Sarge," Gilbert grinned, "we wouldn't do that."

"Yeah, sure," Lyons scoffed, "okay, get into position."

Ears nodded and moved from the window to the door. He took a deep breath. His mouth was dry, but he felt no fear. In fact, his hands were steady, although he had a knot in his stomach. He sensed Lyons moving up behind him.

"Want me to go first?" Lyons asked softly.

"No, I'm fine with it."

"Scared?"

"Not really. A bit nervous about going out, but don't think I'm scared." He paused. "Sorry about Schultz."

"Yeah, well, that happens. Had no way of knowing that gun was there. He was a good man and I hate to lose him."

"I didn't get to know him too well yet," Hank nodded, "but I liked him."

"I know. That's why I'm having Beck and Gilbert go after the gooks. They did know Schultz and they have a good reason to get the bastards."

"Good idea, Sarge."

"Ready?"

"Yeah."

"Beck -- you two ready?"

"We're ready, Sarge. Take care."

"Okay, Hank," Lyons sighed, "whenever you want."

"Here goes!" Hank grunted. He pushed himself through the door and ran in a crouched posture, his rifle held in one hand. Gunfire erupted almost immediately and he both heard the rounds whistle by and felt the air move! Puffs of dust rose around him as he ran! The sixty feet seemed like a mile and the gunfire was catching up with him when he slid to a stop behind the cover.

Sergeant Lyons was five steps behind him and he, too, slid behind the cover as bullets zipped past his head. Both men lay still for a couple of seconds.

"You okay, Ears?"

"Yeah. How about you?"

"I'm fine. Worried about Beck and Gilbert, though. Did they get out?"

"Haven't heard any more firing," Hank shrugged. He raised his head slightly and saw Beck and Gilbert sprinting toward the church, apparently unseen by the North Koreans. "They made it," Hank grinned, "getting in position to throw their --" A burst of machine gun fire made him duck!

"Damn! That gook is sure trigger happy!" Hank snorted.

"Well," Lyons predicted, "he won't be doing much more shooting after this."

Two explosions erupted from the church followed by several rifle shots. Lyons raised up and saw Beck wave to him.

"They got them," Lyons noted, "let's go." He stood and lurched toward the church. Hank followed a few steps back, his eyes moving across the area. As the two men got closer, Gilbert emerged from the church.

"It's clear inside," Gilbert announced, "only four of them."

"Good job," Lyons commended.

"Piece of cake," Gilbert grinned.

"Hell, you trained us, Sarge," Beck added, "you shoulda known we could do it."

"Yeah," Lyons nodded, "you're sure the church is clear?"

"It's clear," Gilbert repeated, "we ain't gonna leave no gooks behind us. We made sure they were all dead."

Lyons nodded. He glanced back at the body of Schultz. It hurt to lose a man. Hurt more because he had told Schultz to step outside and look for the platoon. If only I had -- no, the if only's are for those who want to make excuses. While he regretted losing Schultz, he had done what was necessary and what he needed to do. The loss of Schultz was, unfortunately, a part of warfare. No excuses were necessary nor desired.

"Okay, let's get back to the brewery. We'll wait there for Lieutenant Pitney and the platoon to come up."

The four men started back toward the brewery. Halfway there, Beck looked to rear and saw the platoon. "Here comes the Lieutenant and the others," he announced.

"Figures," Lyons nodded, "well, let's get inside where he told us to wait." He glanced toward the approaching group of men and realized one or two men were missing.

Beck and Gilbert dragged Schultz' body inside and laid him next to the door. Then the four men eased into comfortable positions against the wall and took their helmets off. It seemed the normal thing to do. They all looked up when Lieutenant Pitney entered. Only Sergeant Lyons stood.

"Lieutenant," he greeted, "we were just wondering how we might advance and take the hill."

"Understand, Sergeant," Pitney acknowledged, "but your team has done well. Take a rest while we secure the objective."

"Whatever you say, sir."

Pitney glanced at the body, then at the other three men. "You lose a man?"

"Yes, sir. Schultz got hit by machine gun fire from the church over there."

"The gooks still there?"

"No, sir. We wiped them out. Only a couple of men, I guess. Right, Beck?"

115

"Yeah, Sarge," Beck answered nonchalantly, "four men and a machine gun is all. We got them."

Pitney sighed. "I guess that's war. We lost two back at Cemetery Hill."

"Sorry, sir."

"That's okay, Sergeant. I'll get you a replacement as soon as I can. In the meantime, the four of you can function adequately, can't you?"

"Of course we can, Lieutenant, but I'll miss Schultz."

"I know. Anyway, you guys stand down now. We'll take the hill and then you can rejoin us on top."

"Very well, sir," Lyons nodded. He watched the platoon advance past the brewery and then turned to the others. "Take ten, you guys. The cavalry has arrived to seize the objective."

"The nerve of that ass!" Ears blurted, "he just wants to take credit for what we did."

"Can it, Ears," Lyons retorted, "you know how officers are."

"It don't matter none, Ears," Beck shrugged.

"Right," Gilbert agreed, "let the Lieutenant feel good for a few hours. Least he ain't no coward."

"Well, that's true," Hank nodded, "not like the other one I was under."

"We'll get plenty of action soon enough," Lyons added, "I still feel bad about Schultz. Damn! How was I to know -- what gets me, I ordered him to go out."

"It goes with those stripes," Hank stated firmly, "just one of those things, I guess. We'll all miss Schultz and we'll learn from this incident not to do it again."

CHAPTER TWELVE

As the boats neared Blue Beach, Sergeant Kimball could tell the sea walls were high without looking through his binoculars. According to the briefing, there was supposed to be an exit somewhere near the squad's landing spot, but nothing was apparent. The only thing he could see was what appeared to be a large landslide about a hundred yards to the right.

Kimball shrugged and raised his binoculars. His gaze swept the entire beach. Nothing indicated a breach in the sea wall or an exit. He moistened his lips and turned to check on the members of his team.

Granger was fondling his BAR, his eyes bright with the anticipation of firing it again. The man did not seem to be scared or nervous, just excited.

Beside him, Masters was engrossed with Corporal DeWitt and Martin. He had a slight scowl on his face as if he didn't understand what they were talking about. He didn't seem to be nervous or afraid, either.

Kimball shrugged and concentrated on DeWitt and Martin. DeWitt seemed to be doing most of the talking and he was moving his hands about, clearly trying to explain something. Martin appeared to be a bit seasick -- or just, well, woozy. Kimball eased closer so he could hear the interchange of words.

"This here boat," DeWitt was saying while demonstrating with his hands, "moves much like a bull does, only not as violently. Y'know, up and down, rolling side to side at the same time, bouncing you forward and back constantly, twisting its body around."

Glenn nodded, his lips pale and taut, his face showing a greenish tint. "I, I, don't wave your hands around like that, Barry! Please! I, I think I'm gonna barf!"

"Nonsense," DeWitt snorted, "That's all inna mind. Just like ridin a bull. Y'hafta think y'can do it n'ya will. Remember -- up and down, sideways, rolling about -- it's really easy!"

Glenn rolled his eyes and tried to ignore the moving hands. He swallowed and tried to stare at the horizon, but the motion of the boat made him feel worse.

Kimball chuckled and turned away, put his binoculars on the shoreline again. A smile crossed his face. Sergeants were not supposed to have binoculars. Lieutenant Gilford, in fact, had wanted to take them away from him. Only the fact he had personally purchased them at a pawn shop in San Diego kept Gilford at bay. Gilford could not confiscate private property. The same was true of the Colt 45 pistol he wore on his rifle belt. Usually, only officers wore pistols. The pistol came from a gun shop in Los Angeles and it was in better condition than a government issued pistol.

"Two minutes!" the Navy Coxswain warned.

Kimball nodded, and again examined the sector. Suddenly, he realized the area that appeared to be a rockslide was probably the exit that was supposed to exist. He shifted his glassed to it and studied the jumble of rocks and dirt. Clearly, scaling the wall would be easier than scrambling over that mess. The Navy was supposed to provide cargo nets, but, even so, his squad would have to scale the wall before the nets could be put in place. Apparently, those who had proposed using the nets hadn't thought of that. It was typical upper echelon planning. The nets were piled in the rear of the boat.

He turned around to address the others. "Check your weapons! Lock and load!"

Even as he spoke, the boat slowed perceptibly. The surge of the wake rolled forward, lifting the boat slightly and propelling it against the sea wall. The Coxswain revved the engines and managed to hold the boat firmly in place despite the movement of the water.

"Let's go!" Kimball shouted, "Go! Up and over!"

He scrambled to the top of the still closed ramp and stretched his body upward! As tall as he was, he could not reach the top! "This ain't gonna --."

Suddenly, hands grasped his legs and thrust him upward! His hands grabbed the top and he pulled himself up! A quick look around showed no defenders nearby, so he turned back. Below, Martin and DeWitt were looking up at him with wide grins.

"Give us a hand, Sarge!" DeWitt yelled.

Kimball nodded and reached down, his rifle nearly falling from his shoulder and striking DeWitt. He pulled the rifle back and DeWitt grabbed his outstretched hand. With Martin pushing from below, Kimball pulled DeWitt up. Then Martin extended his hand upward.

"No!" Kimball shook his head, "Granger!"

Martin hesitated and scowled, then nodded. Clearly, Kimball wanted the firepower of the BAR on top. He turned, grabbed Granger's arm and pushed him forward against the ramp.

Granger appeared a bit confused at first, an angry scowl crossing his face. He started to protest, then saw Kimball's hand reaching down. He stretched his arm out, grasped the hand and was drawn up.

Kimball nodded and noticed the others were doing the same thing. He reached down for Martin's hand and, with DeWitt's help, lifted him from the boat. Quickly, the team members moved into defensive positions. Kimball nodded his approval. He had trained these men -- all but Martin -- and they were responding now with professionalism. Even Martin knew what to do and did it without being told.

He scanned the area ahead of them. There were a few scattered buildings that could have been used as defensive positions amid the fields. But, mostly, it was open land and no defenders were in sight.

"Okay," Kimball directed, "let's get the nets out and anchor them for the others to use."

DeWitt and Martin immediately moved to the edge and reached down for the nets. Even Granger started to move back to help.

"Not you, Granger," Kimball shouted, "you watch the front for enemy activity."

From below, Masters started to lift the nets. The men grabbed them and draped them over the rocks and began staking them in place. Kimball watched and saw the work was proceeding properly. When it was done, Masters scrambled up the net and the men nodded to Kimball and grinned.

"Very good, guys," he commended, "now we can move inland. Let's go."

He beamed proudly as the team rose and instinctively shifted into a wedge formation. Then he moved close to Martin.

"Feeling better?"

"I'm okay, Sarge," Martin replied with a frown, "why do you ask?"

"Back on the boat, you looked a bit green around the gills."

Glenn laughed. "You mean when DeWitt was talking to me about bull riding?"

"Yeah. Thought you were going to get sick."

"I almost did," Glenn nodded, "the way he was waving his hands about -- it was making me dizzy and my stomach was about to erupt. I sure didn't want to lose that good breakfast."

"I know," Kimball agreed, "that was one good steak."

He looked ahead when the team paused on a slight rise. Nothing seemed to be stirring in front of them, so he turned to see where the rest of the platoon was. The lead fire team was about a hundred yards back and moving toward them. The rest of the platoon was in column formation, along with the other platoons. He saw Lieutenant Gilford coming and motioned the others down.

"Take five," Kimball directed. He then raised his binoculars and scanned the front. Nothing seemed to be moving. It was starting to rain and was beginning to get dark already.

"Good job, Kimball," Lieutenant Gilford greeted, "any problems?"

"No, sir. Looks clear up ahead."

"Yes, well, I'll take a good look see."

"Very well, sir," Kimball shrugged, "what now?"

"We'll consolidate our position on our objective, Sergeant," Gilford replied, "which may be difficult, considering that it's starting to rain and getting dark. But, we'll do it anyway."

"Aye, aye, sir. Do you want us to remain on the point?"

"No, Kimball, I'll put someone else up there. You can take the left flanking position for now. I may change that in the morning, of course."

"Whatever you want, Lieutenant."

The landing had gone well for the 3rd Battalion. Harry Schein had looked at the other boats taking the 2nd Battalion in and knew Glenn Martin was in one of them. The thought made him feel kind of lonely. It wasn't that he was alone. Just that he really didn't know the guys in his team very well yet.

Brady, of course, was quite bitter. So much so that it was impossible to tell how he would act in any given situation. His stubborn persistence at the briefing was disconcerting. If he was that way under fire, demanding they do the impossible -- well, it could get hairy, despite the fact that Brady seemed to be a good Marine.

The other guys seemed okay enough. Nugent,

Edwards and Mason had all turned out to be friendlier than he expected. At least, he felt at ease around them even though none of them had seen combat. Of course, he had only seen a bit.

Their assignment had been to secure the exits in their sector and they had done that quickly and efficiently. Of course, there was little opposition. Four or five enemy had fired at them and then retreated into the buildings and disappeared. It was just enough to relieve the normal tensions and apprehensive fear one has going into combat. No one, be it a veteran or a boot, approaches combat without being scared. At least, no normal person does. There's just something inherently abnormal about willingly placing oneself in a situation where someone is shooting at you with murderous intent even if you can shoot back. All the training in the world isn't gong to eliminate that sense of idiocy.

Then, of course, it had started to rain as nightfall came. Moving over hostile territory in the rain and at night wasn't his cup of tea. Especially when it was dark as hell and almost impossible to see ten feet. The team had stumbled and fallen, tripped over each other, clawed and cursed at one another as they advanced toward what the officers said was their objectives. Then, once on their objective -- or what they thought was the objective assigned to them -- they had to dig in. The ground was hard and digging a deep enough foxhole was difficult and tiring enough in good weather and soft soil. Doing so in the rain was much more difficult.

Harry wiped the rain from his face and peered into the darkness. It was impossible to see anything. He could hear Mason breathing hard not too far away, but the man was essentially invisible. In the distance, he could hear some rumbling that sounded like trucks or tanks. The sound seemed to be coming closer.

Good grief! Harry thought. If tanks attack us, we ain't got nothing to stop them!

He felt Mason move up next to him and glanced in his

direction.

"Y'hear that?" Mason hissed.

"Sounds like trucks or tanks," Harry whispered.

"Damn! We don't have nothin t'stop no tanks!"

"Knock it off, you guys!" Brady directed from his foxhole, "keep quiet! Mason, get back into your damn hole and stay there."

"Okay, but --don't y'hear them tanks?"

"I hear them," Brady snorted, "and everyone for a hundred yards around has heard you. Look, they're at least a mile or so away. So just relax and be quiet. If they do advance, they'll hit the guys on the roadblock first. Then, if that happens, you can start worrying. Okay?"

"Okay, Sarge," Mason muttered.

Harry nodded. It made sense. The roadblock was the most vulnerable position and it was on the right flank of the platoon. So, the tanks would have to blast through the whole platoon to reach his position. He eased into his hole and tried to ignore the falling rain. His eyes closed and his thoughts began to wander.

A smile crossed his face as he recalled telling his girlfriend he was going to enlist in the Marine Corps. Joyce Swerzer -- she was a right pretty girl, a tawny blonde with blue eyes, about his height -- five-seven -- and just a bit on the plump side. They had been going steady for two years; he had fallen for her early on. Joyce had a graciousness that was hard to find and a quick, contagious smile that seemingly radiated joy. At the Harvest Dance on a Saturday night, he maneuvered her to a shadowed and secluded area and then he told her.

"I'm going to enlist in the Marine Corps Wednesday," he stated flatly.

"You're going to what?" Her voice held a tinge of alarm.

"You heard me," Harry smiled, "things are done on the

farm and I want to see a few things before I get hung up in farming and all. So I'm going to enlist."

"What do your parents think about it?" Joyce asked.

"Haven't told them yet."

"Oh. Well, why the Marines? Wouldn't the Air Force or the Navy -- maybe the Army -- be better?"

"No. I want to be a Marine," Harry insisted.

"Well, what about college? You wanted to go and study agriculture, you know."

Harry shrugged. "I can do that later."

"I suppose, but -- well, we were planning on getting married, weren't we?"

"Of course!" Harry exclaimed, "when I get out. Or maybe sooner. I'm not going to make a career of it, you know. It's only for four years. If you wanted, we could get married while I'm in the service. Then you could come to where I'm stationed."

"No, I don't think so," Joyce reflected, "that costs too much money."

"I suppose you're right," Harry conceded.

"You know I am," Joyce asserted, "we should save as much as we can to pay for your education."

"I know. But I'm still going in."

"You're certain it's what you want to do?"

"Yes, definitely."

"Okay," Joyce sighed, "then I'll support you. I guess I can wait a few years for you. It won't be fun. I'd like to get married, but -- . Well, I can save up some money for us and you can save, too. You don't need to spend all you get."

"I won't," Harry grinned. He stared at her for a moment. "I really love you, you know. Any other girl would have told me to buzz off and refuse to wait. I, well, I didn't want to ask you to wait. After all, you might find someone you like better while I'm gone."

"Not likely," Joyce snorted, "you're pretty special to me. Look, Harry, I don't like it. I'm worried about it. I mean, what if there's another war? It could happen in four years. If it does, you'll be right in the middle of it! I, I don't want to lose you."

She turned away. He could tell she had tears in her eyes and didn't want him to see them. He swallowed the lump in his throat. He hated to see her cry and the tears in her eyes made him feel like a heel.

"I'll be okay," he stated defensively, "that's one of the reasons I chose the Marines. They get the best training there is. Besides, there won't be another war. Where would it be? China is the only place it could happen and we won't be sent into China."

Harry scanned the area, peering intently into the darkness and the heavy rain. He couldn't see more than ten or twenty yards, if that. If there were any enemy troops out there, they could certainly sneak up on him.

He smiled. After that Saturday night, Joyce never questioned his decision and she offered him full support. That had really cemented the bond between them. It also made it easier to convince his parents. But, they were well situated and had plenty of help to manage the farm. They were concerned, of course, just as Joyce was. But they agreed to support him and to watch over Joyce while he was gone.

Then, along came this war to fulfill Joyce's deepest fear. It was ironic, in a way. No one had expected it, not even the government. And no one would ever have predicted an outbreak of hostilities in such a remote place as Korea. Problem was, the government was clearly not prepared for it and neither was the Marine Corps. That was why he and his buddies had been shipped to Korea as a stopgap measure to help prevent the North Koreans from taking the entire peninsula. Harry sighed deeply and shifted his position, tried to ignore the rain trickling off his helmet and poncho.

"You still awake, Schein?" Mason whispered.

"Yeah."

"Me, too. Can't relax. Still worried about them tanks."

"I wouldn't be too concerned, Mason," Harry shrugged, even though he knew Mason couldn't see him in the dark, "like Brady said, we got the platoon between us and them. Besides, they ain't gonna do too much in this rain."

"Somehow it don't help much to know that," Mason snorted.

"I know." Harry glanced toward Brady's position and saw the man rise and move toward him. In the darkness, he was only a shadow. "Hush up, Mason," Harry warned, "Sarge is coming."

Brady eased up beside the foxhole and sighed. "Well, since you guys can't keep quiet, I got a job for the two of you."

"Hell, Sarge!" Harry protested, "we haven't been talking that much!"

"Like hell!" Brady snorted, "anyway, Lieutenant says we have to make contact with the company to our left. He hasn't heard from them -- doesn't even know which company it is, which is stupid. His orders don't specify who is supposed to be there."

"Sounds dumb to me, too," Harry agreed, "but how do we fit in with the grand scheme of things?"

"I want you and Mason to scout out our left flank and find out who's there. That's all."

"In this rain?" Harry protested.

"Yeah, in this rain and tonight. Right now, in fact. Okay?"

"Oh. Sure, Sarge," Harry replied with a glance toward Mason's hole, "uh, are we all using the same password?"

"I would think so. It should be one of our companies, I would think. They just haven't made contact with us yet and haven't notified regiment of their location."

"So the two of us just mosey over there, go up to their Lieutenant and tell him he's been naughty and should contact our Lieutenant or regiment, right?" Harry questioned.

"Well, yeah, something like that," Brady confirmed, "if you want, I can get you a radio. Then you can call us directly. Does that make you feel any better?"

"Not really," Harry sighed, "but maybe it will be okay. As long as they don't shoot us." He shook his head. What Lieutenant is going to listen to a couple of Privates? Hell, any officer would laugh at us!

"You do have the password."

"I know, Sarge, but they won't be expecting us. Maybe they're going to shoot first and ask for the password later."

"Marines don't do that," Brady snorted, "wait a few minutes and I'll get the spare radio for you."

Harry nodded and watched Brady move away. He turned toward Mason's hole. "Hey Mason! You hear what Brady said?"

"I heard. Sounds dumb, especially in this rain. But he's the boss."

"I know. You got a girl back home?"

"Actually, I got several of them. They all write to me now and then. Why?"

"I was just thinking about mine. I only got one. She's a real doll. We were thinking of getting married when this damn war broke out. Now, it won't be until I get out, most likely."

"That's nice, Harry," Mason hissed, "now mine, they don't know about each other, so I'm safe. I'll probably make up my mind and settle on one when I get back. They're all in different towns, so I don't have to worry about them finding out about each other. Unless I screw up and put the wrong letter in the right envelope. Almost did that once. That could have been a disaster."

"I guess so," Harry laughed, "well, here comes Sarge with the radio. You ready to go?"

"As ready as I'll ever be," Mason snorted.

"Okay, Schein, here's the radio," Brady explained,

"just scout over that way about one or two hundred yards. If you don't find anyone in that distance or run into any trouble, come on back. Understand? Remember, keep the radio as dry as you can."

"Gotcha, Sarge," Harry acknowledged, "c'mon, Mason, let's take a stroll in the rain."

"Be careful!" Brady cautioned, "we don't know what's out there."

"Now's a hell of a time for you to think of that," Schein snorted disgustedly, "but we'll take care." He took the radio from Brady and crawled from his foxhole. Mason was waiting a few feet away.

Brady watched them move quietly into the darkness and felt a sense of pride as the disappeared. He knew they were both good men and were well trained. He scanned the front as he moved back to his own foxhole. Nothing was happening and the rumbling everyone thought was tanks had ceased. Hopefully, it would be a quiet night. He eased into his foxhole and settled in as best he could.

Suddenly, a flash of light and a loud explosion shattered the stillness! Brady stiffened and stared toward the left where the sound had come from! It appeared to have occurred about fifty yards out -- exactly where he had sent Schein and Mason! They couldn't have traveled any farther than that!"

For a moment, he was too stunned to act. Then he crawled from his foxhole and called to Nugent. "Nugent, come with me! We have to check that explosion out!"

The two men hurried toward the area where the explosion had occurred. About sixty yards out, they came upon Mason sitting on the ground, his left arm dangling loosely and his left leg torn and bloody, his boot missing! He was shaking uncontrollably and staring at the gaping hole in front of him.

"Mason! It's me, Brady!" Brady questioned, "where's Schein?"

There was no response. Mason simply kept staring at the hole. Brady knelt beside him and only then did Mason turn his head. It was clear even in the darkness that he was in shock.

"He -- he just -- he just went up in a big flash and explosion! Just disappeared! My god, Sarge! How -- what was it?"

Brady looked at the still smoking and gaping hole and swallowed. He closed his eyes and exhaled. "A mine, Mason, a damn land mine. You're apparently in a minefield. Let's get your arm and leg taken care of and get you back to the medics. We can safely go back the way we came in. Okay?"

"But Sarge! Harry! We need to get Harry back to safety! He must be hurt bad! We can't just leave him here!"

"Mason, Harry's dead. No way could he have survived that blast. There's nothing we can do for him now. I'm sorry. We can recover his body in the morning. You're bleeding and losing blood. We need to get you to a doctor fast!"

CHAPTER THIRTEEN

The task of clearing a building in the dark was daunting. Sergeant Lyons wiped the sweat from his brow and eased through the open door into the building. There was something about the darkness of the room and the possibility of enemy soldiers lurking in the area that made one a bit nervous. Facing the enemy in daylight was bad enough, but when you couldn't see them, it was really weird. It was darker inside the room than it was outside! Lyons could hear the others easing up behind him and hoped they wouldn't get excited and shoot him.

They were on the southern end of the runways at Kimpo Airfield. It had taken most of the day to advance that far. The opposition had been minimal -- only a few isolated outposts that resisted and fought it out with them. In fact, large numbers of North Koreans had surrendered without a fight. This led to the conclusion that the enemy they had encountered so far was nothing more than rear area and administrative personnel forced to man the trenches.

Those few pockets of firm resistance, however, had slowed their advance. It was late afternoon before they had reached the outskirts of the airfield and almost dusk before they were directed to clear the buildings and establish a defensive perimeter for the night. Therefore, the buildings had to be cleared after dark and it was a daunting task.

Lyons saw a shadowy figure to his right and stared at it in an attempt to identify who it was -- one of his men or a North Korean. Then the figure turned its head and he saw the profile of the figure's prominent ears. He then realized it was Hank Brown. He took a deep breath and slowly turned his head to his left. The figure there did not move and Lyons felt sweat beading on his brow.

"Don't see nothin," Gilbert whispered.

"Oh, it's you," Lyons sighed.

"Who else?" Gilbert snorted softly, "Beck is right behind you, covering your ass."

"Yeah, right," Lyons nodded, "guess we're in good shape then."

"Should be," Brown noted, "ain't heard nothin moving anywhere in here yet, except us."

"Don't mean much, Ears," Gilbert countered, "best keep listening. It's quiet enough and we should hear them if they move."

"Well, y'ain't gonna hear nothin unless you guys shut up!" Lyons snapped.

"You're right, Sarge," Beck stated from behind, "but you guys stay where I can keep track of you. Don't want to shoot any of you. Okay?"

"We'll try, Beck," Lyons replied, "any doors ahead?"

"See one on my side," Brown noted, "it's closed."

"Another one over here," Gilbert added, "it's also closed."

"Let's check out the one on the right first," Lyons suggested. He saw Brown ease toward the door and moved to cover him. Brown stood to the side and glanced back.

"I've got you covered, Hank," Lyons offered.

"Here goes!" Brown breathed. He grasped the knob, turned it and pushed the door open. Nothing happened.

Lyons saw Hank glance at him and then step through the open door. He held his breath and could hear movement in the other room where Hank had gone. Then, after a few seconds, Brown reappeared.

"It's clear, Sarge. Another door on the other side that's also closed. Couldn't hear nothing through it."

"Let's check out Gilbert's door next." Lyons turned and eased to a position from which he could support and cover

Gilbert. "Okay, Gilbert. Got you covered."

He watched Gilbert repeat Brown's movements and actions. Again, there was no reaction to the door opening. Lyons held his breath as Gilbert searched the room. Then Gilbert reappeared.

"Clear," Gilbert announced, "no other door in there."

"So far so good," Beck snorted.

"Yeah," Lyons agreed, "okay, let's clear the right side now. Beck, you make sure no one comes through the door to the left or the one behind us. We're going to go to the right. We may come out somewhere else, so, if we do, don't shoot us."

"Gotcha, Sarge," Beck acknowledged.

It required nearly an hour to clear the building in the dark. No enemy soldiers were encountered. Reassembled, the team decided to take up positions outside the building for the remainder of the night. Except for some shooting to the east along the road to Seoul, the area was quiet.

By dawn, the team was ready to take the airfield with the rest of the platoon. The men moved out shortly after dawn and advanced toward the main terminal. There was only sporadic resistance and, within hours, they had secured the airfield well enough to allow a few planes and helicopters to land.

The achievement did not allow for much rest by the troops, however. They were ordered to seize the high ground overlooking the Han River and to move eastward toward Yongdong-Po.

Sergeant Lyons oriented his map and noted the position of Hill 99. It was a bit over two miles to the east and his team, along with the rest of the platoon, was ordered to take it and hold it. He shook his head, expressing his irritation. It would have been much easier for his team to take the hills along the Han River. Any counterattack was almost certain to come from Seoul or Yongdong-Po. The orders to take his team to Hill 99 actually placed them in a real hot spot.

There was little resistance as the platoon advanced to and up Hill 99. Sergeant Lyons and his team had the point and they easily overcame what opposition was there. The platoon followed and, after a fashion, established themselves on the crest. Then they watched as another company moved up, ostensibly to reinforce them. A few minutes later, just as the other company arrived, Lieutenant Pitney emerged from their midst and approached Lyons. He met Lyons' gaze and shook his head in apparent disgust.

"We gotta move, Sergeant," Pitney stated ruefully, "they actually want us over on Hill 60 instead of here."

"Why us, Lieutenant?" Lyons questioned, "hell, we've been doing most of the fighting around here. That's even a worse spot than here! If they counterattack, we'll be in the thick of it."

"I know, Sergeant," Pitney acceded, "but that's where they want us. Direct orders from Captain Rhodes."

"Okay, sir," Lyons sighed, "but my guys need some rest."

"Understand, Lyons. I'll see what I can do. You've already lost one man, right?"

"Yes, sir. Private Schultz. A good man, too."

"They're all good men, Sergeant. Hate to lose any of them. Well, carry on. Get your men over to Hill 60 and dig in. I'll be over as soon as I can get there."

"Aye, aye, sir." He watched Lieutenant Pitney move to the next squad, then noticed Brown had been listening. "What do you think, Ears?"

"Don't matter much, Sarge," Hank replied, "one hill is as good as another, I suppose. Maybe, being closer to the road, we'll get our supplied sooner."

"What supplies?"

"Hell, I don't know. Just thought that someone might be kind and considerate enough to bring some hot chow up for us. Y'know -- so we don't have to eat these shitty rations all the time."

"Fat chance of that happening," Lyons snorted, "shit, they don't care about us none. The only important thing to them is that we fight to keep the damn gooks away from them. That way, the rear area pogies can sleep in their clean sheets and cots without worrying about nothin. Except sendin us to places where we might get shot up. Then they'll have something to write home about."

He paused and glanced toward Beck and Gilbert. They, also, had watched the interchange with the Lieutenant with interest, although they were too far away to have heard much. "Okay, you guys!" Lyons called, "get ready to move out!"

Beck looked at Gilbert and raised his eyebrows. A scowl covered his face. "Move out? We just got settled in!"

"The man said to move out," Gilbert shrugged, "there's no rest for the wicked, I guess. We should have stayed at that damn brewery."

"Why? No booze there," Beck snorted.

"You're right!" Gilbert laughed, "so guess it don't make no difference where we go now."

Both men scrambled to their feet and were ready to move out by the time Lyons and Brown approached.

"Where we going now, Sarge?" Beck asked.

"Over there," Lyons snapped with a wave of his arm, "to Hill 60. Near the road."

"Why in hell are they putting us there?" Beck replied, "there ain't nothing there that isn't here."

"Beck, you've been in the Corps long enough not to question orders."

"Well, year, Sarge, but --."

"So just saddle up and get your ass in gear. We're going to Hill 60. Okay?"

"Right, Sarge," Gilbert nodded with a warning look at Beck, who had opened his mouth as if he were going to argue the point. Beck met Gilbert's eyes and shrugged before shifting the pack on his back.

About two hours later, the team and the rest of the platoon were dug in on Hill 60. As it was already late afternoon, the men settled down, hoping the evening and night would be quiet. They ate their rations in silence, each eyeing the road below them. It appeared obvious that if any attack occurred, it would likely be along the road. The thought was disconcerting.

"Hey Ears!" Sergeant Lyons finally asked, breaking the silence, "you got a girl back home?"

"No," Hank replied, "never had the time to get involved."

"No time for women?" Gilbert exclaimed, "you ain't a homo, are you?"

"Of course not!" Hank retorted indignantly.

"Good thing," Gilbert chortled, "we wouldn't be safe around you if you were."

"Why is that, Gilbert?"

"Cuz Beck and I are such handsome fellows," Gilbert laughed.

"Who in hell ever told you two that you were handsome?" Sergeant Lyons challenged.

"I dunno his name. Some queer guy back in the States -- in Oceanside, I think."

"And you believed him?"

"Sure we did, Sarge," Beck grinned, "we all wanta be liked, you know. And if we're handsome, we'll be liked."

"Uh, sure, Beck." Lyons shook his head in wonder, then looked at Beck again. "How long have you gone without a woman, Beck? I don't dare ask Gilbert."

Beck pursed his lips as if in deep thought. "Been a long time, Sarge," he answered seriously, "you see, I have a girl back home."

"Home -- that's Flagstaff, Arizona, isn't it?" Hank asked.

"That's where I live," Beck nodded to Hank, "but she lives in Winslow. It's a bit east of Flagstaff."

"I see," Hank grinned, "so, how did the two of you meet?"

"Well, it's a long story," Beck hedged.

"We're not going any --."

"Say, Gilbert," Lyons interrupted, "didn't you once say you had a dame up in Maine?"

"She ain't no dame, Sarge. Society type. High society, in fact. Maybe even a bit snobbish in her own way. Well, to be honest, she is quite a snob. Her folks have lots of money and prestige, as well as a gorgeous place right on the ocean. Lots of influence, too. She was horrified when I enlisted in the Corps. Almost told me to take a hike, but then, for some reason, she reconsidered. Don't know how it's going to work out when I get back. She got mad as hell when I didn't try to get into officer school. And, y'know, she hear me talkin like I talk to you guys, she'd be utterly shocked."

"Really? Why? We don't talk no different than people up in Maine, do we?"

"Sarge -- her people and some of my family, too, is all proper like. Know what I mean? No ain't's, no cuss words, no calling no woman a dame. All proper like with good grammar. It's all yes and no, not yeah or naw. In fact, it's yes sir and no sir for me. Complete sentences with verbs and that stuff. You don't say I'm gonna do this or go there. It's I'm going to do this or that and I'm going to go over there now. I have to really watch myself when I go on leave. Takes the whole flight home just to tell myself not to cuss or say anything crude. And when I slip up -- I never hear the end of it!"

Lyons laughed. "See, Ears, you ain't so different. I s'pose you have the same problem."

"In a way, Sarge," Hank nodded, "only in Alabama, I gotta speak with an accent or be looked at like a traitorous Yankee. You know -- y'all, that sort of stuff."

"Yeah, the south is still that way, ain't it?"

"Sure is, Sarge. And Blacks -- have never understood

why there's so much antagonism toward them in Alabama. The guys on our team were great guys, yet they were treated badly. Just don't make no sense at all. Is it that way up in Maine, Gilbert? Or in Arizona?"

Gilbert nodded. "Not the same, Hank, but it's there. I think it's more insidious, if that's the right word for it. Lots of hypocrisy up in Maine. Lots of it."

"It's pretty much the same in Arizona," Beck added, "but it's getting better. Of course, we have the Indian or Native American population and the Mexicans to contend with, so it's a bit different. Most people don't really worry much about the Indians or Mexicans, although a lot of people don't like the Mexicans. But Blacks -- well, maybe with more of them coming into regular units now, things will improve for them. Sure hope so. Those I've known are pretty good guys."

"Yeah," Sergeant Lyons agreed, "hopefully it will get better for them. Most of the Blacks I've known are great guys to have around, like you said. There's a few who aren't so great -- just like there's a few, maybe more, whites who ain't so good. Have to look at people as individuals, not as white or colored or whatever. At any rate, however, things ain't gonna improve here unless we quiet down. Startin to get dark, so take your positions and can the chatter. Got a long night ahead of us.

For the most part, the night passed quietly. There was some shooting back on Hill 99 and to the left near the airfield. It was impossible to tell what was happening, although the flashes and explosions lit up the sky some. The most disturbing event was an artillery barrage off to their left, just east of the airfield. It lasted a good half hour and kept them awake for a long spell.

As the day dawned, Sergeant Lyons spotted a large force of enemy soldiers moving across the rice paddies toward the airfield. They wee moving quietly, but seemed to disdain any cover that might hide their presence. He watched them for a few moments and then checked the road to see if any armor was advancing. Seeing no tanks, he contacted Lieutenant Pitney.

"Lieutenant, there's a large group of gooks advancing toward the airfield -- moving across our front. They're crossing the rice paddy and should be right in front of you, about three hundred yards out."

"Where -- okay, I see them, Lyons. Good job. I think we can hold them in check, but you can fire on them, too. I'll call in artillery and mortar fire first."

"Lyons nodded. "Very well, sir. Our fire would hit them on their flank -- would you rather we advance and engage them down there?"

"No, not until the artillery hits them. Don't want you and your men to get hit with our own artillery fire."

"Right, sir," Lyons agreed. He turned to his men -- all three had their weapons trained on the gook unit. The range was close to four hundred yards, but Marines are taught to shoot at long range if necessary. He signaled his men to hold their fire for the time being.

After a few minutes, the artillery came whistling overhead and impacted on the enemy force. The firing was extremely accurate and the fire for effect literally saturated the area! The enemy apparently panicked and they were running in every direction. Then someone imposed some discipline and the enemy began an orderly withdrawal. The damage, however, was already done. Casualties were quite heavy.

As the force cross their front, Lyons gave the signal for his men to open fire. This seemed to confuse the enemy even more and the orderly withdrawal turned into what justifiably could be called a rout. Enemy soldiers were running wild in efforts to find a haven.

Lyons laughed with the others as the enemy soldiers disappeared into the distance. "That was almost a turkey shoot," he offered.

"Yeah," Hank agreed, "it was fun."

"I got several," Gilbert added, "like hittin them things

at the carnival."

"More fun than that," Beck countered, "yet you feel kinda bad for them guys. They didn't have a chance. Sure glad it wasn't us in that spot."

"Well, it was great regardless," Lyons stated, "hey, guys, here comes the Lieutenant."

"Good job, Lyons," Pitney smiled, "and you men did great. Hit them hard. Now, I want you to be the point as we move toward Yongdong-Po. We've been directed to occupy Hills 80 and 85. Okay?"

"Guess so, Lieutenant," Lyons agreed.

"Okay. We'll move out in an hour. So get some chow in you. Got enough ammo?"

"Beck? Gilbert? Brown? Enough ammo?" Lyons questioned.

"We're fine, Sarge," Brown answered for all of them, "got plenty."

"We're okay, Lieutenant."

"Good. Be ready to move out in an hour."

"Very well, sir." Lyons turned to the others. "You guys hear?"

"We heard," Beck answered, "another couple of hills."

"Right. Get some food and rest."

An hour later, Lieutenant Pitney returned. He shook his head as he approached Sergeant Lyons. "Change of plans, Sergeant."

"In what way, sir?"

"We aren't gonna take the two hills. Someone else is. We've been selected to move to the river. A recon outfit and some others are going across tonight. If they can establish a beachhead, then we'll follow in the morning. At any rate, we'll be here for a few more hours, possibly all night. They don't need us for the crossing tonight. So rest easy a while longer."

"Okay, Lieutenant." He paused and tried to read

Pitney's mood. "Uh, sir, any chance of getting someone to replace Schultz? I mean, the other platoons and teams got men to bring them up to strength. I could use another man."

"I know, Lyons," Pitney nodded, "your team hasn't really been attended to properly. I'll see what I can do."

"Appreciate it, sir."

"I know, Lyons. It's not easy to get someone. Probably have to steal a clerk from division, if I can get anyone at all. Just hang tough. I'll try."

"That's all I can ask for, Lieutenant."

Pitney nodded. "You're a good Sergeant, Lyons. I know I can rely on you and your team under any circumstances. That's one reason you spend so much time on the point -- you and your team. All good men and I'm really thankful to have you and the others in my command. Makes my job easier." He paused and considered Lyons for a moment. "I'll do my best, Lyons."

"Thank you, sir."

CHAPTER FOURTEEN

The advance from Inchon to Yongdong-Po involved heavy fighting. After moving through the small town of Sosa, the Marines encountered stiffening resistance and then it was discovered that the main road was heavily mined. The loss of two tanks to the mines removed one of the assets the Marines had counted on. Then artillery and mortar fire from an unknown source slowed them even more. Air strikes were called in to eliminate the artillery, but even the planes could not locate the source of the fire. Neither could the observers flying overhead.

Added to all this was a measure of confusion created by Army units that were sent in to protect the flanks of the advancing Marines. The Army claimed to be holding hills which the Marines were trying to occupy against heavy resistance. Even direct communication could not resolve who held what hill.

All of this was academic to Sergeant Kimball and his team. They had advanced along the road with the others and had taken the point when it was their turn. Fortunately, no one had become a casualty. Now, huddled behind a high dike which joined Hills 52 and 43, he found all the SNAFU's rather amusing. The action they had engaged in, however, had turned out to be a bit harrowing.

He glanced at Martin, who was looking out across a rice paddy that was nearly chest high. Lieutenant Gilford was mildly surprised when he spoke to him concerning Martin. After all, Martin was the new guy, a replacement who had not trained with them. Even so, Martin had proven his worth by his actions.

Kimball smiled knowingly. He had recommended Martin for a Bronze Star after Martin had, single-handedly, held off nearly a company of North Koreans. It had happened after the lead tank, which was far ahead of the point, hit the mine which blew off a track. The North Koreans, seeing that the tank was disabled and unable to fight back effectively, decided to charge it. Martin apparently saw what was happening and realized none of the guns on the tank could be brought to bear on the advancing North Koreans. So he charged out with his rifle blazing!

His audacity surprised the North Koreans, of course, and everyone else in the team. Alone -- no one else on the team knew what was going on and the action was over before they realized what he was doing and why -- he had forced the North Korean company to retreat! It was perfectly obvious they had been trying to capture the tank crew and Martin's action prevented that. Then, as the tank crew evacuated the disabled tank and returned to the protection of the point, Martin provided cover for them from enemy fire with his rifle. It was an act of bravery worthy of an award.

Lieutenant Gilford questioned everyone in the tank crew as well as the others on the team -- actually, anyone who may have witnessed the even. Then he went back to the rear without speaking to anyone else.

Kimball glanced at the others. DeWitt seemed reflective, his back against the dike. Granger was fondling his BAR as usual. Masters had one of his boots off and was massaging his foot.

Kimball made sure no one was watching, then pulled a letter from his blouse pocket. The paper was well worn -- he had received the letter just before they sailed from San Diego. It was from a girl he had met while on recruiting duty in Chillicothe, Ohio, and shortly before he was to be transferred. He really hadn't expected much to come from the meeting. Actually, he had asked her to have dinner with him that evening. She refused, of course. It really hadn't upset him very much. After all, who wants to date a Marine Sergeant? An officer, perhaps, but not an enlisted man.

Then he got the letter. How she obtained his address was beyond him. Maybe someone in the recruiting office gave it to her. Anyway, in the letter, she apologized for not having dinner with him and said she had thought it over and had wanted to see him again. But, when she returned to the office, he had already been transferred. She asked him to write to her and to call or visit her when he returned to Chillicothe.

Kimball swallowed the lump in his throat. He had never been very lucky around girls or women. Most seemed to think he was arrogant and full of pride -- a show-off of sorts. He had never been very articulate and had trouble expressing himself sometimes. This was the first time in his life he had ever had a girl ask him to call of visit her. The act really touched him.

He had written her twice since receiving the letter, asking her to send him a picture of her and telling her he'd be pleased to visit her when he got back from Korea. So far, no other letter from her had arrived, but that was to be expected. Took time for mail to cross the Pacific Ocean and half the country. And maybe she was taking her time to reply.

He re-read the letter now, a smile gracing his face as he did. Maybe something special would come from it, maybe not. He read the letter again, then shrugged. Chances were he would never hear from her again. That was the way it was with him.

Kimball refolded the letter and placed it back in his pocket. From what he remembered, she was a very pretty girl. Dark hair, green eyes, a bubbly sort. His first thought when he had seen her for the first time was "that's for me!" Then, when she turned him down, well -- he more or less expected it.

"You okay, Sarge?"

Kimball looked up. Martin was staring at him strangely. "Yeah, I'm okay. Why?"

"Well, you look kinda melancholy or something, like you're thinking about something deep or emotional."

"Now ain't you the perceptive type," Kimball laughed. He paused and met Martin's gaze. "Yeah, I was," he admitted, his face sobering. "I was thinking about a girl I met a couple of days before leaving Chillicothe."

"Your girlfriend?"

"No. She actually refused to have dinner with me."

"I'm sorry," Martin nodded, "some girls are like that, you know."

"Yeah, I know. She was quite nice, though. Got a letter from her just before we shipped out. Just read it again. The umpteenth time. I guess I'm being kind of foolish, hoping something might come of it."

"It's happened before, Sarge," Martin encouraged, "many times. A girl just says no without thinking and then changes her mind. They do that a lot."

"What are you, Martin? Some kind of counselor? I haven't heard from her again."

"You wouldn't have yet. Takes time."

"Perhaps you're right," Kimball shrugged, "that's what I was trying to convince myself of to justify not hearing." He looked around, indicating he wanted to change the subject. "Wonder when were going to move out?"

"Who knows? Same old story. Hurry up and wait."

"Maybe, except the Lieutenant is coming now. Hopefully he had some news." He stood and waited for Lieutenant Gilford to come up.

"Kimball, your team gets the point again. Be ready to move out in ten minutes."

"Aye, aye, sir," Kimball nodded.

Gilford glanced at Martin. "By the way, Martin, you've been recommended for a medal. Likely a Bronze Star. Good work."

"Me?" Martin gasped, "for what? I haven't done anything to merit that."

"Kimball told me about what you did back on the road -- to help those tankers. He commended you and I passed it up to Battalion. We'll see how it goes from there. But keep up the good work."

"Yes, sir," Martin swallowed. He glanced at Granger and DeWitt and shrugged.

"Hey Martin!" Masters called, "you deserve it."

"Yeah," DeWitt agreed, "you were brave enough to act while the rest of us just sat on our butts and watched. Take the medal if they give it to you. You earned it."

"I was so damn scared I couldn't move," Granger added, "can you imagine it? Me? Scared shitless."

"No, I can't imagine it, Granger," Martin snorted, "the whole thing just caught you by surprise. You're not scared of nothing."

"Yeah, that's it!" Granger grinned, "won't do that to me again. Not as long as I got this here BAR. Y'know, you got smarts, Martin. They should've made you an officer."

"Okay, okay," Kimball snapped, "if you guys is through bull-shittin each other, get ready to move out."

"We're ready, Sarge," DeWitt shrugged, "hell, we've been ready since we got here. We do have time for a quick smoke, don't we? Lieutenant said ten minutes."

"Take your damn smoke and be quick about it."

"Thanks, Sarge," DeWitt smiled. He drew a tattered, squashed pack of Lucky Strikes from his pocket, extracted a crumpled, bent cigarette and replaced the pack. Then he carefully straightened the cigarette before lighting it.

Sergeant Lyons raised his eyebrows as he assessed the young Marine Private following Lieutenant Pitney. The man couldn't be more than eighteen -- perhaps even less than that! His boyish face and short, blond hair made him look like a high school kid. Lyons glanced at the others and saw that they, too, were evaluating the kid.

"Here's a man to take Schultz's place," Lieutenant

Pitney announced, "name is Louis Kenyon, Private. He's young, but has been in the Corps about six months or so. Came in with divisional headquarters as a clerk. Sorry, Lyons, but he's the only man I could get. Kenyon, this is Sergeant Lyons. He'll be your team leader. Okay, Lyons?"

"I guess so, Lieutenant."

"Good. Introduce him to the rest of your team and then come over there," Pitney stated, pointing to a small group of Sergeants, "we'll have an NCO meeting."

"Right, Lieutenant," Lyons shrugged. He waited until Pitney walked away and then turned to Kenyon. "Welcome to the group, Kenyon," he smiled tightly, "had any good training?"

"Just what everyone gets before shipping out."

"Okay. How old are you, anyway?"

"I'm seventeen, Sergeant."

"Seventeen," Lyons mused, "must have enlisted right after your birthday."

Kenyon grinned. "I did, Sarge. Wanted to get in the Corps and get out of my hometown."

"Why?"

"Wasn't too popular in high school," Kenyon admitted with a sheepish grin, "so I just wanted to get away."

"Any reason for not being popular?"

"Don't really know, Sarge. Was good in math and science Guess a lot of my classmates thought I was an intellectual and a softy. Didn't go out for sports or nothing. Was going to go to college, but, with the war, thought I'd join up."

"I see. Why the Marine Corps?"

"Well, as I said, everyone thought I was a weakling, you know. So I wanted the toughest branch and figured that was the Marine Corps. I think I was right."

"No regrets?" Lyons questioned.

"No regrets, Sarge. Of course, I haven't really done anything that could be called tough yet. They assigned me to the division staff as a clerk right out of boot camp."

"You'll get a chance to show your stuff here, Kenyon," Lyons replied.

"I hope so, Sarge. Want to do what I can and show them back home that I'm no weakling."

"I see," Lyons nodded, "well, the rest of the guys -- the one with the large ears is Hank Brown. Goes by the nickname of Ears."

"He doesn't mind it?"

"No. Pinned on him in boot camp. The other two are Gilbert and Beck. Go on over and introduce yourself. Have to go to the meeting. They all saw you coming with the Lieutenant, so they know why you're here."

"Okay, Sarge."

Lyons turned away without comment and started toward the meeting. Why do I get the people who can't fight? Well, can't say it's always true. After all, I did get Brown and he's a good Marine. He eased up the edge of the group of Sergeants Lieutenant Pitney was talking to. Pitney glanced at him and nodded.

"Okay, everyone is here. The straight scoop. We're going to cross the Han River this morning. We'll go in LVT's and land near the town of Haengjin -- hope I pronounced that right. While most of the unit will attack the village and then move north, we are to take Hill 125 to the east. We'll take the hill and hold it until relieved. It's an important position because it gives us a pivot point for the swing east. Any questions?"

"Is the hill fortified?" a Sergeant asked.

"We don't think so," Pitney answered, "the Recon Team that was over there last night didn't run into much of any opposition."

"Why didn't they stay there and hold the hill?" Lyons questioned.

"I've heard they ran into heavy fire from the area of the village -- and, I suppose, some from the hill. In addition, some of the boats came under fire and they lost control of them. They drifted downstream quite a ways. So, they pulled back."

"They couldn't effect a crossing at night, yet they want us to do it in broad daylight?" Lyons snorted, "sounds crazy to me, Lieutenant."

"I don't understand, Lyons."

"It's about like General Burnside at the Battle of Antietam, sir. He had a bridge across the creek, however, but, even so, he sent his men across in the face of devastating fire. His men were slaughtered by Lee's army."

Pitney shook his head and seemed at a loss for words. "This -- this -- it's not -- what are you talking about?"

"The Civil War, sir," Lyons snorted, "everybody knows about the Battle of Antietam Creek."

"This isn't the Civil War, Sergeant. Are you sure you're okay?"

"Sure I'm okay, sir, and I know it's not the Civil War. But the brass seems as crazy as Burnside was."

Pitney shook his head and scanned the faces of the other Sergeants. "Well, all I know, Lyons, is that they directed us to effect a crossing of the Han River at this point and we're going to do it. Are you implying that you don't want to take your team across?"

"Hell no, Lieutenant! Lyons snapped with a grin, "I just think they're crazy."

"Oh," Pitney scowled, "well, crazy or not, we're going to cross. I was going to have your team on the point. Should I assign it to someone else?"

Lyons scanned the faces of the other Sergeants. They clearly were amused by the exchange. Most of them liked Lieutenant Pitney, as he did, but, even so, it was fun to see him befuddled once in awhile. "Not necessary, Lieutenant. We'll take the point. Kinda like it out there anyway."

Pitney sighed in relief. "Very good, Sergeant. You'll have support. A heavy weapons team and a mortar section will back you up. And about three or four more men for when you try to take the hill. Of course, we'll be there to back you up, too -- the rest of the platoon -- if you run into any trouble."

"Right, Lieutenant. When do we load up?"

"As soon as the boats are ready. Get your men down close to the river right away."

"Aye, aye, sir," Lyons acknowledged. He nodded to the other Sergeants and walked back to his team. Kenyon and Brown were chatting and he got in on the last few words.

"That's interesting, Kenyon," Brown was saying, "you know, Sergeant Lyons and I are both southerners, too. Oh, here's Lyons now."

Kenyon grinned and turned toward Lyons. "I'm from Mississippi, Sergeant."

"That's good, Kenyon," Lyons smiled, "that makes three of us. The other guys are Yankees. But they're good guys and we all get along real well."

He paused and his sweeping glance took in Gilbert and Beck. "Listen up! We're going to go down to the river and load up in an LVT. That will take us across the river. Then, once we land, we're going to turn to the right and take Hill 125 and hold it until the Lieutenant tells us to move. We're supposed to have the support of a heavy weapons team and a mortar section, plus three or four more men. At least, that's what the Lieutenant said. The rest of the guys will take the village of Haengji and then swing east, pivoting around us. So the hill is an important position. Understood?"

"Understood, Sarge," Gilbert replied.

"Okay," Lyons nodded. He turned to Kenyon. "You comfortable with your weapon, Kenyon?"

"I think so," Kenyon answered, "I can shoot pretty well, you know. My Dad and I went hunting when I was in high school. Did quite good on the range, also."

"This is different, but you'll probably do all right. Got enough ammo?"

"Cartridge belt is full, plus eight in my rifle," Kenyon nodded.

"In good shape, then," Lyons grinned.

"Got some grenades, too."

Lyons stared at him for a moment, then shook his head slightly. "You'll be okay, then. All right, guys, let's move out."

There was some fire from the North Koreans as the LVT's crossed the river, but nothing substantial. Most of the fire seemed to be coming from the vicinity of the village and the crest of a ridge that ran up to Hill 125. Sergeant Lyons studied the hill and the approach to it. There was precious little cover for the troops. He saw Brown staring at it and moved up beside him.

"Doesn't look like much cover up there," Lyons stated.

"Not much at all. Kind of reminds me of Pickett's Charge."

"Yeah, kind of hopeless, too. You know, I've been thinking about what you said regarding Lee and Longstreet. Beginning to believe you're right. Longstreet was pretty smart."

"He was, Sarge," Brown grinned, "and a better offensive General than Lee. Of course, no one in the entire war on either side was as good as Lee in establishing a defensive line."

"I'd agree to that. By the way," Lyons chuckled, "I almost had Pitney up in arms when I mentioned Antietam Creek and General Burnside this morning. You know the Recon group tried to cross last night and got pushed back. Why we're going over now. Anyway, I told him this crossing was like Burnside charging across Antietam Creek."

"Hope not," Brown snorted.

"Naw, be a piece of cake," Lyons laughed, "hell, we got heavy weapons and mortars with us now." He glanced at the rapidly approaching shoreline. "Get ready, guys," he called.

The LVT ground up onto the shoreline, the ramp dropped and the men spilled out. Three men who came on another LVT landed and looked around, apparently confused. Lyons saw them and nodded.

"You guys looking for Sergeant Lyons?"

"Yeah, Sarge. That you?" the tallest man replied.

"I'm Lyons."

"Lieutenant said we should go up the hill with you and your team. Supposed to give you some support."

"Okay. Don't have time for formalities," Lyons stated, "what's your names?"

"I'm Pete," the man stated, then nodded toward the other two. "He's Lewis and this guy is Dennis."

"Okay, got it. Any combat experience?"

"Been fighting since we landed at Inchon," Lewis stated defensively, "and doing okay. Our Sergeant got shot up pretty bad yesterday and was evacuated. So we're kind of at loose ends until they get a replacement to take his place. Lieutenant didn't think any of us had enough combat experience to run the team. Anyway, the Lieutenant also thought you could use some help in taking the hill. So he sent us over."

"Good. We can use the help. Rest of the team -- Hank Brown, Kenyon, Gilbert and Beck. Kenyon is new, too. You guys stick close and don't take no chances. Keep an eye on me for directions, hand signals, whatever is needed. Let's move out."

Behind them, Lyons noted the heavy weapons and mortar men milled about for several minutes, seemingly uncertain what they should do. Even so, Lyons led his men toward the bare slopes of Hill 125 quickly. As soon as they started up the slope, the enemy opened fire!

Lyons hit the deck amid a hail of bullets! He glanced around -- everyone seemed okay, but it was impossible to tell. He knew from experience that to stay where they were was to invite death. With a twisting motion, he looked toward the base of the slope.

The mortar crew and the heavy weapons teams, although still confused, were beginning to set up their weapons despite the heavy fire. It was difficult to even move under such an intense barrage. Lyons saw three men fall wounded or dead. The heavy weapons team acted as if they wanted to advance up the slope, but the enemy fire forced them to seek cover.

A burst of submachine gun fire raked the ground just in front of his face, forcing him to hug the deck. Beside him, Gilbert, Beck, Brown and Kenyon also were unable to move! The three new men were behind him. Lyons rolled over and saw a slight depression about ten yards to his right.

"This way!" he yelled just before he leaped up! He scampered across the slope almost on all fours! Behind him, the others copied his movements and followed. The firing seemed to lessen when they all reached the depression. Lyons did a quick visual check. No one seemed to be hurt.

"What are we going to do?" Kenyon sobbed almost hysterically, his hands trembling so much he nearly dropped his weapon, "what are we going to do? We're pinned down and they're going to kill us!"

"Shut up, man!" Lyons snapped angrily, "we're gonna advance and take the hill. You guys -- you all okay?"

One by one, Brown, Gilbert and Beck answered in the affirmative. Pete acknowledged that he, Lewis and Dennis were all right. Kenyon was still shaking, his eyes glazed.

"You okay, Kenyon?" Lyons demanded harshly. He reached out and grasped Kenyon's shoulder and shook him.

Kenyon turned toward him, seemingly terrified, his eyes wide and unseeing. Then, slowly, his gaze focused and studied Lyons' face for a moment.

"Are you okay?" Lyons repeated.

"Huh? Oh, yeah, I'm fine, I guess. I, I don't know what came over me. I'm okay now."

"Good," Lyons grunted.

"Sarge," Brown offered, "when I was scampering over here, I noticed a slight wash about twenty yards further on. I'll dash over to it and draw some fire away from you guys. When I go, you can probably advance to those rocks up ahead about ten yards or so. They'll give you good cover and maybe you can engage them from there."

"Then what?" Lyons questioned.

"Then I'll climb up the wash and flank them on top."

"Sounds good, Ears," Lyons nodded, "but take Beck with you. Maybe the new guys, too."

"Probably be better if I went alone," Hank shrugged, "can move faster."

"Yeah and get cut-off from behind or shot without someone to cover your ass. Beck, you and the three new guys -- Lewis, take your two men and go with them. Brown, when we get tot he rocks, you guys can start climbing. We'll lay down as much fire as we can. When we hear you firing near the crest, we'll charge up the slope. Make sense?"

"Sure Sarge," Hank grinned, "that's exactly what I had in mind."

"Yeah, right." Lyons turned to Kenyon. "You too scared to fight, boy?"

Kenyon raised his eyes and met Lyons' questioning gaze. For several long moments, their eyes were locked. Then Kenyon looked down at his hands. They were no longer trembling. "I, I'm sorry I got scared, Sarge. I, I can fight now. I'll be okay."

"You certain? If you're not certain, stay here. Otherwise, you'll be in the way and likely will end up dead. I don't want that to happen. Be sure, boy."

"I, I'm sure, Sarge. Just kinda got to me -- first time and all."

"I know," Lyons grinned, "first time gets to all of us. Did you hear what we plan to do?"

"I heard," Kenyon nodded, "he -- Hank and the others

-- are going to the small wash. Then the rest of us are going to advance to the rocks. Right?"

"Right, Kenyon, and we're going to give them covering fire as they climb the wash." He took a deep breath, then turned to Hank, Beck and the other three men. "Whenever you guys are ready. Good luck. You guys be careful, now."

"We'll be fine, Sarge," Beck snorted, "hell, they ain't very good shots anyhow."

Brown met Lyons' gaze and nodded. "Thanks Sarge, for being so supportive and helpful. Appreciate it. We'll get the job done." He turned to Beck and the others. "You guys ready?"

"Sure am!" Beck enthused.

"We're ready, too," Pete nodded.

"Okay, let's do it!"

Hank pushed himself up and darted across the slope. Almost instantly, gunfire erupted from the crest of the hill! Hand ran crouched, his long legs eating up the yards! He half fell into the small wash and rolled to a shooting position. The few rounds he fired seemed to help Beck, who almost dived into the wash. Behind Beck, Pete, Lewis and Dennis scampered to safety.

"Made it!" Hank exulted. He glanced back -- Lyons, Gilbert and Kenyon were crawling toward the rocks under heavy fire. Occasionally, they were able to fire back.

"Let's give them some covering fire," Beck suggested.

"Right!" Hank agreed.

All five men leveled their rifles and began shooting almost blindly at the crest. There were no real targets at which to aim. But, apparently, their fire had some effect, for the volume of shooting from the top immediately dropped off. Brown smiled when he saw that the rest of the team had reached the rocks.

"Time for us to advance," Beck sighed.

"Yeah, I guess so," Hank agreed, "not as much cover

here as I thought. My best guess is that we should go straight up this wash. Looks like it leads almost all the way to the top and provides some cover for us."

"Sounds good to me," Beck nodded, "I'll lead the way."

"Oh no you won't!" Brown retorted, "it was my idea and I'm going first. That's my job."

"Well, it was your idea," Beck conceded, with a glance at the others, "so I won't argue with you. Lead on, kind sir."

"Now you're talking," Brown grinned, "just follow my dust. You other guys ready?"

"We'll be right behind you," Pete grinned.

The five men started climbing along the wash. It was difficult to climb when holding a rifle in one hand. After about ten feet, Hank paused and slipped his rifle over his shoulder and head.

"Can't climb otherwise," He explained to Beck.

"Difficult. At least no one is shooting at us yet. I'll cover you."

Slowly, the group worked their way up the narrow wash toward the top. From below, they could hear the machine guns of the weapons team firing and the mortars had been hitting near the crest since they had started climbing. Hank paused to catch his breath and assess his position. He was about ten yards or so from the top and slightly behind the crest facing the others. Beck was right behind him and the three new men had stopped on each side of the wash.

"Should we make a dash for the top from here?" Brown asked.

"A bit far, isn't it?" Beck questioned.

"Perhaps, but they might hear us and react if we try to get closer. Charge from here and I don't think they'd have time to react even if they do hear us coming."

"Whatever," Beck gasped breathlessly, "just five us a few seconds to catch our breath."

"Okay," Brown nodded. He turned to face the top, his

eyes widening when he heard the cry from above! He saw the North Korean's head pop up momentarily and then drop down just as he rolled the grenade down the wash toward them!

"Damn!" Hank cried out, "grenade!" He tried to catch the grenade, but it bounced off a rock and fell to the ground in front of him! Frantically, he tried to pick it up -- two more grenades came rolling and bounding down the wash! Hank saw them and dropped to his knees to hold them in front of him!

Sergeant Lyons heard the three rapid explosions followed by the firing of an M-1 rifle. He grinned and waved Gilbert and Kenyon ahead. Fearlessly, the three men began firing as they advanced up the slope. Suddenly, there was no return fire!

Lyons ran the last few yards, firing at anything that moved. He topped the crest and saw the North Koreans running down the reverse slope. He and the others shot a few and then the men were out of range. Overhead, an aerial observer circled the hill. Within seconds, artillery fire rained down on the fleeing enemy.

Lyons, Gilbert and Kenyon watched with cruel satisfaction. It was gratifying to take the objective and send the enemy running in a panic and then be able to watch them being torn to pieces by artillery.

Suddenly, Lyons remembered Brown, Beck and the new men. "Where's Brown and the others? They should --."

He turned and saw Beck and the three new men climb out of the small wash. A frown crossed his face. "Where's --." He stopped when Beck shook his head, lowered his eyes and awkwardly wiped at them.

"He -- grenades," Beck mumbled tearfully, "they dropped them down the wash! Ears -- he protected us! He's dead. The damn bastard fell on the grenades and -- they blew up! He shoulda let me go first."

Lyons' heart sank and all he could do was stare at

Beck. Hank Brown -- gone. Dead. It was almost too much to bear. First Schultz and now Brown. How many more would die needlessly? He turned away, his mind already forming the words he would put in his recommendation for a medal for Brown.

CHAPTER FIFTEEN

The news that the Seventh Marines were finally unloading at Inchon spread like wildfire through the ranks. Now the division was complete and could function as it should. That thought was heartening to the troops and bolstered their morale. The enemy was proving to be stronger than anticipated and more reluctant to let them advance. It should be easier with the whole division in the action.

According to the original planning, the Seventh would consolidate, cross the Han River behind the Fifth, and then protect the left flank. This would give them time to get accustomed to the area and to work out any glitches that might arise. After all, they had not functioned as a unit before. It also meant that the battle for Seoul would fall almost entirely on the First and Fifth Regiments, who already were bloodied.

As the advance neared Seoul, it became more evident that the North Koreans were bringing in trained, seasoned troops. Resistance was stiffening everywhere and the fighting was becoming more savage. Casualties on both sides were rising and the Marines in the advance echelons were taking a beating.

The North Koreans had heavily fortified a series of hills north and west of Seoul. Filled with caves, revetments, bunkers and other defensive installations, this complex had been used by the Japanese in World War II as a training area. Then it was taken over by the South Koreans for the same purpose prior to the invasion from the north. As far as it could be determined, the area was well supplied and the terrain was very favorable to the defenders.

To the south, the First Regiment consolidated in

Yongdong-Po prior to crossing the Han River there. Plans called for the First to advance into Seoul from the south and for the Fifth to move in from the north. It was hoped the North Koreans would abandon the city in favor of fighting elsewhere. However, as the Marines neared the city itself, fighting became fierce. Clearly, the North Koreans intended to fight for every building, street and block of Seoul.

At Headquarters, some staff officers advocated by-passing the city and moving on. This would isolate a large army and make them useless. This concept, however, was rejected and the vicious battle continued. In the line of the advance were the American, French and Russian Consulates as well as a couple of South Korean palaces. Besides, it would not be a wise political move to by-pass the capitol city of Korea at this time. The State Department and President Truman's office wanted the city freed regardless of the costs.

Casualties were high as the units advanced into the city. A major fight developed at a roadblock established by the North Koreans. Several Russian tanks were destroyed and, eventually, the roadblock was breached. However, the enemy was prepared for that. They simply retreated to another roadblock a few hundred yards back and continued the battle as before.

After awhile, the Marines learned how to deal with the barricades. Tanks rotated so every team on point had two tanks with them. IN addition, air strikes were called in on all barricades. The air strikes proved to be the deciding factor and, soon, the advance quickened.

To the north, resistance was also quite heavy. Finally, the Seventh Marines were called in from their flanking assignment to carry on the attack. They were given the task of advancing along the Pyongyang-Seoul Highway to enter the city near the Sodaemun Prison. Opposite the walls of the prison, the lead elements came under heavy flanking fire.

Sergeant Roletto changed the advance of his team to

protect the flank. He watched critically as his men moved into position professionally and without hesitation. A slight grin twisted his lips -- after all, he had trained them. All but Murphy.

His eyes sought out Murphy. So far, the man had shown good judgment and had obeyed orders without question. He liked that in a man. Clearly, Murphy had been a bit arrogant when he first came to the team. Still was to a slight degree. Even so, it now was clear that Murphy had received some good training somewhere along the way. He was proving himself to be a valuable addition to the squad.

Roletto turned his head when Corporal Martinez fired a single shot. The man was good with a rifle, very good.

"Got one," Martinez announced.

"Yeah, well, get some more," Roletto snorted, "where they shooting from?"

"Along the street and up to the archway up there, Sarge," Murphy answered before Martinez could, "they got pretty good cover. They're even on the roof tops."

"Perhaps we should just lay low until the rest of the guys --."

"Shut up, Walter," Roletto snapped, "we'll fight our own battles."

"Sorry."

"Dammit, Thornquist!" Banks growled, "must you always say you're --."

"Knock it off, you guys," Roletto directed, "and start shooting."

"Here comes another team!" Martinez noted, "and they got machine guns!"

"Hey, Lieutenant!" Roletto offered, "we don't --." He stopped when the one Sergeant charged inside a nearby house and opened a hole in the wall with machine gun fire! Then the man began firing. Soon, several machine guns were firing down the street. They didn't stop the enemy from shooting back.

After a fashion, the Marines were ordered to advance. Roletto lead his team along one side of the street and another fire team moved on the other side. Movement was extremely slow and cautious. Firing by the enemy was heavy and most of it came from upper stories of the buildings and the roof tops. At length, the two teams were recalled. Even as they withdrew, the enemy firing was intense. Back on the road, the teams gathered together in bunches. Roletto scanned the dirty faces of his men and nodded with pride. All of them had done well under fire, especially Murphy.

He grinned. First time I saw Murphy, I knew he was a fighter. A bit arrogant, but ain't we all? He's a good man to have on the team.

"Your men did well, Roletto."

Roletto turned his head and stared at Lieutenant Kenton. "They did, sir."

"We're going to fall back along the road to the high ground for the night," Kenton explained, "too exposed here. Then we'll see what we can do tomorrow."

"Very well, Lieutenant."

"You satisfied with Murphy, the new man?"

"Yes sir. Very. He's a good Marine."

Lieutenant Kenton nodded and smiled. "I'm glad for you, Sergeant. I thought he would be."

The night passed slowly for everyone. Sporadic artillery and mortar fire rained down on them, inflicting even more casualties. Sergeant Roletto and Murphy huddled near a wall with the rest of the team. There really was nothing anyone could do except cringe a little whenever a shell exploded nearby.

"You know, Murphy," Roletto stated during a lull in the barrage, "you never said much about how you got out of New York and into the Corps. Not many manage to escape the gangs and all. I know it was difficult for me to get out in one piece. You did mention you tried to get into the movies.

What happened? Didn't they want a he-man like you?"

"Wasn't that, Sarge. I was just too damn arrogant then. Wouldn't listen to them, to their advice that I get some training in acting. Just being a he-man wasn't enough."

"Still are arrogant to some degree."

"I know I am. I'm working on it, though."

"Being in combat changes a man's perspective, don't it?" Roletto asked.

"Yeah, it --." A few shells exploded near the wall, causing him to stop talking. When the dust cleared, he looked at Roletto. "You know, being in combat even for a short time before I joined your team taught me a lot. No man can do it all by himself. Have to be part of a team. I never really understood that before. Doesn't matter whether you're the boss or just a peon, it's being part of the team that counts."

"That's true, Murphy. Combat takes a lot of arrogance out of everyone. Did it for me and it will for you, too."

"Yeah," Murphy snorted, "but I, well, gotta tell you about one of my escapades. You know, back in New York, and even since, I was -- well, I had a reputation as a real whiz with the women."

"You?" Banks questioned from the side, leaning forward so he could look at Murphy in the dim light.

"Yeah, me," Murphy acknowledged, "I'd pick them up, take them to bed and then leave. In reality, I was a real heel."

"Lots of guys in the services are that way," Thornquist quipped dryly, "ain't they, Martinez?"

"Sure are. I mean, all of us are a long way from home, so we act more recklessly and without the usual restraints."

"Exactly what I mean," Murphy asserted, "anyway, I met this young woman in Long Beach -- shortly after I got back from a few days leave. She was a real nice, polite, naive kid, a real doll -- know what I mean?"

Before anyone could answer, another barrage jolted the area. Everyone ducked down as dust and dirt flew around them and the earth shook violently.

"So you met this real doll," Thornquist queried after the dust settled, "then what?"

"Right. She was something else. Not at all like some of the girls I knew in New York. She was a decent gal. I think she fell for me right away. Completely. We went to dinner and then we drove -- she had her own car. I didn't have any wheels. We went to this spot on the hill where everyone goes and we started neckin."

"Wow!" Banks exclaimed, "you did work fast!"

"I know," Murphy snorted, "almost too fast. I, well, she was totally mine. Seemed to trust me completely. I coulda done anything I wanted to. I started takin her clothes off and she didn't protest or nothin. Just pressed close to me, a bit nervous and trembling some, but yet calm and collected. So much so I began to wonder if she'd done it all before. Know what I mean?"

"We know," Roletto replied impatiently, "go on."

"Well, I started feelin bad about it all, about what I was doing. You know, taking advantage of her and all. I mean, she was too young to be a pro."

"Some of them girls start real young," Banks stated knowingly.

"Maybe, but there was something more, well, wholesome about her. She was, or seemed to be, so innocent and naive. So, finally, before we went too far, I decided to stop. She seemed very relieved at that point, but I really think she would have let me go all the way if I pushed her."

"Maybe you should have, Murph," Martinez shrugged, "some of them gals expect it."

"No, I'm glad I stopped. Anyway, after she got her clothes back on, beats all if she didn't ask me if I wanted to go and meet her parents. So, what the hell, I agreed."

"Wow!" Thornquist gasped, "that was fast! Do you think she might have -- I mean, if you had done it?"

"No maybe about it," Murphy laughed, "want to know

who her father was?"

"Does it matter?" Banks shrugged with an air of indifference.

"It does. He was a Major -- in the Corps. Stationed at Pendleton and on the General's staff."

"Good grief!" Thornquist exclaimed, "if you had -- man, you'd be married now and maybe saddled with a wife and kid!"

"Or rotting away in some brig somewhere -- at hard labor."

"I think it's a good story, Murph," Roletto added thoughtfully, "I don't know much about psychology or whatever, but it showed that you have a decent bone in your body. Maybe a lot of them."

"He's got a point, Murph," Thornquist noted, "at least you showed yourself to be a nice guy. Not many guys in the Corps -- in any branch of the service, for that matter -- would do what you did. That gal ought to be grateful."

"You're a stronger man because of it," Banks noted, "have you seen her since?"

"No, we got shipped out a week later, which probably was for the best. But, you know, it helped change my thinking about girls and taking them out. I don't feel like I have to take them to bed right away now. Except, of course, the women we pick up in Japan. We know they're pro's."

"You never know, Murphy. That relationship might have blossomed into the love of the century," Roletto joked.

"With a Major for a father-in-law? No way!"

"Know what you mean," Roletto nodded, "hey, guys, it's startin to get light. Better chow down now so we'll be ready to go when the Lieutenant is ready."

An hour later, the team moved out. Again, they were on the point. The opposition seemed to be much lighter than the day before. A few firefights broke out, but they were easily handled. The team functioned well together and cooperated with other teams as necessary.

Roletto was really impressed at how quickly they had melded themselves into a cohesive fighting unit. He knew it wasn't necessarily any reflection of his ability to lead. Good men had a way of quickly learning how to use the tools they have in such a way as to survive -- a fact true not only in combat, but in other walks of life. Good men realized that coordination and teamwork was needed to achieve goals.

He admitted to himself that, at first, he had been somewhat worried about Murphy. Being a street bum from New York, Murphy had street smarts, to be sure. But men with street smarts tended to be loners. Thankfully, Murphy was not a loner. He heard a shout from Martinez and snapped out of his reverie. Ahead was another group of Marines!

"How in hell did anyone -- we're the damn point!" Roletto muttered. He stared at the troops in confusion.

"We've broken through, Sarge!" Martinez announced, "these guys is with the First!"

"Hey! Okay, man!" Roletto exulted, "hey guys! We've broken through!"

They had just taken up their assigned positions along the river bank when Lieutenant Trowbridge approached. The Lieutenant was furious and he wasn't hiding his feelings! His face livid, Trowbridge cursed and ranted loudly, then glanced at Sergeant Greenberg. The Sergeant was half-grinning, fidgeting with the sling on his rifle and looking at him with obvious amusement.

"What are you grinning about, Sergeant?" Trowbridge angrily demanded.

"Nothin, Lieutenant," Greenberg replied, "except -- well, I ain't ever seen you so upset before. Fact is, I ain't ever heard you cuss like that. Is somethin wrong?"

Lieutenant Trowbridge stared at him for a long moment, his eyes studying Greenberg's face to make sure the Sergeant wasn't mocking him. They had been together for a long time -- Greenberg had been in the first command he had been assigned to. Greenberg probably knew him as well as he knew himself, maybe better. He took a deep breath and lowered his eyes.

"It's the brass, Greenberg. They don't seem to think we're good enough to get into the fight in Seoul. So they gave us the assignment of guarding this stupid ferry crossing. While the rest of the regiment is fighting their way into Seoul, from the north, and getting into the action, we get to sit on our asses here and defend this stupid, insignificant ferry crossing. It's insulting! That's why I'm cussing. My platoon is as good as any other, better in fact. We should be in the thick of the fighting."

"Suppose they is doing their best, sir," Greenberg shrugged, "be awful hard for us t'get into position real quick like to help in Seoul. At least, being here, we can make sure no gooks mount an attack on this flank. So maybe they did right by us, sir."

Trowbridge studied the ground for several moments, assessing Greenberg's words. Then, with a smile, he raised his eyes and met Greenberg's gaze. "Yeah, Sergeant, I guess you're right. Hell, there's going to be a lot of fighting ahead and we'll get our share of it eventually. I shouldn't have ranted on like that. Not officer-like, so they say. It isn't conduct befitting an officer to cuss and carry on like I did. I'm sorry."

"Everyone's gotta let of steam once in a while, Lieutenant," Greenberg shrugged, "even officers. Least, I think officers is human, too."

Trowbridge laughed. "Okay, Greenberg, you win. I can't stay angry now. I sure hope I'm human. Hat to be so arrogant as to think I was better than enlisted men or anyone else just because I wear this bar." He paused and glanced at the terrain surrounding their area. "Your men positioned well?"

"Yes, sir."

"They all okay? Plenty of ammo and food?"

"Enough ammo, sir, but I doubt if any of them would call them rations food."

"Not very tasty."

"No, sir."

"I know. Wish we could get some hot chow up here. By the way, how is the new man fitting in?"

"Tilton? He's okay, sir," Greenberg replied, "won't really know until we see how he does under fire. In a real battle, that is. He's been under fire before around Pusan. Don't know enough about that action to say if it was a real battle or not. So far, he's done okay."

"Wanted to get you another Jewish boy, you know," Trowbridge offered, "but none were available."

"That's okay, sir," Greenberg smiled, "Tilton may be a Christian, but he's a good one. Not like some I've known."

"Good. Well, I gotta check on the others. Take care, Greenberg."

"Yes sir." Greenberg fussed with his helmet as Lieutenant Trowbridge walked away. Then he turned to check on the members of his team.

Withrow was behind the line, leaning against a rock and reading the letter he had received from his girlfriend for the umpteenth time. It was the one he received just before shipping out, breaking off the romance. His face reflected the self-pitying mood he was in. Greenberg simply shook his head and turned away.

Tobin was watching the rice paddy off to the right. He sensed Greenberg looking at him and twisted around, then nodded and grinned, gave Greenberg the okay sign. "Lieutenant have anything interesting to say?"

"Naw," Greenberg replied, "he was just a bit upset at the brass for not lettin us go into Seoul with the rest of the regiment."

"Geez," Tobin snorted, "I'm kinda glad they put us here for now. Nice to have some peace and quiet."

"Yeah, guess so," Greenberg agreed. He spotted Franklin on the left, watching a small draw that led away from the river. Although Franklin appeared to be half asleep, he knew the man was alert to any movement in or near the draw. That was the type of man Franklin was.

He turned and walked to Tilton's position in the center. Gary was scanning the area in front of him intently. He turned abruptly when Greenberg approached and then silently nodded. Then he turned back to the front.

"Something is brewing out there, Sarge," he stated softly without turning his head, "I've seen movement in the brush several times. Haven't been able to identify what, though. Each time, it's a bit closer."

"Animal?" Greenberg questioned with a frown.

"Don't know," Tilton shrugged, "but I don't like it. They're good at sneaking up on us, you know. Back on that ridge near Pusan, they snuck up real quiet like whenever they attacked."

"At night, though, wasn't it?"

"Most of the time. Occasionally, they would try it in the daytime." Tilton paused and glanced at Greenberg's face. "Guess you think I'm worried about nothing. Maybe I am. Still don't like it. With all that cover, they could get real close. If they're in any great number, we'd have a tough time stopping them if they get too close."

"I guess they could manage to get close," Greenberg admitted, "but, on the other hand, they -- there, something moved off to the left! Looked like a man!"

"I saw it, too, Sarge," Gary breathed, "bothers me. Do you think you'd better alert the others? I'm kinda worried."

"You're right," Greenberg grunted, "I'll get the other men shifted over here for support. Nobody's mentioned any activity out in front of them." He eased back and moved toward the other men.

Gary watched him go, then turned back toward the front. A shot rang out and the bullet chewed up dirt not far from his head! He shrank down to lessen the target he presented, but kept his rifle trained on the area the shot came from. When the North Korean rose up to fire again, Gary squeezed off a round. The man slumped back.

Behind him, Gary could hear the other men rushing to defensive positions around him. He fired again at a moving target, tried to ignore the bullets spraying around him. For what seemed like an eternity, he fired and fired, reloaded and fired some more! Then he realized others were also shooting back and the North Koreans.

He felt someone slide up beside him and glanced over. It was Sergeant Greenberg. The man ignored him and continued firing with a cool, calm demeanor. Gary nodded -- it was what he would have expected from Greenberg..

The North Koreans kept advancing. When men fell, others took their placed and continued the assault. Gary could feel the tension in his body, the soreness in his shoulder from firing so long. He lost track of how many shells he had fired. Then, finally, it seemed like the charging North Koreans diminished.

"They're falling back," Greenberg announced.

"Looks like it," Tilton sighed.

"Anyone hit?" Greenberg asked of no one in particular.

"We're all okay, Sarge," Franklin answered, "but we sure did a number on them gooks."

"I think we did," Greenberg acknowledged, "thanks to Tilton, we were forewarned. Good job, guys." He saw Lieutenant Trowbridge approaching and gave him the okay sign. The lieutenant nodded and veered away to check on another team. A few minutes later, he returned and approached.

"That was quite a charge, Sergeant."

"Yes, sir. If it wasn't for Tilton, we might have been caught flat-footed."

"I don't understand."

"Well, sir, Tilton was watching the center and he saw the men advancing long before they got close enough to attack. He alerted me and we got into position to hold them off. Otherwise, they might have gotten real close."

"Good. Tilton might just be a good man to have in the group. He do okay in the fighting?"

"Yes, sir, did right well. I'm glad I had him here."

CHAPTER SIXTEEN

With the capture of Seoul and with their primary supply line cut, the will of the North Korean Army around Pusan wilted. In short order, the Eighth Army broke out of the Pusan Perimeter and started advancing north. It appeared that General MacArthur's gamble had paid off. There were now two major questions: would the United Nations forces advance beyond the 38th Parallel and would the troops be home by Christmas?

As if in response to the former question, the higher echelons of command immediately began laying plans for the invasion of the North Korean country. The foremost and most popular of these plans called for the First Marine Division to be extracted from the front, loaded aboard ships at Inchon, and taken to the east coast for an amphibious landing at Wonsan. For, although the primary supply line through Seoul and down the peninsula had been cut, the enemy could still head north along the east coast. It was considered imperative that the large number of enemy heading north be headed off and captured. Most were traveling in unorganized groups and posed a grave threat to civilians and military alike.

So the Marines were extracted from the front and replaced by Army, United Nations troops and South Korean Marine and Army units. The loading of the Division and its supplies was originally scheduled to be completed in four days. Given the capricious tides at Inchon and the number of Marines involved, that time frame was completely unrealistic. So the date of the proposed landing was pushed back.

In the meantime, the Marine brass was given their assignment and began their detailed planning. It was then discovered that no maps of the proposed assault area were available and that intelligence on the beaches, tides, roads and other important details were sadly lacking. So various staff units were put to work in a near-frantic effort to obtain the vital information and maps.

The Photo Section of the Marine Air Wing was directed to take aerial photos of the region and, from them, put together a mosaic from which adequate maps could be produced. Given the lack of aircraft available for this type of work, it became a gargantuan task. Regardless, information on the road network and exits from the beaches had to be developed.

Divers and Frogmen from the Navy were assigned to investigate the beaches and determine where it would be best to land the troops. Any obstacles placed along the shore by the enemy had to be identified and eventually destroyed. Also, any hidden defense emplacements had to be located.

In the meantime, the Marines were stuck aboard ship. All they could do during this period of enforced inactivity was hope the problems would be solved soon so the landing could take place. Otherwise, it seemed as if the war was passing them by.

Eventually, a large mosaic was constructed from the thousands of photos and planning for the landing could be resumed. Then it was discovered that South Korean forces would take Wonsan before the Marines could possibly effect a landing. That was a direct slap in the face to the thousands of Marines aboard the ships. The Army and, possibly, even the USO would get to Wonsan long before them. Of course, everyone in the ranks blamed Dugout Doug for the fiasco.

Once aboard ship, Glenn Martin made a determined effort to contact Harry Schein, whom he knew was somewhere in the Third Battalion of the 1st Regiment. With no other information to go on, the attempt was doomed to failure. No one seemed to know or be able to find out which platoon

Schein was with. In fact, no one appeared to even know who he was! Glenn was getting quite frustrated when Sergeant Kimball stepped in.

"Look, Glenn," Kimball advised, "it's hard to locate an individual without going clear to the top. Even then, the chances of finding him are almost zero to none. Just hope you'll run into him somewhere, maybe in Japan if they give us R&R leave."

"Yeah, I guess you're right, Sarge," Martin nodded, "it's just -- well, five of us went through boot camp together and came over here before they split us up. We're going to meet after the war and, I just wanted to see him."

"And you will," Kimball encouraged, "like I said, perhaps you'll meet in Japan. There's talk some of us will be going to Japan soon -- Kyoto or Tokyo -- for a week or so. That would be neat."

"Always wanted to see Japan," Glenn enthused, "we didn't get to stop there on the way over. Went straight to Pusan."

"I hear the Japanese girls are something else."

"You don't think they'd harbor any ill will toward us, do you?" Glenn asked.

"I wouldn't think so. Hell, it's been five years or more. Sure we fought the Japanese in War Two, but we're almost like saving their butts now. I mean, them North Koreans, if they take all of Korea, could invade Japan next. Especially if the Chinese Reds butt in and help them."

"You think they will?" Glenn questioned.

"Don't know. Suppose it's possible. All them Communists tend to stick together. But, if they do, maybe old Harry Ass Truman will let the Chinese Nationalists invade China proper."

"That would be something else," Glenn snorted.

"Hey Murphy!" Sergeant Roletto called, "got a visitor."

"Yeah? Who?"

"I dunno," Roletto snorted, "I ain't your receptionist. Go on back, fella."

"Thanks," Gary Tilton smiled. He stepped past Sergeant Roletto and looked around for Murphy. Then he saw him propped up against the bulkhead. "Hiya, Murphy!"

"Hey! Tilton! How y'doing, man? You over your sea sickness?"

Gary laughed. "You bet. Got my sea legs at last. You guys have a rough time in Seoul?"

"Wasn't bad. How about you?"

"Same," Gary nodded, "we had one big fight -- was assigned to protect a ferry crossing on the Han. They wanted to take it back. We kept it. That's about it."

"Well, we were slated to go in on the flank and almost got ambushed. But we managed to hold our own. Had a good firefight, though." Murphy paused, his eyes searching Tilton's face. "You know anything about the others?"

"No," Tilton shook his head, "I was hoping you might have heard something."

"Nothin," Murphy shrugged, "and with them being in other battalions, probably no way to find out anything. I'd also like to find out about Sergeant Parker. He's one man I learned to respect, you know. Along with you and the others, of course."

"I know, Murphy," Tilton nodded, "we all liked Parker. Kinda strange, us being in the same regiment and all. I guess Harry and Martin are in the First. Ears, I think, went with Parker to the Fifth."

"Both the First and the Fifth saw a lot of action, from what I've heard."

"Yeah, well, we'll see our share once we get to Wonsan. Probably be a worse landing than Inchon."

"Ain't you heard?" Murphy frowned.

"Heard what?"

"The Koreans -- the South Koreans have already taken

Wonsan. We'll be makin a landing, okay, but behind our own lines."

"You're kidding!" Gary gasped.

"No way! They got there faster than anyone thought possible. From the scuttlebutt going around, the USO shows are going to get there before we do."

"That would be insulting, to say the least!" Gary replied, "good grief! Ain't the top brass got any pride at all?"

The stateroom was small, but neat. Sergeant Parker noted that with one sweeping glance. A small, built-in desk was against the left bulkhead while the bunk was against the right. Colonel Dickins was seated at the desk, half turned away from the door. An empty chair was between the desk and the door.

"Sergeant Parker reporting, as ordered, sir," Parker announced.

Dickins turned around and nodded, his eyes searching Parker's face. "Good, good, Parker," Dickins smiled, "sit down, man. Be at ease."

"Yes sir," Parker grinned. He moved to the offered chair. *So this is how a battalion commander travels. Pretty nice. Much better than us enlisted men.*

"I suppose you're wondering why I called for you."

"Yes, sir, I am. Did I do something wrong?"

"Oh, heavens no, man!" Dickins chortled, "not at all."

"Then --"

"I have some real good news for you."

"My discharge, sir?" Parker asked with raised eyebrows.

Dickins laughed. "Not quite, Parker, not quite. Remember Colonel Bowman? Colonel Lucius Bowman?"

"Yes, sir. Quite well, in fact. He commanded the provisional battalion a bunch of use came over in., Before the division was ready to sail."

"That's the man."

"Is he all right, sir?" Parker queried.

"He's fine, Sergeant. A good Marine. You may recall he was sent back to Camp Pendleton to establish a training program for replacements."

"Yes, sir, that's what he told me."

"He got his star a few weeks ago."

"That is good news, Colonel!" Parker smiled, "if anyone deserved it, he did. A good man to serve with and have in command."

"That's what a lot of others have said," Dickins agreed, "I've never had the privilege of meeting him, but I have heard a few things."

"Is that why the Colonel called for me, sir? To tell me the good news about Colonel Bowman?"

"Well, partly," Dickins admitted, "you know, a General has a bit more pull than a Colonel, if you know what I mean."

"I would think so, sir. At least a lot more than a Lieutenant or a Sergeant."

"Right. You are aware, also, that good Sergeants are hard to come by over here. Seems we've been losing a lot of NCO's lately, especially in the battle for Seoul. a lot of Sergeants were casualties."

"I know that, sir."

"Well, to make a long story shorter, Parker, Bowman -- General Bowman now -- has requested that you be transferred to his command at Camp Pendleton. He also wants to promote you to Lieutenant."

"Me, sir?" Parker gasped. He was at a loss for words and could only stare in shock at Colonel Dickins.

"Yes, you, Sergeant. Bowman apparently put a lot of stock in you. He declared you to be more valuable to the Corps as a training officer than as a field leader. The high brass apparently agreed with him. You're scheduled to leave tomorrow from Kimpo Airfield for a flight to Tokyo. From there, you'll go by commercial flight to Los Angeles and then to Camp Pendleton, where you'll report to General Bowman. Your orders have been cut. The Sergeant outside has them for you. The war's over for you, Parker. You're going home."

"Pardon me, sir, but do I have any choice whatsoever?"

"Don't want to go?" Dickins questioned.

"I'd love to go, Colonel," Parker smiled, "but I do have responsibilities here, too."

"Your team of men?"

"Yes, sir. They're young and inexperienced. Learning fast, but still --."

"The entire Corps is young and inexperienced, Parker, the whole Corps. But, we'll take care of your men. However, as I said, we are a bit short of qualified line Sergeants right now. Could one of your men take over and do a decent job?"

"I think so, sir. Private First Class --."

"I must tell you, Parker," Dickins interrupted, "that I have already discussed the matter with Lieutenant Bradford. He has made his recommendation from among your team. By the way, he really hates to lose you, but agrees with everyone else that it's better for the Corps. You see, we desperately need trained men over here and soon."

"I understand, sir," Parker nodded, "the one man I was about to mention -- PFC Lofton -- is, in some ways, a natural leader."

"And you think he should take over the fire team?" Dickins asked, his eyes questioning.

"No, sir, I don't," Parker asserted, "he's a born leader, but he isn't ready yet."

"Perhaps you had better explain yourself, Sergeant."

"Yes, sir. Lofton is too rash. He doesn't listen to instructions and goes his own way rather than follow orders explicitly. Some independence is good and the Corps allows that. But not the way he exercises it. He'd end up getting himself or the others killed or both."

"I see," Dickins mused thoughtfully, "how about the

others? Worrell, Hall or Jackson?"

Parker barely suppressed a grin. *So he has been well briefed by Lieutenant Bradford.* "Good men, Colonel. I believe Owen Worrell is the best man to take over. I knew his brother in War II before he was killed in action. His younger brother, Owen, is much like he was. Owen is levelheaded, calm under fire, and he listens to orders and advice. I would trust the men with him, sir."

"I see. And you aren't naming him because you knew his brother, are you?"

"Absolutely not, Colonel. Worrell is well qualified. He is inexperienced, admittedly so. But he learns fast, sir."

"That's very interesting, Parker," Colonel Dickins nodded, "most interesting. Lieutenant Bradford essentially said the same thing."

This time Parker could not suppress his grin. "That's gratifying, Colonel."

"Exactly. Why didn't they promote you to a commissioned rank earlier?"

"I don't know, sir. Besides, that's up to the Corps."

Dickins nodded. "Yes, I suppose it is. We'll see about that. One more thing, Parker. Do you want to tell the men or do you want Lieutenant Bradford to do it?"

"I'll tell them, sir. Lofton will, I think, take it better if I explain things. Besides, I think I've earned their respect these last few weeks and if I tell them, it might sink in."

"I was hoping you'd say that, Parker," Dickins replied. He made a few notes on a pad, then put his pen down. For a second, he just stared at the paper, then he stood and extended his hand to Sergeant Parker. "Sergeant, I want you to know you've earned my respect, also. If you can instill that spirit of courage, that sense of honor and duty in the men you train, you'll be worth a dozen Sergeants over here. Good luck."

"Thank you, sir."

The plane was loaded with wounded men being

transferred to hospitals in Japan. Most of them had received serious wounds that could not be treated in the field stations and no hospital facilities were ready yet in Korea. It was rumored a hospital ship would soon be arriving to handle the casualties.

Sergeant Parker settled back in the canvas jump seat alongside the forward bulkhead and sighed. It felt good to know he was leaving the war zone, leaving combat behind. Of course, he would be training men to fight. There was much he could teach such men. He glanced at the wounded man on the stretcher in front of him. The man was sleeping -- or drugged -- which probably was for the best. Although there were canvas bunks along both sides of the fuselage, this man's stretcher was on the floor. All the bunks were filled.

His thoughts drifted to the men he was leaving behind. Worrell, Lofton, Hall and Jackson. He wondered if they would be coming back whole, wounded or dead. One never knew in combat.

A slight smile touched his lips when he thought of Lofton. The man was upset when told he would not be taking over. At first, he didn't want to listen to the reasons why. Then he calmed down. Although it was obvious he wasn't completely satisfied, he did, finally, accept the fact.

Worrell, on the other hand, really didn't want the job or the responsibility. He had to be convinced he had the ability to lead. It took some doing and the fact he received a promotion to Buck Sergeant helped convince him. It seemed that Hall and Jackson were relieved that Lofton was not taking over. They knew what he might do. They wanted someone like Worrell. And Lieutenant Bradford. His recommendation was surprising. It wasn't as if the Lieutenant had been with the team very much. Yet, he seemed to know the men quite well.

Parker leaned back and smiled. It was good to be going home in one piece. He took a deep breath and heard the man on the stretcher moan. Parker looked at him and he seemed to be hurting.

Parker's eyes sought the Corpsman. The man was near the center of the plane. He was a husky, muscular man and Parker wondered why he had chosen to become a Corpsman instead of a fighting man. Not that the man's decision really mattered much. Everyone in the Corps respected those who tended to the wounded. The Corpsmen took as many chances or more than any Marine ever took even though they never carried a weapon. It took a lot of courage to expose themselves to enemy fire to help a wounded Marine. Many a wounded Marine was able to recover because of them.

He caught the Corpsman's eye and nodded toward the wounded man. The Corpsman approached quickly and knelt beside the man and checked on him.

"He seems to be okay, Sergeant," the Corpsman nodded, "still under sedation. With all the drugs in him, I don't think he's hurting. Just dreaming, I guess."

"Looks to be hurt real bad."

"Yeah, he took a lot of shrapnel, but he came through the surgery in good shape. The doctors got most of it out of him. They said they'd get the rest once he gets better. He's a tough hombre." He glanced at the man and smiled slightly. "He'll be fine once he gets some rest and some good care."

"I'd say he's getting good care now," Parker declared.

"Well, thanks, Sergeant. We do what we can."

"Anything I can do to help?"

The Corpsman shook his head. "No, Sergeant, nothing. Just relax. You've earned that right."

Parker nodded. "Well, they certainly have earned it more than me," he commented with a glance at the other wounded, "so, if I can be of any assistance at all, please let me know. I feel kind of useless just sitting here and doing nothing."

"Okay, Sergeant. Uh, you're a line Sergeant, right?"

"Yes."

"Thought so. Not many in a staff position would care that much about these guys. So you just relax. We'll take care of these guys. You enjoy your trip. And thanks for asking. You heading home?"

Parker nodded. "Being sent back to join a training command. As a Lieutenant, I guess. At least that's what they told me. Rejoining a General I used to serve with. He requested my transfer."

"Well, good luck Sergeant. I think you'll make a good officer."

CHAPTER SEVENTEEN

Winter was beginning to set in when the Marines finally went ashore at Wonsan. Initial plans had called for the division to attack to the west after landing and join up with the Eighth Army, which had advanced to the north of Pyongyang. The rapid succession of events and the unexpected victories following the landing at Inchon altered even these plans before the Marines when ashore. New plans and directives developed by GHQ called for the Marines to relieve the Republic of South Korea forces, defend the Kojo area and patrol the routes to the west. In addition, one regiment was to advance northward to the Yalu River, which forms the border with China.

Although there was much talk about the war ending soon and troops being sent home by Christmas, not everyone was optimistic. Early rotation was, of course, highly desirable for everyone and the troops were quite hopeful. But a few ranking officers both in staff positions and in line units realized the situation could change quickly. These few admitted the Chinese or even the Soviets could send assistance to the North Koreans. There was talk at GHQ about allowing the Chinese Nationalists to invade China from Formosa, but few expected the Truman administration to permit that.

Glenn Martin scanned the area just south of the town of Wonsan, noting it was cleaner than Changwon in the south around Pusan. The beaches were white and the water seemed clear. The flat plain around the landward side of the populated area extended out almost three miles. It was all flooded rice paddies. He shrugged and spotted Sergeant Kimball.

The Sergeant apparently was talking to some villagers

with the help of a Korean Army interpreter. The interpreter looked like a college educated man. He wore rimmed glasses and his hair was short, his body well conditioned. The conversation seemed to be quite animated, the interpreter waving his hands and shaking his head vigorously. Glenn wondered what was going on, so he ambled over.

"Sergeant, they are saying many of the young men in villages are actually North Korean soldiers disguised as civilians. They claim the men have threatened them and made them keep quiet. But, they say, now that you Americans are here, they feel free to speak out. What they are saying is not true, of course. Our people have checked everything and everybody completely and have sent patrols out thousands of yards. We have uncovered nothing. No enemy, no armaments. These civilians know nothing. They are just simple, frightened farmers. They know nothing of war or the military. Before the war started, they were oppressed and they fear a return to that situation."

Martin listened to the interpreter and thought he was using pretty good English. Most South Koreans, even educated ones, did not speak English that well. Glenn shrugged and nodded to the older villager who was standing nearby. He appeared to be the village elder or whatever they called them in Korea. His clothing was much like that some of the men on the pier had been wearing when the unit arrived in Pusan. The pajama-like clothing was loosely fitted and the man's black hat seemed out of place.

The man grinned and revealed a few missing teeth. From what Glenn could discern from the conversation between Kimball and the interpreter, the elderly man was concerned about the younger men who had accompanied him and the other older villagers to the site.

Martin smiled back to the old man and turned away. He had wondered about the presence of so many younger, military aged men, too. He moved to the side so he could watch Sergeant Kimball and the interpreter.

Kimball glanced at Glenn before replying to the interpreter. "Well, this area was in North Korea before the war. I just wonder why the North Koreans would allow so many young men to remain out of the military. They're a Communist regime -- they don't do things like that. They require that everyone who is fit serve in the military."

"I tell you -- it is not a problem, Sergeant," the interpreter insisted, "they are civilians who are most happy to be out of the war. They swear that when the North Koreans were recruiting, they did not come to this village. I strongly emphasize, sir, they are not military."

"Yeah, sure," Kimball snorted, "thanks for your assistance." He clearly remained unconvinced and shook his head in wonder as the interpreter walked away. Then he turned to Martin.

"Hey, Martin!" he called, "go tell everyone to get ready to move out. We're going south -- to Hill 128, near Kojo. We'll be overlooking a couple of villages called Pangdong-ni and Habongdong-ni."

"Okay, Sarge," Glenn nodded. He strolled over to where DeWitt, Granger and Masters were waiting.

"What's up?" DeWitt asked.

"Sarge says we're going south -- to Hill 128. Supposed to overlook a couple of other towns as well as a large rice paddy, I guess."

"He say that?" DeWitt questioned.

"No, but what else is there around here?"

DeWitt laughed. "See what you mean. Sure a lot of men of military age in these towns."

Martin nodded. "Sarge is worried about it. The interpreter says it's okay, but the locals say they're enemy soldiers in civilian dress. I'm inclined to believe the locals."

"Me, too," DeWitt agreed. He drew out a map. "What hill we going to?"

"Hill 128."

"Oh, here it is. Long way out there. At least five or

six miles. I don't like it."

"Don't like what, DeWitt?" Granger tuned in.

"We're going out about five or six miles -- to a hill. That's to damn far."

"We'll have support, won't we?" Granger questioned.

"I suppose. Hope so, anyway," DeWitt snorted, "here comes the Sarge. He'll fill us in on the details, I hope."

"You guys ready to move out?" Kimball asked.

"Pretty much, I guess," Martin shrugged. There wasn't much to do to get ready to move. All their gear was in their packs.

"Then belay the order," Kimball grinned, "we're staying here tonight. Going out in the morning."

"What about all these young guys, Sarge?" DeWitt wondered.

"Interpreter says it's okay. Frankly, I don't like the situation. I mean, if they are military, then we have the enemy all around us. I don't trust the South Korean military types. They seem pretty sloppy to me and too trusting. These older people -- they keep saying the young men are North Korean soldiers. I tend to believe them. So stay alert as much as possible."

"Where do you want us to bunk down?" Martin inquired.

"Right here seems pretty good. We don't have any guard responsibilities tonight, but, even so, we need a defendable spot. This seems to fit the bill. Going to be cold tonight. Had ice on the water this morning, you know," Kimball reminded them.

"Yeah," Granger snorted, "hear it gets real cold up here in the north."

That night, the temperature dipped well below freezing. Several of the men discovered that the zippers on their sleeping bags had a tendency to get stuck when the air was that cold. By early morning, a directive was issued to the extent that anyone in a squad on watch was not to zip up their sleeping bags. Most of the men scoffed at the order.

The next morning, the entire company was loaded aboard either a train or trucks and taken to the area around Kojo. There were no attacks and no interruptions along the thirty-nine mile route. Once in the Kojo area, Sergeant Kimball's team was told to take up positions on Hill 128. The company CP was set up near Kojo to the north.

The hill was almost seven miles further south and faced the sea. It overlooked the villages of Pangdong-ni and Habangdong-ni. The hilltop was almost a circular area, with gentle slopes leading downward. On the north side was a smaller area that formed a kind of spur that curved to the west a good fifty yards before sloping sharply downward. The men took a good look around, then began the task of digging in.

Almost before they got established, villagers came up to greet them and brought them gifts of fresh eggs. The men welcomed the gifts, but were unsure of the visitors. Although most were elderly, there were a large number of young men of military age among them. The older villagers seemed happy to have them there; the younger ones appeared resentful. It was eerily similar to the situation near Wonsan.

"I don't know," Kimball commented to Corporal DeWitt, "I got the feeling they're casing our positions."

"Strange you should say that, Sarge," DeWitt replied, "Martin was just saying the same thing. You think they're planning an attack?"

"Could be," Kimball nodded. He saw Granger and Masters huddled together and walked over.

"What do you think, Sarge?" Granger asked when Kimball got close, "they figuring on driving us off the hill?"

"Why do you say that?"

"Seems strange for these guys to come up here with eggs for us without some reason," Granger explained.

"I tend to think Granger is right," Masters added.

"Here comes Martin," Kimball noted, "let's see what

he thinks." He waited until Martin joined the group. "These guys think the gooks are casing the place for the enemy, Martin. What's your opinion?"

"Well, let me tell you about my experience back around Pusan." He paused and glanced at everyone to see if they were listening. "We were raw -- no doubt about that. First taste of combat for most of us. But our Sergeant -- Parker was his name -- he was out of War Two. Had lots of experience. Anyway, the first night we used the foxholes the Army guys had dug. Had our choice of holes to snuggle into. Was more of them than us, you know. Anyway, it worked out well and saved us a lot of work."

"Don't see how that applies here," Granger snorted, "ain't no foxholes here except the ones we dug."

"Let me finish," Martin continued with a scowl, "so we stayed in them foxholes for two nights. Got attacked the second night. Lots of artillery and mortars, a mass charge by the infantry. So Parker, he came around and told us to change holes. There were still plenty of unused ones to go around."

"So what happened?" Kimball frowned.

"The next night, the gooks snuck in. They're real good at that, you know. Didn't hear them coming until they was real close. I swear to God, they went straight for the foxholes we had been in during the firefight. Somehow, they seemed to have mapped them out. If we had stayed in them original holes -- curtains."

"Okay," Kimball replied, "but how does that relate to --."

"I get the feeling the gooks are casing our positions. If they are, we should change our positions. As a safety factor if for no other reason. You asked what I thought and that's it. We should move."

"I guess it makes good sense," Kimball mused, his eyes searching the terrain of the hill, "rest of you guys think we should?"

"Better safe than sorry," Granger grunted.

"Agree," DeWitt nodded, "ground up here ain't so hard we can't dig another hole."

"Masters?"

"Good idea, Sarge. I think Martin makes sense."

"So do I," Kimball offered, "as soon as they get off the hill, we'll do it. However, I'm doing something different. We'll move onto the spur to the north. Ain't as high as the top of this hill, but, if they do attack, we'll be flanking them. Also, the slope is much steeper and no one will come up behind us. We'll spread out facing south."

He paused and studied their faces. "We'll also pair up. One man awake and outside a sleeping bag at all times. Understand?"

"It's supposed to get really cold tonight, Sarge," Masters complained, "we'll freeze outside a sleeping bag!"

Kimball glared at him contemptuously. "You read the order about the sleeping bags. What's your preference? You want to be warm and dead in the morning or a bit chilled and alive? You know them bags are death traps. We get attacked and that damn zipper sticks, you're helpless and you'll be dead before you can get it unstuck. So wrap up, but don't zip up. Do you hear me?"

At dusk, small fire fights broke out all around the hill. A truck was fired upon and what was reported to be an enemy group was observed and taken under fire. The reports of large groups of enemy soldiers were unconfirmed. Darkness settled in on an uneasy group of Marines.

Sergeant Kimball gathered his men around him in the dark after they had situated themselves on the spur. "Okay, here's what we're gonna do. Martin and DeWitt will take the first watch. Granger -- you and Masters will take the second. You guys suspect anything, get me immediately. Any questions?"

"We know the drill, Sarge," Martin replied.

"That's right," DeWitt agreed, "you guys just be sure

to relieve us on time."

"Don't worry, DeWitt," Granger snorted, "we'll let you get some beauty sleep tonight."

Kimball suppressed a slight grin even though he knew the men could not see his face. He was proud of these guys and knew they would stand by each other. He stared into the darkness and wondered if they would be attacked. Everything indicated it.

Shortly before midnight, Martin roused Kimball from his light sleep. "Heard something out there, Sarge," Martin explained, "I don't like it. Should I get Granger and Masters up?"

"No," Kimball stated, "let's see what happens first." He stood and followed Martin back to his post. His eyes scanned the slope leading to the top of the hill and saw nothing. "You sure of what you heard?"

"Yeah," Martin nodded, "I've been here long enough to recognize an enemy advance. They're coming. How many, I don't know."

"Well, maybe you should --."

A bugle blared and shots split the air! Several grenades exploded harmlessly on the top of the hill! The flames from the muzzles of the enemy weapons flashed in the night from three sides as the enemy advanced up the gentle slope! DeWitt moved closer to Kimball and Martin, his eyes wide.

"Get the others up," Kimball directed.

Martin turned to wake up Granger and immediately saw that the man was cursing and struggling to get out of his sleeping bag! Realizing that Granger would not be able to help immediately, he grabbed Granger's BAR and turned back. The rushing hordes were visible now in the dim light.

"Open up on them!" Kimball ordered.

The three men opened fire, pouring a hail of lead into the flank of the advancing enemy. The fire from the flank seemed to confuse the enemy and it took several minutes before they realized the Marines were not on top of the hill! Then, however, they shifted the point of their attack and came toward the spur!

Something hot and painful hit Martin's left shoulder and he felt the warm flow of blood down his arm. Even so, he continued to fire the BAR at anything that moved in front of him. The enemy kept advancing despite the heavy defensive fire from the three men. Then, suddenly, the advancing horde seemed to part and sweep around the spur! In a matter of minutes, the only firing that could be heard came from the north, close to where Hill 198 was located.

Shortly before midnight, a well-coordinated attack began on Hill 198. The enemy crept close over familiar terrain and launched their attack without warning. Amid bursting grenade and automatic weapons fire, the Marines were wrenched from their slumber. The men who were on watch fought valiantly against overwhelming numbers while men caught in their sleeping bags were trapped when their zippers stuck. Numerous positions were overrun by a determined enemy.

At the company Command Post, it was reported that Sergeant Kimball's team was overrun and the flank turned. That fact suggested that a withdrawal might be necessary. For the remainder of the night, the enemy made numerous probing assaults, trying to locate weak spots and areas where they could flank the defenders.

Finally, units were consolidated by withdrawing to the railroad tracks and establishing positions on either side of them. Then mortar fire was called in on the villages from which the attacks were believed to have originated. With the coming of dawn, following intensive air attacks on the village, reinforcements were sent in. The troops returned to Kojo and made a house to house search, netting a few snipers and stragglers. The city had largely been destroyed by the post-dawn air attacks.

The second day following the attack, Sergeant Kimball and his team made their way back to the lines. The uniforms of the four men able to walk were tattered and dirty. The faces of the men were drawn, dirty and tired looking. One man was being carried on a makeshift stretcher and two others appeared to be wounded. After getting a Corpsman to look after the wounded, Sergeant Kimball reported to Company Commander Captain Skelton and Platoon Leader Lieutenant Gilford.

"What happened, Sergeant?" Skelton demanded.

"They were upon us before we could blink, sir," Kimball replied, "Martin was on watch and heard them coming and, if it hadn't been for his advice and suggestions, we'd all be dead."

"What do you mean by that?" Skelton inquired.

"Well, sir, Martin was with that provisional battalion that fought near Pusan before joining the Division."

"Yes, I know that."

"Well, he suggested a trick they used there. Taught to them by a Sergeant who served in War Two -- Parker, I believe." Kimball paused to catch his breath.

"Go on."

"Uh, yes, sir. The gist of it, sir, was that they changed foxholes after a vicious firefight and assault. He said they figured the enemy had the old ones zeroed in, so to speak. That is, the enemy knew which holes they were using. So he suggested we do the same -- did new foxholes -- after those so-called civilians visited us on the hill."

"I see, Sergeant. Good idea," Skelton nodded with a glance at Gilford.

"Well, anyway, sir, we did it a bit different than they did. There was a small spur extending out on the north side of the hill and I directed our men to deploy there. We were below the high ground, but we flanked the enemy charge. Worked like a charm, Captain. Those bastards did have our positions mapped out, but we fooled them and, when they attacked, we blasted them from the flank. Wiped out a whole bunch of them."

"Why didn't your team fall back with the others? Gilford asked.

"Couldn't, sir. They swarmed around us and by-passed our position. If we had tried to withdraw, we'd have had to move through the entire enemy force."

"Well, how did you manage to get out alive?" Captain Skelton asked.

"Once the enemy surged by us, we went the other way. Took up positions in one corner of a rice paddy that had good cover and fields of view and made a stand there."

"They attack you later?" Lieutenant Gilford inquired.

"Yes, sir, Lieutenant. Several times," Kimball shrugged, "and we fought them off. Martin and DeWitt were fantastic in both actions."

"Were they both wounded?" Skelton asked.

"Yes, sir. But they fought well even after being shot -- DeWitt once and Martin twice. If it wasn't for Martin -- again, sir -- he must have wiped out an entire platoon by himself, sir. Sure glad I had him on my team. I'd like to recommend both men for an award, sir."

"Why is that, Kimball?" Gilford snorted.

"Well, Lieutenant, two of my men -- against orders -- had gone to sleep in their sleeping bags. When the attack hit, their zippers jammed and they couldn't fight. Martin saved their butts by holding off the enemy with Granger's BAR until he could help Granger get out of his sleeping bag. Same with Masters. He got stuck and Martin's actions saved both men from certain death."

"I see. Martin badly wounded?" Gilford wondered.

"He got hit in the left shoulder first, then, later, in his left hip. He still fought with us, but had to be carried back. DeWitt got grazed by a bullet along his head. Then later he got hit in the shoulder."

"You told us about Martin's exploits, Sergeant," Skelton noted, "how about DeWitt's?"

"He was fantastic, sir," Kimball grinned, "he and I were holding off the enemy and essentially protecting Martin's flank on the inside of the spur, where the enemy could advance from the top of the hill. DeWitt was grazed by a bullet in the initial assault, but came to in a few minutes. Man, was he angry. When three enemy charged us, he fought them off -- hand-to-hand, sir, with only his knife. Then four more charged. I was shooting out the other way -- holding off at least ten men -- but I saw DeWitt take them on. He's a former cowboy from Montana and he showed them gooks how to fight. Then he got hit in the shoulder. Was still able to fight and shoot, however."

Captain Skelton smiled and nodded. "Very good, Sergeant. Give us a write-up about both men and I'll forward it. You and your men did well. How about a write-up for an award for you? You earned it."

"No thanks, sir. They did most of the fighting. But, I thank you, sir."

"I suppose Martin will have to be evacuated," Lieutenant Gilford asked, glancing at the approaching Corpsman.

"I'm afraid so, sir," Kimball nodded. He turned to face the Corpsman and raised his eyebrows questioningly.

"I've already called for an evacuation helicopter, sir," the Corpsman noted.

CHAPTER EIGHTEEN

Four days after landing at Wonsan, the Marines of the Seventh Regiment were at Hamhung, some seventy road miles to the north. Despite deep concerns regarding stretching the regiment seventy miles along a single road in hostile territory, the orders still stood for the regiment to advance north. The concerns of regimental and divisional staff were based on the fact that the nearest friendly troops were over forty miles distant on one flank and almost seventy miles on the other flank. In addition, the enemy activity around Kojo weighed heavily on those in command. Clearly, they did not want a repeat of that.

Several patrols were sent out to check on road conditions and enemy dispositions. Limited resistance had been met, but rumors were rampant about the presence of Chinese troops in the hills. Republic of Korea troops were adamant that an army of Chinese were waiting for the Marines to advance. Marine intelligence was not certain and higher echelons seemed willing to ignore the possibility. MacArthur's GHQ staff was of the opinion that the Chinese would not dare to interfere.

As the advance continued, the resistance stiffened and, soon, it was confirmed that the Marines were in contact with the 124th Division of Communist Chinese troops. With this confirmation, the battle plans changed. To the Marines on the single road leading north, the situation now required them to be especially wary of being cut off and surrounded. Enemy troops apparently were not only in front of them, but on their flanks and behind them.

To prevent the enemy from cutting the road behind

them, the staff decided that a fortress of a hill known as Hill 659 had to be occupied. The hill was a distance of about fifteen hundred yards west of the road, which, in itself, was not a threat. But the fact was that any emplacements on the hill threatened not only a vital bridge, but a tunnel which, if destroyed, would cut off the supply line to the Marines, as there were no by-passes or other roads available.

So a platoon of Marines was immediately dispatched to take and hold the hill. These Marines made a valiant attempt to take the hill, but were beaten back with high casualties. Clearly, the enemy held Hill 659 in force and that was frightening to those in command. Because of its importance, another attempt was to be made to wrest control of the hill from the enemy.

Sergeant Greenberg scanned the faces of his men For the first time, he realized how young and innocent they seemed. They're just boys, he mused, young kids fresh out of high school! Of course, I'm not much older. But these guys -- I can't believe I've led them into battle.

His eyes settled on Tobin. The man looked almost angelic, his clear skin somewhat flushed and radiant. He could just as well be heading toward the synagogue as preparing to do battle against a determined enemy. Greenberg took a deep breath and shifted his gaze to Tilton.

Tilton appeared almost like an advertising poster boy. His face was clean and shaven, his uniform a bit rumpled, but neat. Anyone who didn't know better would expect him to step in front of a camera and strike a pose. He had matured since joining the group and actually seemed to be the most sober one of them all.

Then there was Franklin. The hot-tempered knife fighter watched him with a slight, knowing smile. It was as if he knew something the rest of them didn't. And, yet, he, also, looked more like a choirboy than a Marine. Somehow, he didn't appear as fierce as usual on this day.

Even Withrow had somehow pushed aside the self-pitying, maudlin emotionalism that had plagued him since the ship had sailed from San Diego. Now, he was calm and apparently at peace with his inner being, if that made any sense. Clearly, he must have forgotten that his girl had dumped him just before he sailed. He, too, had matured on the battlefield.

Greenberg took a deep breath. I've come to love these guys. Together, we've faced perils that have been far greater than anything any of us could have imagined in our wildest moments. These guys have stood by me, have fought beside me, have done what I demanded of them. They have made me very proud to be associated with them. I love them as much as a man can love anyone -- even a woman.

He closed his eyes and lowered his head. Now, I have to order them into a battle where we all might end up dead or, at the very least, casualties. How can I soften the words so as not to horrify them? How can I describe for them the terrors they will soon be facing? Maybe it would be better if I said nothing and just let them find out when the assault begins. No, I can't do that. It wouldn't be fair to them nor compatible with the love I have for them. I have to tell them the truth.

He swallowed the lump in his throat, ignored the heaviness in his heart. Lieutenant Trowbridge had explained what had to be done. The Lieutenant had told him and the other Sergeants that they had to take and hold Hill 659. The hill dominated the valley through which they had to advance and through which all of their supplies had to come. If the enemy were to put artillery or rockets on the hill, they could blast away the bridge and close the tunnel that was vital to keeping the road open. If the enemy did that, the regiment would be cut off from any source of resupply and vulnerable to annihilation.

Already, as Lieutenant Trowbridge had explained, one platoon had tried to take the hill. They had not succeeded, had only gotten halfway to the top. Their casualties had been high.

Very high. Only four men returned unscathed. There was only one path to the top. The rest of the hill was composed of nearly vertical cliffs.

The enemy knew that, of course. They also knew the Marines had no recourse but to make a direct assault if they wanted to occupy the hill. To attempt to go around and take the hill from behind was not feasible, although they, the enemy, had an escape route down the reverse slope. Therefore, the enemy had every gun on the hill zeroed in on the path. They had mortars registered on the path and they could shoot their rifles from covered positions. They could throw or roll grenades down on any advancing troops. No one knew if they had also mined the approach along the path. No one in the initial assault had advanced far enough to find out. The assault appeared suicidal and, yet, according to the brass, it had to be done.

Of course, no one had given any thought to calling in an air strike on the hill. When one of the Sergeants suggested that line of action, Lieutenant Trowbridge simply said it was not possible to do it, that it was too close to the road and would endanger troops on the road. Hell, it was fifteen hundred yards away! Greenberg shrugged. He was only a Sergeant, but he knew better. However, the officers seemed to be locked into a direct assault and that was what was going to be done.

Greenberg silently said a short prayer -- it was a Jewish prayer, but he believed it would apply to the Christians as well. After all, they all worshipped the same God. Well, maybe Franklin didn't. The man had always refused to listen to him or the Chaplain and had never wanted to talk about his beliefs or lack of them. So he wasn't sure about Franklin.

"Okay," He stated, "listen up. We got a dirty job to do. Lieutenant Trowbridge says it has to be done. Directive from higher up, I guess. No question about the fact its a necessity. One other platoon already has tried to do it and they got kicked around and had lots of casualties. Some of you may have seen their wounded being carried back. Not a pretty sight to see."

He paused and scanned their faces. They were listening carefully, which pleased him.

"There's two platoons going up at once this time. Only one path, but its wide enough, so they tell me. The other platoon will be on the left and we'll be on the right. We're going to take the hill -- Hill 659 -- and we're going to hold it. We'll go as far as we can as fast as we can, get within grenade range and toss some grenades at the enemy positions. When they explode, we're going to charge to the top before the Chinese have a chance to react and continue shooting or retreat. Understand?"

"Sure, Sarge," Franklin nodded, "but can we get rid of some of this heavy gear before we start up? Be a tough climb with all this extra crap."

"Of course. Drop it and carry extra ammo and grenades, instead. And some water."

"Who's gonna be on our left?" Tobin inquired.

"Another platoon. Don't know which one. Lieutenant didn't know."

"Oh, okay," Tobin shrugged.

"When -- how soon do we go?" Tilton questioned.

"In about fifteen minutes or so."

"That soon?"

"Yeah, that soon, Tilton. Any problems with that?"

"No, not really, Sarge," Tilton sighed, "I just thought I'd write a short letter home if there was time."

"Sorry, Tilton. I'd like to do that, too."

"Uh, rations," Withrow asserted, "they will bring us rations once we take the hill, won't they? I mean, we don't have to carry them, do we?"

Greenberg laughed. "The Corps won't let you starve, Withrow. They'll bring us some rations. Maybe even some filet mignon and red wine when we take the hill. Hey, you guys, this is serious business and it is critical. The enemy could cut us off and -- well, want you to know it's going to be rough. Very rough. The enemy has the trail zeroed in with everything they have. We have to advance through it regardless of what they throw at us and -- ."

He choked up and looked at their faces again. "I want you guys to know -- haven't said much about it, but, well, dammit! I love you guys. Really love you. Take care up there." He turned away to hide the mistiness in his eyes and began fidgeting with his gear. He walked a short distance away and stood with his back to them.

Tilton glanced at Tobin and frowned. Withrow looked at both of them, his eyes puzzled. Franklin snorted and seemed confused.

"What's with the Sarge?" Franklin finally asked, "he ain't never acted like this before."

"No, he hasn't," Tilton shrugged, "but, hey, you guys know him better than I do."

Tobin shook his head. "If I didn't know better, I'd say he turned away so we wouldn't see the tears in his eyes. He was a bit emotional, you know."

"Tears?" Withrow questioned, "Sarge is too tough for that."

"Maybe not. Maybe what we're getting into is pretty bad," Tilton offered, "might be a rough attack."

"Yeah," Franklin nodded, "he did say another platoon got beat up pretty much."

"He did, but we've been in rough attacks before," Withrow stated, "you don't think he's getting sentimental on us, do you?"

"I don't know," Tobin replied, "could be."

"Well, hell, Tobin, you're Jewish, too. If you don't know, how in hell are we --."

"It ain't a Jewish thing, Withrow," Tobin snapped.

"Whatever it is," Tilton added, "we all better keep an eye on him up there. Franklin, why don't you stay close to him and watch him. If he shows any sign of breaking, drag

Lest We Forget

him down. For damn sure, we don't want to lose him."

"Good idea, Tilton," Franklin nodded, "I'll do that."

"Yeah," Tobin agreed, "we can take care of the rest, but someone has to watch Sarge."

"Makes sense," Withrow grunted, "hell, we love him as much or more than he could us. Right, gang?"

"Right, Withrow," Franklin asserted.

"Don't say nothin to anyone," Tilton warned, "especially not to Lieutenant Trowbridge. Okay?"

"Definitely not the Lieutenant," Franklin snorted, "shit, he might make Sarge sit this one out and we need him."

"Okay, then," Tilton nodded, "we'll do what we can to take care of the Sarge. Hopefully, it's a temporary thing."

"Let's go get some more ammo and grenades," Tobin suggested.

"And get rid of these heavy parkas and stuff," Franklin added, "I want to be able to move easily."

"Right," Withrow nodded, "and I'm almost out of grenades."

"Shall we take the Sarge with us now?" Tilton asked.

"No," Tobin replied, "let him be for now."

Shortly after the two platoons started up the hill, machine gun and small arms fire swept the front ranks. Clearly, the Chinese defenders had the path covered and their fire was both accurate and devastating. Even so, the Marines kept climbing along the path. Then a curtain of mortar fire rained down and the advance slowed as dust, rocks and bodies suddenly filled the air!

"Keep going!" Lieutenant Trowbridge shouted, "keep going! Run through! Keep moving!"

The Marines surged ahead, seemingly oblivious to the hail of murderous fire. On the left and right, men fell to the deadly fire. Those who were not hit kept advancing relentlessly toward the top. When within grenade range, the depleted attackers paused long enough to throw their grenades.

They didn't wait for them to explode before pushing on. Everyone knew that to stop and stay where they were was to die. The only way to stay alive was to keep moving!

Sergeant Greenberg urged his men on constantly, exposing himself brazenly in order to keep them going. He saw Withrow, who was ahead of him, vanish in a mortar blast that blew dust and debris over everyone. Perhaps even pieces of Withrow -- there was no body that remained when the dust began to settle as the men surged ahead.

Tilton was clearly hit in the thigh and stomach, blood streaming down his pants leg. But he kept hobbling forward, dragging his leg with each step. Tobin looked at Greenberg with eyes wide with horror, but he, too, kept moving. Franklin was beside Greenberg, firing and reloading as he matched the Sergeant's steps, constantly cursing the enemy blasphemously.

Greenberg had no time to think about his love for him men. He, too, was busy firing and moving ahead, scrambling over the rocks and bushes. Yet he had to watch out for them as best he could and he glanced at them whenever possible. He saw Tilton limp a few feet ahead, firing his rifle, his face etched with a grim fear and determination. Then, the grim face and head seemed to explode into a bloody mishmash and Tilton's body slumped to the ground!

Sergeant Greenberg turned away, his stomach retching -- he didn't see Tobin nearly cut in half by the machine guns of the enemy. He took several blind, stumbling steps -- an enemy grenade landed in front of him, bounded off his legs and stopped at his feet! He bent down to pick it up and throw it back -- it exploded in his face!

Franklin felt the shrapnel from the grenade tear through his arm! He stared at what was left of Sergeant Greenberg, tried to ignore the horror and forced himself to keep moving. His legs numb with fatigue, his mind stunned by the ghastly devastation, he stumbled over the crest of the hill. The enemy was retreating down the back slope and Franklin started throwing grenades at them. Tears streamed down his face as he cursed them for killing his friends. Without thinking, he instinctively threw his grenades even after the enemy was beyond range.

Finally, he sensed some others beside him. He stared at them -- five other men including Lieutenant Trowbridge -- were on top! All of them had been hit somewhere and were stained with blood. Hopefully, he looked for a friendly face -- he saw none!

"Captain! We're on top!" Trowbridge was shouting into the radio, "but there's only six of us. Get some help up here quickly! We have little ammo left and we need medical help!"

Franklin turned and looked down the path. It was littered with bodies, among them the other members of his team. He couldn't spot them or identify anyone, but he knew they were there. Almost two entire platoons lay in grotesque positions along the path. With a heavy heart, he sank to his knees, his body trembling, his rifle laying beside his knees. He began to sob openly and covered his face with his hands. All of them -- Greenberg, Tobin, Withrow, Tilton -- all of them gone in searing minutes! All slain in a hideously cruel and senseless assault on a damn, barren hill. His body shook spasmodically as he sobbed in horror. Then, the voice of Lieutenant Trowbridge penetrated his thoughts. When he looked up, he heard the bugles heralding a counterattack.

Instinctively, he checked his supply of ammo. Two clips left. Sixteen rounds. No grenades.

"Franklin!" Lieutenant Trowbridge shouted, "go get what ammo you can find off the dead! Now! Hurry!"

Franklin stared at the Lieutenant. His initial reaction was one of shock, disgust and horror. He wanted to shoot the man! How dare the Lieutenant ask him to defile the memory of dear friends lost in battle? How dare he order him to go and rob the dead of their last shred of dignity by taking their ammo from them?

He turned away and stared at the bodies. Greenberg

had tried to tell him about God, but he hadn't wanted to know. But, if Greenberg and the others were in good with a God, then why did the God let this happen? Why did He take them all on this damn barren hill in a God-forsaken, stinking country they hadn't even heard of six months earlier? Why?

"Franklin! Move it! We need more ammo!"

Franklin opened his mouth to tell the Lieutenant to go to hell when he suddenly realized it wasn't God's fault! Nor the Lieutenant's and not even Greenberg's! In this situation, Greenberg would be yelling at him too! He pushed himself up, waved a hand at the Lieutenant, and staggered down toward the bodies.

As he approached them, he wondered. Were they the lucky ones? Maybe they were blessed by being killed now, so they wouldn't suffer anymore. Franklin shook his head. I don't know. Maybe that is it. Maybe I was spared so I could think a bit more about a God. I just don't know. One thing is certain -- we need more ammo or all six of us are going to join these guys and I ain't quite ready to do that. So, sorry guys.

CHAPTER NINETEEN

Word of the assault on Hiss 659 and its disastrous results filtered through the ranks. A few Marines were jubilant that the Chinese had been met and defeated. Others could only dwell on the fact that two platoons had nearly been wiped out and a third decimated. The number of casualties was sobering.

When Lieutenant Kenton told Sergeant Roletto's fire team about what he had heard, Jim Murphy listened closely. After the Lieutenant had finished, Murphy leaned forward.

"The survivors -- do you know their names, sir?"

"Uh, no, Murphy, I don't. They didn't tell us all of their names. All I know is one platoon was wiped out except for one man and the Lieutenant and only four from the other platoon made it. They were all wounded."

"Oh."

"Why do you ask, Murphy?"

"I had a good friend in that battalion. A real good friend. I'm worried about him, sir. He could have been in that assault."

"I see," Kenton nodded, "all I know, Murphy, is that the one man on the right who made it up the hill and wasn't killed -- he was with a fire team led by a Sergeant Greenberg. Everyone else in that platoon was killed."

"Greenberg, sir? A Sergeant Terry Greenberg? A Jewish man?"

"Well, now that you mention it, I believe it was him. I think that was the name they gave us."

Murphy stared at him. "My, my friend was in that fire team, Lieutenant. Name was Tilton, Gary Tilton. PFC

Tilton."

"I don't think that was the name of the man that made it, Murphy. Let me see -- in my notes -- here it is! The survivor's name was Franklin, not Tilton." He paused and noted Murphy's downcast expression. "I'm sorry, Murphy."

"Thank you, sir," Murphy mumbled. He turned away and stared across the adjacent river. So Tilton is dead. Damn but it hurts to know that. He was such a nice, quiet guy. Was seasick on the way over and we all kidded him about it. Perhaps too much. Shit, I always thought he'd be the one to make it. Damn! Wish I had been friendlier when he visited me on the ship. Also wish I knew about the others. Schein, Martin, Brown and -- Tilton dead. Wonder if any of the others are. The First and Fifth had a rough time in Seoul. Thankfully, we missed most of that. Why couldn't the brass have let the five of us stay together? He turned when Roletto moved up beside him.

"Sorry, Murphy," Roletto stated softly, "was Tilton the kid that visited you aboard ship?"

"Yeah, Sarge, that was him."

"Nice looking kid. Seemed real young. Well mannered and all. Out of the midwest?"

"He was. Iowa."

"Fit the mold."

"I always thought he'd be the one to make it, Sarge," Murphy sighed.

"You just never know, Murphy. God figures all that out. When it's your time, you go. That's just the way it is."

"You're beginning to sound like a damn Chaplain," Murphy snorted, "you learn all about that crap in Little Italy?"

Roletto looked at him and grinned. "You can learn a lot about life and God and other things on the streets of New York, Murph. Actually, though, I went to church with my parents."

"Figures. I never went to no church. Don't believe in all that crap."

"Hopefully, you'll understand some day," Roletto stated clearly, "faith gives you a reason for living, a purpose for life as well as something to lean on. You can believe --."

"I believe in me. I rely on myself," Murphy sneered, "my own guts, my abilities, my rifle -- what I can do for me. I don't go out of my way for no one. Period. Over and out."

"I'm truly sorry to hear you say that," Roletto sighed, "I was beginning to believe our team was becoming a cohesive, coordinated unit that I could rely on. I guess I was a bit premature in that. I'm really sorry you feel that way, Murphy."

"Well, I -- I didn't mean the guys I'm serving with, Sarge. Not you and the others."

"I think you intended it about everyone, Murphy," Roletto stated bluntly, "us, the Corps, everyone. Well, regardless, get squared away. We may have a battle brewing tonight." He spun around and walked away.

"I think the Sarge is kinda pissed off," Martinez quipped.

Thornquist rubbed his jaw thoughtfully, then turned to Murphy. "You're wrong, Murph. No man can stand alone. Take my folks, for instance. They're high class snobs, you know. Lot's of money and influential positions, all that. But even they know that, once in awhile, they need some support. Hurts them deeply to have to ask for it, but --."

"Stuff it," Murphy growled, "I ain't interest in no sob stories."

"Yeah, okay," Thornquist nodded, "but here, we have to work as a team. One guy gets out of line, we all suffer. If we're going to get through it, we --."

"Uh, hey, guys," Banks interjected, a worried look on his face, "we still got a war to fight -- with real enemies trying to kill us. We don't need another war in our own fire team."

"Buzz off, Banks," Murphy snapped.

Banks glanced at Martinez and rolled his eyes.

"C'mon, Banks," Martinez grinned, "let's find a

quieter, more peaceful place to chow down."

Murphy watched them walk away, then turned to Thornquist. "What are you hangin around for?"

Thornquist smiled. "It's a free world, Murphy. I do what I want to do. Right now, I'm comfortable here and I'm staying here. If you don't like that, it's too damn bad. You can go find yourself a rat hole to crawl into like the rat you are. I really don't give a damn if you stay or go fuck yourself somewhere else. Just stay out of my hair."

Murphy stared at him for a long moment. He was tempted to start something, then remembered the reputation Thornquist enjoyed. He took a deep breath and nodded. "Okay, I'll buy that."

Thornquist snorted and turned his back toward Murphy to show his contempt. "Shove it," he grunted.

The enemy attack started close to midnight. Two Russian tanks rumbled down the road and through the roadblock. The Marines manning the roadblock thought they were friendly vehicles until it was too late. The tanks fired up the company command post and the roadblock, causing many casualties before they began to withdraw.

Almost simultaneously, using the tanks' actions as a diversion, enemy infantry suddenly attacked along the perimeter. Several outposts were overrun and casualties there were high. The Marines could hear the Chinese enflaming each other into a feverish pitch as they pressed the attack with flares, bugles and whistles, swarming toward the main line of resistance.

Sergeant Roletto shrank into his foxhole a bit deeper when the flares brightened the landscape. He saw the hordes of Chinese soldiers advancing toward the line, their AK-47 rifles at the ready. Then grenades came flying toward him and he ducked even deeper. After the grenades exploded, Roletto raised up and opened fire. He could hear the others firing beside him and knew they were doing what they could. Clearly, the enemy held the advantage in both numbers and firepower. The question to be resolved was whether they had the will to fight.

After a few minutes, it became evident the enemy charge had stalled. As the smoke cleared and flares again brightened the area, the enemy could be seen straggling back into the hills. Those that were left alive, that is. The area was littered with enemy dead and dying.

Roletto crawled from his foxhole and moved to the position occupied by Martinez. "You okay, Martinez?"

"I'm fine, Sarge."

Roletto nodded and shifted to Murphy's foxhole. "You in good shape, Murphy?"

"Yeah, Sarge. Hey, look, I'm sorry about what I --."

"It's past, Murphy," Roletto snorted, "forget it." He moved to Thornquist's hole.

"Thornquist, are you --."

"I'm okay, Sarge," Thornquist replied, "and so is Banks. We're both doing fine and have plenty of ammo and grenades."

"Okay," Roletto acknowledged, "they'll be back. I hope we're more ready for them this time. Hang in there, guys."

He had just gotten into his foxhole when Lieutenant Kenton appeared.

"Sergeant, you team all okay?"

"Yes, sir. We're fine. Why?"

"Rest of the teams got hit pretty hard," Kenton explained, "look, we need to go out and hit them hard"

"Us, sir?"

"Yes, you and your team. We can hear them setting up four or five machine guns and possibly mortars on the hill out front. About eighty to a hundred yards out. If they succeed in getting those set up, we'll have to pull back. I don't want to do that. This area is more defensible than any back there." He paused and stared at Roletto's form in the darkness. "What I want you to do is lead your team out there to destroy those machine guns and mortars. There's no one else available now and won't be until morning. I know it's a long way out, but it has to be done. Can you do it?"

"We can do it, sir, but who's going to hold our positions here?"

"I'll shift some other men over here to hold it until you and your men get back. If we -- you -- can hit them soon enough, there may not be another attack tonight."

Roletto watched Kenton crawl away, then gathered his men around him. He didn't feel good about this assignment, but decided not to say anything to his men.

"Lieutenant wants us to sneak out and destroy a machine gun and mortar nest the Chinese is puttin in on the hill out there about eighty to a hundred yards. He thinks they're puttin in four or five guns and maybe some mortars. So we're gonna have to do it. We'll go in team formation, hit them with grenades and rifle fire, wipe out the nest and then run like hell back here before we get cut off. Questions?"

No one said anything and Roletto could not see their faces in the dark. It was impossible to tell how they felt about the assignment.

"Okay. Everyone got enough grenades and ammo?"

"We're well supplied, Sarge."

It was Martinez who spoke. The others grunted their agreement.

"Good," Roletto acknowledged, "we'll go when the guys who are gonna watch our sector get here."

"Who will it be?"

Again, it was Martinez who spoke.

"I don't know," Roletto replied. He heard a movement behind him and turned. Three shadowy figures appeared out of the darkness. For a moment, he stared at them, wondering if they were Marines and who they were.

"You Sergeant Roletto?" one of the men asked.

"Yeah."

"Good. We're supposed to watch your sector. Lieutenant Kenton sent us over."

"Just you three?"

"The three of us are all anyone else could spare, I guess, Sergeant. They all got hit pretty hard. Each of us is from a different team. We'll do what we can to hold your area for you."

"I see. Well, then, spread out. One of you here in the center and one on each side, about ten yards out. Guess that's the best we can do. You guys know the password?"

"Yes, sir," one of the men grunted.

"You don't say sir to a Sergeant."

"Sorry. Guess the last action kind of shook me up a bit."

"Yeah, well, don't get so shaken up that you shoot us when we come back. You understand me?"

"We understand, Sarge."

"Okay," Roletto snorted, "here we go, you guys. Key on me as much as possible. I know it's dark, but try to stay as close as you can without bunching up. Anyone got anything shiny on? Pockets got anything in them that will rattle or make a noise?"

Hearing no response, he shrugged and moved forward, stared into the darkness toward the enemy positions. "Then let's get the job done," he sighed.

The team moved away from the line in low, crouching postures, each man keying on the one next to him. Quietly, they crept toward the hill, careful not to stumble into a Chinese outpost. It seemed strange to be moving through an area controlled by the enemy and not to encounter either an outpost or a listening post.

The sounds of the Chinese setting up the machine guns and mortars was enough to guide them. Apparently, there was no effort by the Chinese to keep quiet or conceal the fact they were putting the machine gun nest there. That thought made

Roletto smile. The Chinese were so confident that they were sealing their own fate.

Halfway to the hill, Roletto heard some Chinese speaking to his right. He smiled knowingly. It was commonplace in any army. Men had to talk when isolated on a battlefield at night. Yet, it was the most dangerous thing to do.

There was just something about being in a foxhole at night, usually alone, that affected men. Often, they had someone -- a buddy or just another soldier -- nearby, so it probably wasn't loneliness. Was it an unconscious fear? A dread of the unknown? The inability to see if an enemy was approaching? Or just the seeming emptiness of the night? Whatever it was, the soldier in the foxhole was most affected by it. He had seen men actually develop the shakes in a foxhole, trembling so much they could not function effectively. Some had their nerve broken and they were sent back to the rear area as basket cases. Some wept unashamedly, but remained in their foxholes while others simply closed their eyes and ignored everything but the sounds. How one would react to the situation was unpredictable.

Roletto knew they easily could have sneaked over and killed the men who were talking. That, however, was not the objective of this foray. Perhaps they could get the men on the way back. There would, of course, be no surprise then. Not after they blew up the machine guns and mortars with grenades and killed the crews. After that, everyone in the area would be alert. There might even by enemy flares fired to light up the battlefield. That wouldn't be good. If flares were fired, all they could do was lie still until the light faded. If they moved, it was likely they would soon be dead.

The sounds were getting louder and Roletto paused. The others moved up close to him. He scanned their darkened, shadowed faces, unable to see them clearly. "Not far now," he hissed, "have to watch for them Chinese off to the right on our way back."

"And those on our left, too," Martinez added, "didn't you hear them?"

"No," Roletto admitted.

"At least eight or so, I'd guess," Martinez stated.

"I only heard the two off to the right."

"Probably more there, too," Martinez cautioned.

"Well," Roletto sighed, "let's spread out and go get the machine guns and mortars. Any questions?"

No one spoke up.

"Then let's go. You know what to do."

The men spread out and crept forward. As they moved even closer, they could easily hear the metallic sounds of the machine guns and mortars being assembled. Sergeant Roletto glanced toward the others. As far as he could tell, they were all in position at the base of the revetments where the guns were being placed. He raised his grenade and pulled the pin, saw the shadows of his men mimic his action. With a deep breath, he tossed his grenade over the top of the revetment. A cry of alarm sounded from the top, but it was too late! The five grenades exploded almost as one, the blasts wreaking havoc among the Chinese!

Sergeant Roletto charged up and over the lip of the position and began firing at anything that moved. He heard the others firing beside him. For what seemed like several minutes, they were the only ones shooting. Then the Chinese began shooting back. Quickly checking to be certain the machine guns and mortars were damaged beyond repair, Sergeant Roletto moved around the revetment, ignoring the wild enemy fire. It was obvious all the Chinese manning the revetment were dead and the guns destroyed. He waved to his men to start pulling back.

As he leaped over the edge and tumbled down the slope, a stinging, burning sensation hit his left leg! He fell and rolled to his feet, only to fall again! Then he realized his left leg was not responding well. He reached down and felt the sticky blood seeping through his pants leg!

Frantically, he looked around -- the others were far ahead, apparently out of sight, hidden in the darkness! He could see flashes of gunfire off to either side. With a firm resolve, he started crawling. Then the pain hit him and he instinctively groaned and nearly passed out. Stubbornly, he fought off the pain and kept crawling while bullets burned the air above him. He glanced ahead and saw what appeared to be the four men of his team about thirty or forty yards away.

He tried to call to them, but the noise of the battle was too great for them to hear. So far, no one was even coming close to hitting him with their shots. The Chinese were concentrating their fire on the others and their shots were too high to threaten him.

Roletto crawled ahead, stopped and lowered his head when flares lit up the slope. He heard Chinese cries all around him, but figured they hadn't spotted him yet. Then, strangely enough, the firing stopped! He heard the shouts of alarm -- from his own people!

"Where's Sarge?"

The voice, although distant, sounded like Corporal Martinez' and Roletto smiled in relief. They knew he was still out on the battlefield. He hoped they wouldn't do anything foolish like trying to rush out to rescue him.

"I see him!"

That voice sounded like Murphy's! Stay where you are, Murphy! Don't chance it! I'm okay for now!

"He's wounded! I've got to get him back! Can't leave him out there!"

That, too, sounded like Murphy. Roletto raised his head slightly and saw Murphy dash from the protection of his own lines! He wanted to shout to him, to tell him to stay where he was until things quieted down, but it was too late. Murphy only was able to cover about twenty yards before he was cut down in a hail of bullets! Roletto lowered his head and closed his eyes. He heard footsteps approaching -- a burst of automatic rifle fire hammered his body, ripping his back to pieces!

CHAPTER TWENTY

I never returned to Korea. After three months in the hospital, split between Japan and Hawaii, I was released back to active duty. As I had accumulated leave, I decided to spend it in Hawaii rather than to return home. For some reason, I just did not think going home to Washington State at that time was wise. My parents likely would not have understood the changes wrought in me by my combat experiences. My girlfriend, Carol Myers, and I had lost contact with each other and so I had no reason to go back home to see her and did not even know if she was still there in my home town.

Most of my leave was spent lounging on the beaches of the islands and soaking up the sun. I located an inexpensive, small apartment and, in essence, became a beach bum. I met a few people I liked and quite a few I didn't. The Hawaiians were like a different breed of humans, the 'cousins' being somewhat arrogant and cliquish. We didn't get along.

After my leave, my orders directed me to report to Camp Pendleton, California. There, I was assigned to a Fleet Marine Force unit that was being used to train troops for fighting in Korea. It was interesting duty, although seeing so many young and naive men coming out of boot camp brought back a lot of memories. Sad and depressing memories. It became difficult duty and I came to hate my work.

It was here that I was reunited with Sergeant, now Lieutenant, Parker. Between the two of us and the survivors we managed to locate and obtain specifics from, we were able to discover and reconstruct what had happened to the four other men I considered my best buddies. The information gleaned from them as well as our own experiences, served as the basis for this story. Without that information, our story could not have been told. Even so, it was a long time before I could bring myself to put it on paper. It saddened me greatly to discover that not one of my buddies made it through the first few months of the war.

Harry Schein was killed outside of Inchon right after the landing. He was not granted much of an opportunity to do anything in the war or to use his training. All because of a goof-up by a company officer who forgot to report his location. It should never have happened.

Hank Brown, the redneck from Alabama, won the Medal of Honor for his sacrifice on Hill 125. His bravery was typical of many Marines who died in the early struggles around Seoul. Most received no recognition whatsoever.

Gary Tilton and all but one member of his fire team were wiped out in the senseless assault on Hill 659. That battle was extremely savage, but the Marines won the day. Individual bravery was commonplace in those days. It is unfortunate that another means of taking or destroying the hill wasn't used. The utter sacrifice of so many men simply did not make sense.

Jim Murphy, of course, sacrificed his life in a futile attempt to rescue the wounded Sergeant Roletto. Both men died needlessly in the effort to protect the flank of the regiment. Other means could have been used to destroy the machine guns and mortars in that emplacement.

For my actions, I was awarded the Bronze Star, the Purple Heart and the Silver Star. I really don't understand the reasons for the awards, except for the Purple Heart. I was simply doing what I was trained to do as a Marine. Apparently, those in higher echelons who decide such matters thought what I did was extraordinary and courageous. That has always puzzled me and continues to do so even today. For I saw greater acts of courage and daring by ordinary men virtually every day. They truly earned the rewards I was given, yet they received little, if any, recognition.

I kept the date the five of us had planned on the ship enroute to Korea. It was the least I could do to honor the memory of my companions and their heroic deeds. Of course, the people at Rossini's were a bit perplexed when I appeared alone after making reservations for five. I ignored them and ordered five drinks.

The Screwdriver was for Harry Schein. It was the only drink he ever ordered. Hank Brown got a Margarita. He enjoyed the Tequila drink very much and never strayed from it. Gary Tilton always ordered a Scotch and Soda, so I got one for him. It is a drink one has to learn to like. The Double Martini was for Jim Murphy. It was a strong drink which Murphy had acquired a taste for both in New York and in Hollywood. For myself, I ordered an Old-Fashioned. I had acquired a taste for the drink in San Diego after boot camp. At home, I seldom had anything but beer.

I was very pleased when now Lieutenant Parker showed up. As a matter of fact, I was getting quite lonely and even a bit depressed before he came. After returning to Camp Pendleton and reuniting with him, I had never mentioned my intention to keep the reunion date the five of us had planned. We had, of course, invited Parker to join us. So it was especially pleasing to me that he remembered the date and the time and the restaurant and showed up when I returned to San Diego from Washington State. It just demonstrates what kind of man he was -- the man all five of us had come to admire and respect. He ordered his own drink -- strangely, I don't recall exactly what it was.

As Lieutenant Parker and I sat at the table ignoring the confused and perplexed waiters, I began to consume the five drinks. It was a strange experience for a non-drinking man, but I felt it imperative to finish all five drinks in memory of my four companions.

When I picked up the Screwdriver and looked into the orange liquid, I saw the stocky form and grinning face of Harry Schein. Tears swelled up in my eyes and his voice seemed to reach out from the filled glass.

"Glenn, I loved that farm in Michigan -- the land, the weather, the people. My folks worked hard to get it established and I was going to make it work out when I went back. That was my intent."

He paused and looked at me seriously. "You know, Joyce was right. I never should have left it. I'd have married her and raised a family. We'd have had a son --." He choked up and couldn't continue.

"You'd have been very happy, Harry. Except, well, I'd never have met you."

"We were great buddies. You had me and Hank kind of worried after you guys went north. That was one helluva fight you guys put up. Glad you made it."

"Thanks, Harry. Wish you could have been there."

"Wasn't to be, I guess. Thanks for coming, Glenn. We all wondered if you would remember. Good-bye, Glenn."

"See ya sometime, Harry," I mumbled. The glass was empty when I put it down and glanced at Lieutenant Parker. He was staring into his own glass and seemed not to have noticed anything. I looked at the waiters -- they were nervously searching for their manager. I figured they could go to hell.

The Margarita was next and I almost eagerly grabbed it if only to let Harry go back to being dead. I usually avoided Tequila and, now, as I raised the salt-rimmed glass, I envisioned Hank 'Ears' Brown watching me and wondering how I would handle the tequila. I took a sip and Hank's face twisted into a knowing grin.

"That's it, Glenn. Not too fast."

I nodded to him and took another, longer sip. "This isn't too bad, Hank. I could learn to like it."

Hank nodded. "You did okay over there, Glenn. Me, I was stupid to enlist. Could have been an All-American if I had stayed in college. That southern pride dies hard, however, and I --."

He stopped and looked at me, his eyes questioning. "Sorry about mentioning dying, Glenn. You know, I never once thought I'd go that way. But when I saw those grenades tumbling down that hill --."

"You know you got the Medal of Honor, don't you?"

He nodded his head and fingered his ear. "Yeah. Don't mean much to me now, of course. What means more is that I got to know you and the others -- at least for a short period of time. We -- Harry and I -- watched you guys, you know. Wish we could have done more to help you. I'd better go now. Thanks for coming to our reunion, man. Means a lot to us."

"Good-bye, Hank." I stared into the empty glass and nodded solemnly. That was like Hank Brown. Always thinking of the -- I took a deep breath and reached for the Scotch and Soda.

Already, the liquor was affecting me. My head felt a bit numb and I wasn't certain I could stand up and walk without staggering. I smelled the Scotch and Soda and a sense of nausea swept over me and I shuddered. A glance at Lieutenant Parker told me he knew what I was experiencing.

"A strong drink," he cautioned.

"I know."

"Take it slow, Glenn. Don't want to have to carry you home."

"I'll be okay. Hell, I'm a Marine." The words came out without rancor or bitterness. Maybe there was just a touch of boasting in them.

"Sure," Parker smiled. He nodded toward the glass. "Who drank the Scotch and Soda?"

"Tilton."

"Good kid. Wasn't he the one who was seasick on the trip over?"

I nodded, took a deep breath and raised the glass, tried to ignore the smell as I took a gulp. At first, it burned my tongue and traced a fiery path down my throat! Then I really tasted it and, strangely, decided it wasn't all that bad. I took another gulp, this time savoring it for a few seconds.

My head was spinning a bit and I looked across the table at the shimmering image of Gary Tilton. He shook his head knowingly.

"Better take it easy, Glenn," he cautioned, "mixing various drinks like this is not a good idea."

"That's what Sergeant Parker just said," I mumbled, my tongue a bit thick and my words slurred somewhat.

Gary glanced at Parker and nodded. "A good man. Wish we could have stayed together. Maybe things would have been --."

I met his sorrowful gaze and swallowed. "It was great when we were together, Gary. We made a great team."

"We did. Hurt when we were split up. You know, Hank and Harry thought you might join them when you went north. They told me you put up a great fight."

"Not like you did later, Gary. The guy who survived from your team told us about the charge. Took a lot of guts to go up that hill."

Gary shrugged. "It was nothing. Just doing our duty." He paused and raised his sad eyes, met my earnest gaze. "At least you came through, Glenn. We all want you to tell our story and let everyone know we did what we could. Glad you came today, Glenn. Semper Fi, man."

"Semper Fi, Gary," I mumbled, the words difficult to speak. I brushed at my eyes and ignored the questioning glance from Parker. I hadn't planned on the reunion being so emotionally stirring. My hand trembled as I drained the Scotch and Soda and immediately reached for the double Martini.

Jim Murphy, the tough guy from New York. A strange one. Hard, impenetrable outer shell, but a heart of gold inside. A fighter, trouble-maker, brash and boastful, but let one of his friends be put in peril and he was there to help. I took the olive from the glass and slowly ate it. From across the table, Murphy watched me.

"You sure you're man enough to drink it?"

"I'll manage, Murph."

"Guess you will," Murphy agreed with a snort, "you always were the strong one of the bunch. Not really the type to enlist in the Corps, but you did well and you can hold your liquor better than some."

He paused and rubbed his chin. "Don't know if they told you, but I really made an ass of myself just before -- well, Sergeant Roletto tried to help me --."

"You don't have to tell me about it, Murphy. Between you and Roletto. I didn't know the man, but he didn't make it, either, you know."

"I know. Talked to him up here and apologized."

The boasting tone was gone from his voice and I looked at him sharply. It wasn't like Murphy to speak like this. "Don't be so hard on yourself, Murph."

"You know, Glenn, it's different now. When we went over there, none of us really knew what we were getting into. We should have been better prepared, received more realistic training. That's why its important for you to tell our story. You have to do it or no one will know."

His voice had a tinge of desperation in it and I stared at him. Then his image began to fade. "Thanks, Glenn. Semper Fi, Man."

"Semper Fi, Murph," I gulped emotionally. There was much I had wanted to say to each of them, but the emotional aspect of it all blurred my thoughts. I blinked the tears from my eyes and turned to Parker. "They were a great bunch of guys, good friends."

"They were, Martin, all of them. Not just the five of you, but everyone who went over there. Marines, Army, Navy, Air Force -- all of them."

"They were," I agreed. I reached for my Old-Fashioned. One more drink -- one more chance to give a toast to my fallen comrades. I owed them much more than that.

"Here's to the fallen," I stated, my voice strangely

clear, "Semper Fi, guys. Lest We Forget."

I tuned back into the ceremonies and tried to casually wipe away the tears that blurred my vision. I silently wished my wife, Carol, could have lived long enough to join us on this day. She would have been a very proud Grandmother, indeed. However, she had passed away a year earlier.

I tensed when the officer-in-charge barked the order for the recruits to pass in review. All of the speeches, the awards and other items on the agenda had been completed. I took a deep breath and watched in awe as several hundred new Marines snapped to attention in one coordinated motion. The rest of the ceremony was anti-climactic.

So, what else is there to say? For the Marines with whom I served and those who came later, Semper Fi. For all veterans who served in any of the branches of the military, Lest We Forget.